Other books by the author
Raven's Realm Series
Raven's Child
Windows to the Soul
Chaos Within
Immortality
Darkness Falls

Women of Ravenwood Series
Fallen
Unspoken Oaths

Gods & Dragons Series
Brothers
Victory
Beyond Valhalla

Immortal Series
Whispers of the Immortal
Tears of the Immortal
Soul of the Immortal
Fall of the Immortal
Echoes of the Immortal
Quest for the Immortal

QUEST
OF THE
IMMORTAL

Immortal Series
Book Six

M.J. Spickett

NORTHERN GEM
PUBLISHING

Northern Gem Publishing (2024)

ISBN: 978-1-998318-07-0 eBook
ISBN: 978-1-998318-11-7 Paper Back
ISBN: 978-1-998318-12-4 Hardcover

www.mjspickett.ca

Library and Archives Canada Cataloging in Publication
Spickett, M.J., 1976-, author
Quest for the Immortal / M.J. Spickett
Issues in print and electronic formats

I. Title.

Art by Margreat Davis

Dedication

To Priya and Ashley, who kept me encouraged and focused while writing. To Jayden, who put up with my craziness and continues to do so as I keep writing. And to Andrew, one of the best editors I've had the pleasure to work with.

AUTHOR NOTE

MJ Spickett is a Canadian Author. Most locations within her novels focus on Canada and England, and, as such, words and spacing may appear differently than they would in America. For example, we like to use "U" and "Z" in many of our words, for example "honor" (US) and "honour" (Canadian), or "organisation" (US) and "organization" (Canadian). We write grey with an "e" not with an "a." My editor is also Canadian and is helping me keep to Canadian standards. As well, although it is normal for Americans to use a single space at the end of a sentence, Canadians tend to double space. This also makes it easier to read and give an extra pause to help readers digest what they just read and better comprehend it. These are not spelling or formatting errors but simply the way we are taught to read and write.

Canadians tend to be a complicated group but that's also what makes us special.

To my Canadian readers…celebrate your uniqueness and continue writing.

Chapter One

The squeal of brakes filled the air as one of the motorcycles took a turn just a little too tight. A momentary fear of merging into oncoming traffic filled Kyra as she slid onto the next street. Thankfully, it was the wee hours of the morning and the streets were relatively quiet. Nonetheless, slowing down cost her precious time and put more distance between herself and the transport she was after. It was absurdly agile inside the confines of the city. Whoever was driving knew their way around much better than her and was able to take the turns with practiced ease. Kyra Griffith was not so lucky. She rarely drove and preferred a much more elegant way to get around than the noisy piece of machinery she was presently driving. The vibrations and noise of the engine grated on her nerves and not even the insulation of the heavy black helmet she was forced to wear helped in the slightest. Why anyone would enjoy such a thing was beyond her. She longed for the simple comforts of her home further north. There she dominated the night.

"We need to keep him from getting to the highway," Tyler called through the radio in her helmet. "If he gets there, we'll lose him."

"You'll lose him," Kyra snapped back at the bounty hunter. "I can move freely on the highway."

"Kyra, we need to keep a low profile," he reminded her or what must have been the umpteenth time.

She growled lowly in response. "If we lose it our 'profile' will be the least of your boss's concerns. Let it hit the highway."

1

"Kyra."

"Trust me. I hunt these bastards back home. The highway is the safest place. Unless you have collateral damage insurance in place," she reasoned.

So far no one had been hurt but it was only a matter of time before there was some sort of accident and someone was killed. Quite frankly she didn't want that on her conscience. If they got to the highway then the truck was unlikely to take very many – if any – sharp turns. And they would be able to get in front of it. From there it was a matter of slowing it down and detaching the trailer from the cab. After that it should be a breeze. At least that's what Kyra told herself. She had done this many times back home, but it seemed to have become more frequent down south to the point that the northern bounty hunters were being called in to help.

Human trafficking was all over the news in recent years. There were always reports on the internet and social media. Hundreds and even thousands of missing people were listed daily. At first look most of the missing seemed normal enough but those with the sight began noticing a similar theme in many of the victims – they were not normal. Sure, they looked human enough, each one as different as can be, from different cultures, ethnicities, and backgrounds. Poor, rich, middle class, it didn't matter. Everyone seemed fair game. They all just disappeared, most weren't fully human. They were hybrids. Some had no clue what they were and lived out their lives believing they were just as human as the rest of their family. Others worked in secret to help protect their kind. Unfortunately, someone had learned their secret and were hunting down and kidnapping the hybrids.

None of the descriptions shared online fit and it was by mere chance that they discovered transports were being used in the larger populated areas. Transports, not just one, which meant whoever was doing this, they knew exactly where to look and how to find them, especially the younglings. It was a frightening concept; one for which they had not been prepared.

In all honesty, Kyra was not suited for these hunts. Her territory was much smaller, the kidnappings less intense. She was used to small towns and cities with few to no cameras. Places where she could go unseen and if she was spotted, treated like a ghost or a drink-induced hallucination. No-one knew her and that was the way she liked it. The north was far less complex than the south.

She and Tyler fell back, giving the truck more distance and simply following it. It pulled further ahead, still going far above the speed limit but no longer posing a possible danger to the public or those possibly trapped within the trailer. As predicted, it turned off on the first exit onto the 401. Kyra cursed under her breath. Of all the highways it had to take, it took the busiest and most hectic of them all. Despite it being the dead of night, the 401 was always busy and hard to navigate without years of experience and patience.

The truck picked up speed. Kyra and Tyler matched its pace. It swerved in and out of traffic, the driver obviously knowing they were still behind him. The blaring honk of horns caused Kyra to cringe as they rang through her ears. There were more cars on this highway at night than there was most of the day on her section of highway 17, and the drivers were not afraid to let their displeasure at the truck driver be known.

"Damn it! I told you not to let it reach the highway," Tyler cursed. "We can't stop it here."

Kyra swallowed back a retort. This was her fault. She should have just done as he said. She wasn't used to working with a partner and she was not one to be talked down to. She was used to being on her own and dealing with these people her way. She wasn't about to change tactics just yet.

"How far does this highway go?" she asked, even though she already knew.

"All the way to Ottawa, and we don't have the gas to go that far."

"Do we have anyone ahead of us? Anyone who can set up a roadblock of some sort?" she said, her mind working quickly. "All we need is to get him off this main stretch and I can deal with the rest."

"No...no, you are not changing out here," Tyler objected. There was desperation in his voice.

"We're running out of options," Kyra pointed out. "We need him off this road. Do we have a way to reroute traffic or not?"

He was hesitant for a moment as he mulled over their options. Kyra waited silently. An itch began moving through her body and up the back of her neck as it often did during a hunt. She had been holding it back far longer than she was used to. Pressure between her shoulder blades began to build. The change was coming, she could feel it. The question was how long she would be forced to keep it under control before it became too much. The thrill of the hunt always made the change come so much easier. There were times when she could barely control it.

"No," Tyler finally answered. He glanced toward her, his dark helmet concealing his face. "We're nearly at the city limits. There should be a lull in traffic. When that happens…do it."

A pleased purr slipped from Kyra. The tension of keeping her true form trapped inside a human body melted away as she slowly began to shift forms. Even the painful cracking and snapping of bones could not distract her from her target. The change was not visible to the drivers around her. No one would notice until it the change was nearly complete. She held on, forcing the more prominent parts of it back. A few more minutes were all she needed. They just needed to make it to city limits.

The vehicles ahead of her began taking different turn offs and disappearing to various locations within the east end of Toronto. The truck continued east. If there were no hybrids trapped in the trailer, Kyra would have been tempted to track it and see where it was taking its victims… but lives were on the line. Kyra waited a few minutes more before gunning the engine and closing the distance between her and the truck. She moved to the right side, out of sight of oncoming traffic. If she was going to change forms the closer to the truck the better. There would be fewer witnesses that way.

She moved to the right side of the truck. It was a dangerous position, one she didn't particularly like. She was relying on Tyler to keep the driver distracted on the left side so she could reach the passenger door unnoticed. The truck picked up speed as the driver tried to keep ahead of them. It swerved toward Tyler, trying to run him off the road then back toward Kyra, trying to do the same to her. For a moment, she had to drop back to keep from being pinned against the guard rail. Sparks flew as the trailer made contact with the metal and for one fearful moment, Kyra feared the truck might go through, further endangering the children trapped in the trailer. She had to stop it before there was an accident.

Waiting for another opening, she sped up to narrow gap between the big rig and guard rail and reached for the passenger door. Grasping the handle, she shoved the motorcycle out of the way, directing it to the shoulder of the highway and over the barrier. It landed in the grass without serious damage.

The driver immediately stepped on the gas, steering toward Tyler once more. Kyra kept her head down as she balanced on the step below the door. Taking a deep breath, she yanked the door open and slid inside, surprising the driver. He drew a handgun and aimed it at her but she moved quickly, kicking it out of his hand before slamming his head into the window, breaking the glass, and effectively knocking him unconscious. When he was no longer a threat, she dragged him out of the driver's seat and took his place.

After waving to Tyler to show him she had control of the truck, Kyra veered away from the busy highway toward a rural, forested area where few would dare follow. She carefully took the truck down to a clearing then turned to the trucker, fighting to keep her anger in check.

"Who are you?" she demanded, her voice a threatening hiss. "What do you want with them?"

She got no answer. The driver lay hunched over on the passenger seat, face drained of colour and foam covering the corner of his mouth. She stared at him in shock as Tyler pulled up beside her.

"He's dead," she breathed.

"What did you do?" Tyler demanded, shoving her aside to climb in the cab. "You killed him?"

She bristled at the accusation. "If I was going to kill him, he'd be in shreds. The Shadow possessing him fled."

"Shadow? Seriously?"

She nodded. "He reeks of it."

"The Shadow-beings haven't been an issue in years. Why would they come back now?"

Kyra shrugged. The Shadows being involved didn't surprise her. They had been a thorn in her side throughout her childhood. They could possess humans, make them do unthinkable things, and once they were done, discarded them like an old pair of worn-out running shoes.

"Did you find anything?" she called to Tyler.

He jumped down and shook his head. "Nothing. Not even a driver's license. Whoever he is, or who he's working for, there's nothing except an old cell phone, and he wiped it before dying."

"Joy," Kyra grumbled. "Well let's get these kids back to headquarters and let the Guardians figure this out."

It took several minutes to unlock the doors of the trailer. They were double locked and equipped with smaller, nearly invisible cameras. Tyler destroyed them before stepping into their view. Once they were gone, they grabbed one handle each, pulled them down, and swung open the doors, prepared for the worse.

Inside there was the sound of sniffles and sobbing as more than two dozen beings sat huddled deep inside. At first glance most were human in form but several of the younger hybrids had lost control of their glamour and reverted to their true form. The older ones were hiding them, those with enough sense to try and encourage them back to their human guise. Kyra paid them little mind as she took in their condition.

"Is anyone hurt?" she called.

There was a hushed murmur for a moment before a young hybrid, maybe sixteen in her human appearance, stepped forward. "No, ma'am."

Tyler did a double take as the young woman jumped down. She stood before him, nearly a head shorter than both him and Kyra. She looked disheveled and a little tired, no doubt the chase having thrown her and the other kids around in the trailer, but she didn't have the frightened wide-eyed look of the others. This wasn't her first kidnapping.

"Zoey?" Tyler asked in disbelief.

The girl brushed a long colourful cornrow back over her shoulder.

"Hi, Tyler," she answered with a small sigh.

She paused as a new truck came careening into the clearing. She gave the other hybrids a single command to stay in the trailer as she took a defensive stance.

"Hey, whoa," Tyler said quickly as the truck came to stop.

A bus followed closely behind the truck cab and came to a stop not far from the trailer.

Zoey let out a slow breath and relaxed. "Sorry, these guys are getting more aggressive and aiming for younger kids. It's getting crazy out there. I never knew how many of us there truly were."

Kyra nodded in understanding. "There were thousands of Celestials, far more running loose than we originally thought."

"Let discuss this back HQ," Tyler said with surprising gentleness.

Kyra raised a questioning brow, but Tyler said nothing to her. Instead, he began directing the hybrids to the bus, both he and Zoey working in tandem with some of the older youths to get the young – some still struggling to return to their human forms – off the truck and onto the bus. Once the trailer was unloaded, it was unhooked from the cab and attached to the new one to be taken to a truck yard where it would be searched then discarded. The original cab and driver would be towed to another site, searched as well before it and the body were disposed of. Kyra wasn't sure how. In the north it would be incinerated but the south handled things differently.

Headquarters was not located in a nice shiny building in downtown Toronto, huddled amongst the day-to-day hubbub of city life as one might have expected. Most of it was situated in a large warehouse behind a cluster of old shops that had somehow survived the modernization of the city. Some dubbed it the "bad part of town" due to its large homeless population, but the homeless could be found anywhere, including amongst the gleaming white towers and office buildings that were more regularly patrolled by police and security. The difference between the "bad part" and the towers was the fact that the homeless were often safer amongst the old shops where the Guardians could watch over them and hide them if they must. Glamour was a powerful tool. Entire neighbourhoods could be warped to look as if the streets were empty, or make it appear more modern. That power didn't work as well amongst the towers and more modern sections.

The bus pulled into the warehouse where the hybrids were unloaded. Guardians hustled to find out their names and their families.

Any who were injured were quickly treated and helped back into their human forms. Kyra huffed softly to herself as she walked past them. The growing number of hybrids made little sense. Most of the Celestials had left the planet over a decade ago, the few remaining classified as rebels, trying to help the humans prepare and fend off a possible invasion. They had normal lives, pretending to be human and mixing in with the surrounding population. Several had hybrid children, half human-half Celestial, but their offspring were accounted for and worked along side them to protect the human race. So, if they were not the parents of these children then who was? How many other Celestials were still on-planet?

This led to her current problem as she stepped into the office, containing the regional director and not one, but three Celestials. All of which were rebels that helped head what the United Nations lovingly called Earth Defense Command. Fun name for the smallest division of their defense program. She cringed at the monitors lining the far wall. On them were a mix of highway security cameras and YouTube, all featuring almost identical images of her commandeering the transport. It looked like a scene from *Fast and the Furious*.

"I can explain," Kyra said before anyone could reprimand her.

All eyes turned toward her and that was a little disconcerting considering Mason had six, two of which were on the back of his head. Nonetheless, Kyra refrained from tugging on her long auburn hair, a habit she often had when nervous. It wasn't her natural colour, just glamour she used to hide her Celestial heritage to appear human. Without it not only would her hair be a glossy, unearthly white, but so would her body. Her skin was as fair as any with albinism. She kept her back straight as she faced White. They had asked for her help, not the opposite way around. She had nothing to fear. If anything, they should fear her. She was a hybrid, they were mere humans. They needed her. She did not need them.

A tall white-haired woman, stick thin and sickly pale, folded her arms across her chest and gave Kyra a cold look.

"I certainly hope so. Your fathers didn't spend the last thirteen years setting up this organization just for you to swagger in here and disrupt it simply because you can't follow simple rules," she drawled with a cold forwardness that would have made any Celestial proud.

8

Kyra inhaled slowly and dug her nails into the palms of her hands to keep her power in check. "We were running out of time."

"Had you followed Mr. Yue's direction, you would have been able to safely stop the truck within city limits, without your little stunt," Director White continued. "Now we have a mass hysteria that terrorists are attacking trucks on the 401. How exactly do you propose we spin this to the public? If anyone figured out what you really were..."

"I don't know. Maybe say they were filming an illegal action scene on the highway that the city had no knowledge of? It happens all the time?" Kyra shot back. She gave a small snort and folded her own arms across her chest in a mock impersonation of White. "Look, we found and saved the hybrids. No one was hurt. They can go back to their families. Everyone is happy."

Wide magenta eyes narrowed. "No, not everyone is happy. We still don't know who these people are, or what they want with the hybrids. Neither you, nor our own team have been able to capture even one driver alive. It means I must endanger our people more by sending someone undercover. I will not do that."

Kyra opened her mouth to respond. Someone undercover wasn't that bad of an idea but White didn't give her a chance to respond.

"We have no idea what these humans are doing to the ones we haven't been able to save," the director continued in a near yell. "Humans are cruel and hateful, but the Shadows are far worse. They will not hesitate to hunt us down and murder our kind, or worse. And now..." She waved at the monitors. "Your stunt not only endangered us but could have exposed you. I want you out of the city and back up north by daybreak."

"What?" Kyra snapped in shock. Her arms dropped to her sides and hands balled into fists. "I came to help. If I hadn't changed forms, we may never have stopped that truck! I saved those kids!"

White turned away, her crisp suit matching her name. "I will arrange for a plane to take you to Sudbury. You can make your way home from there."

"You asked for my help!"

The older woman turned back to Kyra. "And now we no longer require it," she said simply.

With a gesture of her pale hand, she dismissed Kyra and returned to her work.

Furious, Kyra stomped out of the office and back into the warehouse. She couldn't believe this was happening. After everything she had done, they were dismissing her as if she was some unruly child, incapable of holding up her family name let alone completing the mission they had asked of her. That was fine. She would continue her mission on her own.

* * * * *

There were few things Kyra liked about the big city. She normally avoided the subway and most forms of public transportation, preferring instead to walk where she needed to go. Today, she made an exception and took to the tunnels shortly before daybreak and headed to a section of the city she had not been to in a long time. She wasn't ready to head home just yet.

The Royal Ontario Museum had changed considerably since her last visit. The art deco addition was a vast contrast to the old stone building and Kyra inwardly cringed when she first saw it. The silver gleamed in the morning sunlight. While it looked imposing on the outside, the inside was a little more inviting and felt almost like home. The few times her family left the safety of the Ishpatina Mountain Range, her fathers made a point of visiting museums all across Canada and even a few in Britain. The "ROM" was her favourite. It housed many of her family's discoveries from their archeological digs.

Mornings were usually quiet. Toronto and the surrounding area had quite a few schools, many of which made special class trips to the museum. If they were about to attend, they wouldn't arrive for another hour or two. Nonetheless, Kyra avoided the more populated areas. She took a moment to admire the Brontosaurus from the first-floor gallery. It was a sight she always enjoyed seeing, even if it was only the casts of bones from the long dead creature. She gave it a small whimsical smile then headed to the stairs and up to the second floor where exhibits of ancient civilization and temples were displayed. The photographs of ancient temples lined the walls with pieces of stone and cut rock sat on display below them. Artifacts were kept in secure glass displays, the only remains of temples that were now lost to history.

"You know they say the Egyptians are the direct descendants of the Celestials."

Kyra inhaled deeply through her nose and let it out slowly. "Do they?" she asked.

Her body thrummed with energy. She folded her arms across her chest to keep it in check. The last thing she needed was to lose her temper here of all places. Tyler sidled up next to her and studied the displays as well.

"Well, that's what they say at least. Personally, I think they were one of the few races that didn't join the great uprising," he explained.

A small frown tugged at Kyra's lips. "Then they were fools."

"The direct descendent theory holds merits though. Can you imagine an entire country of hybrids?"

Kyra grinned and she couldn't help the small laugh that escaped her. "That is an incredible theory."

"One of my best."

"Well, if the Egyptians were direct descendants of the Celestials they wouldn't have kept to one country, they would have moved outward and conquered other countries until they managed to conquer the world. If anything,…the Romans may have been. Conquering other beings has always been the Celestial way. I suppose humans take after them in that aspect."

He fell silent, unsure how to answer.

She turned toward him and raised a curious brow. Her curiosity grew at the way he was dressed. Normally when they met, he was dressed casually, now he was dressed as if on his way to a corporate meeting. He cleaned up nicely.

Tyler frowned at her then looked back at the display.

"I hit a nerve," Kyra mused. "Are all humans this moody?"

He gave her a dark look. "I shouldn't have come here."

She shrugged but didn't turn away. "No one asked you to. So why did you come? I highly doubt it was to talk about the Celestials."

He was silent for several long moments. Then he sighed, his stiff shoulders finally relaxing. "White shouldn't have sent you away. If I had listened, we could have stopped the truck much sooner. I let my pride get in the way."

Kyra blinked in surprise. "Wow, did that hurt?"

"Shut up."

"No, seriously, you don't normally apologize for anything."

"And hybrids are nothing but trouble yet here we are."

They glared at each other for several moments before Kyra finally grinned. "You could be right...maybe."

Tyler stared at her in confusion. "Which part?"

Kyra didn't answer. She moved off to the next exhibit and Tyler dutifully followed. There were new exhibits, pieces taken from temples that were discovered underground in locations all around the world. The artifacts on display were typical wall carvings and trinkets, nothing otherworldly. Those were locked up in government research labs and kept secret from the public. Nonetheless, Kyra couldn't help but run her fingers over the glass protecting them. A longing to go home filled her. It had been months since she was last in the comfort of her mountain-side cabin. Her fathers provided most of these artifacts. Both had firsthand experience with these temples and the Celestials that had once ruled them. A small frown tugged her lips downward. She had been away from home for far too long. She missed her dads. She missed going on digs with them. It was so much calmer than having to deal with Shadows potentially possessing people and kidnapping hybrids. She missed the quiet of the mountains.

"Are you alright?" Tyler asked, reaching out to touch her but stopping short.

Blinking away tears, Kyra nodded. "I'm fine. I just got lost in thought. Did you say something?"

"No, just watching you."

She gave a snort. "You must have better things to do."

She moved on, no longer interested in the temples, her mind no longer peaceful. Perhaps if she moved on the Mayan exhibit, she would find peace? It was always quiet there this time in the morning. Despite how it resembled the Aztec and underground temples, there was a distinct difference that helped calm her aching heart.

"You look nice," Tyler tried. It took Kyra off guard.

"Are you hitting on me?"

"What? No! I'm just stating a fact." He took a deep breath. "I'm just saying that you clean up pretty good. I'm used to seeing you in jeans and a t-shirt. It's nice to see you in a pant suit. Makes you look less like a teenager and more grown up."

She paused and turned toward him. "Just how old do you think I am?"

He had the decency to be hesitant before answering. "According to your file you're nineteen but spent most of your life living along the Ishpatina Ridge. Before that you lived in a...lab?"

Her brows furrowed as anger filled her. "You read my file?"

He rolled his eyes in annoyance as he caught up with her. He took a deep breath. "That's why I'm here. I need your help."

She searched his gaze to see if he was telling the truth. His eyes were so dark they were nearly black, but she could see the traces of blue that ringed them. He seemed almost desperate and afraid, aspects she was not used to seeing in him.

"Why should I help you? White doesn't want me on this case."

"White doesn't know I'm here."

Her brows rose in questioning.

"These kids that are being kidnapped range from infants to early twenties. They have no combat training, but you, you have training. You could walk into any school and pose as a student," he explained.

He took her hand and led her to a bench. It wasn't something Kyra liked. She avoided being touched and immediately drew her hand away from him as if it had been burned. No such thing had happened, but it was an old habit. Only a few people were allowed to touch her.

"I've never gone to school," she objected. "My dads homeschooled me. Hell, I learned to fly a plane before I drove a car. I have nothing in common with normal teenagers. I'll never fit in."

He nodded. "Perhaps, but you can track Celestials and hybrids." He raised his hands when she began to object. "I'm a hunter; I know these things, just like you do. These people hunting hybrids? They're able to find them and the only logical explanation is they're tracking their energy signature. The question is how and why? Are they Shadows possessing people? We won't know unless we can get someone on the inside. Someone has to be captured. Someone who can handle themselves if things go south."

"And you have no one else willing to do that?" Kyra countered.

She was not about to play the victim for anyone. She had been a victim as a child, raised in a lab then kidnapped by a military group that had been possessed by Shadow beings and taken to another lab to be "harvested." No one knew who funded the group or how they knew she was a hybrid, but she had spent the last year trying to track these people down and saving kids just like her. This wasn't her territory though. Up north things would be easier. She may not have had any luck tracking down who was after the hybrids or why, but eventually she would. She just needed a better plan.

"No-one who can handle themselves like you do," he confessed. "Look, you may have been homeschooled, but you also have military training. Griffith is ex-military and taught you everything he knew before you went to bootcamp with Caldwell. You were top of your class."

She rolled her eyes. "My file."

He nodded in agreement.

A flicker of energy caught both her and Tyler's attention and they glanced up in unison as an eight-year-old boy walked by with a group of other kids. Each looked like a normal human but that energy, the signature of a hybrid, was prominent if not seen by the naked eye. Humans could not see or feel it, not most at least, but for anyone of Celestial descent, there was a vibration of sorts that signaled they were something far more alien. The child glanced at Kyra, sensing her otherworldliness as well, then quickly dashed after his classmates. She watched as he disappeared onto the next floor.

"If I do this it won't be here," Kyra finally decided. She looked Tyler in the eye. "We do this in my territory. Less people, less possible collateral damage, and less chances of being caught on camera."

"Well, the incident on the 401 has been the talk of the town all morning," he teased.

She blushed a little. "Yeah, well…less street cameras."

He nodded in agreement. "Just tell me what you need, weapons, tech…you name it and I'll get it for you."

Kyra watched the class move around the gallery, her gaze never leaving the young hybrid. "Papers. We need to create an entire backstory before I attend any school. Social media, ID, school records...everything a teenage girl would have for transferring schools."

"Alright."

"And this is between you and me. I don't want the Elders or Guardians knowing about this. Completely covert."

He inhaled through his nose and let it out slowly through his mouth. "With deniability. Alright...I have someone who can do that. So where are we setting up shop?"

She took a moment to think. There were a lot of small communities that would work, even a few cities that were dealing with their own crisis. Sudbury would make the most sense, or even North Bay. However, both had the same issues that Toronto had: too many ways out of the city and too many chances of being caught on camera. They needed some place with only one way in and one way out, a place where a major highway could be shut down for a short time without too many people noticing or being immediately affected. There were a few places like that, but she would have to research it first and see what the hybrid issue was there. After all, a small city hidden deep in the wilderness was uncommon, but such a place would be very appealing for the hybrids in hiding.

"I have an idea. Just give me a few days to do a little recon. It's a little out of the way," she told him as she stood. She headed toward the exit. "You know how to find me."

Chapter Two

The greatest archeological find of the century was also one of the greatest controversies in the world. Underground temples had been discovered all over the globe, each with the same strange, almost Aztec-like motif. Most were gone now, destroyed by cults; or by the military, looking to discover the secrets within, or by an alien force freeing the spacecrafts hidden inside. The one hidden in the Ishpatina Ridge, north of Sudbury, Ontario, was one of the few that remained fully intact, untouched, and virtually unknown, except to a select few. For Anthropologist Alexander Jackson, it was his second home. For almost thirteen years, he and his husband, Archeologist Lucas Griffith had spent every chance they could get investigating the temple. The pyramid was huge and every day was a long trek up the stone staircase to enter the structure. What made it distinctly alien was the fact that unlike most human built temples, this was all one structure, made of marble and limestone with large rooms and moving equipment. Despite investigating the temple for well over a decade, they were only a tenth of the way through it. Unlike the previous temples they had been in, this one they were able to take their time with. The set-up was exactly the same as the others, but for once they were not dealing with occultists, mercenaries, military, or Celestial getting in their way or rushing them through it to get to the Vault hidden deep inside. Here the Vault was dormant, shut down, and locked up. The few other people who knew of the temple had no interest the Vault or any other part of it other than making sure no one else ever found it.

With Kyra grown up and off on assignment, Alex and Lucas had more time to explore what had been dubbed the "Sanctuary." Unlike the other underground temples that they had been to, this one had an entire village with it. There were over a hundred stone buildings that were situated in front of the temple, as if facing it in worship. They were the first things Alex and Lucas had investigated when they became the Guardians of the Sanctuary. They were basic, simple living and eating quarters that once upon a time housed entire families. A river ran along the edge of the village, bringing in fresh water from an underground waterfall not far from the temple. It gave the cavern an ethereal feel as the mist filled the chamber, glistening off the marble and turning the artificial overhead lighting an eerie green.

Alex and Lucas were on the fourth floor of the temple, carefully archiving the ancient carvings and engravings set into the stone walls. It would at least another month or two to document every inch of it, but they had time and Alex enjoyed the slow leisurely pace at which they were working. It wasn't like their other digs where they had limited time and governments or agencies breathing down their necks to get it done. In fact, the person who left them in charge of the temple already knew everything about it. She had left them to investigate on their own, asking only that they protect the temple and village, which they gladly did, despite their history with other temples and the Vaults within.

Carefully brushing aside dust, Alex cleaned an intricate engraving on the wall, working slowly and diligently to clear the entire section before scanning it. Lucas was working on another part of the room, doing the same as one of the three quadruped drones moved about the room, scanning the sections that were clean and ready. All the data it gathered was stored in its memory banks, only accessible to them. Lucas had purchased them, as well as several other drones to help protect the site and assist them in their research. They carried what little equipment they needed as well as patrolled the site when Alex and Lucas were above ground, reporting anything unusual in real time with streaming video and audio. They, mixed with the flying drones, made for some of the best security available.

"Any clue what you want for dinner?" Lucas asked. He swapped several tools on the drone stationed next to him, his focus never wavering from the engraving fresco he was working on.

Alex shrugged. "I don't know. I was thinking of going fishing...maybe have a cook out. We haven't done that a while."

A grin lifted his lips as Lucas sighed. They had been together over seventeen years and came from completely different lifestyles, despite their careers almost mirroring one another's. Lucas was more posh, preferring a very upper-class lifestyle even though they lived in the mountains. He didn't like hunting or fishing and instead made sure their freezer and pantry were well stocked with the best food money could buy. Alex was the opposite. He wasn't big on hunting but he liked fishing and having a good fish-fry whenever he could. It had been a long time since they last had one.

"What if I made lamb tonight?" Lucas offered, clearly not interested in fishing.

Alex perked up. As much as he liked a fish-fry, he loved Lucas's lamb. It was one of those meats that had to be cooked just right to not end up greasy or tough. Not only like, but Lucas made the best red wine sauce to go with a rack of lamb. Alex turned away from what he was working on to look at his husband.

"Alright, I'm always up for being spoiled," he teased. "Paint me a picture...a rack of lamb with red wine sauce and..."

18

He bit his lower lip, hoping Lucas would fall for the bait.

Lucas shook his head and chuckled. "First, I would let the lamb marinate in the red wine while I season the little baby potatoes you love so much and…"

Alex's smartphone rang, surprising both of them. Very few people called either one of them, those that did rarely did so during the day when they were usually working underground. Their phones worked underground thanks to equipment previously installed by members of the Canadian Armed Forces in order to monitor the temple.

He leaned against the wall and smiled fondly as Kyra's number appeared on the screen.

"Hey, sweetheart," he greeted, setting the phone to speaker mode.

He shared a look with Lucas as the older man strolled over.

"Hi Daddy," Kyra's cheerful voice answered. "Is Pappy there, too?"

"I'm here, honey," Lucas answered. His face lit up at the sound of her voice.

They were "empty nesters," their daughter now a grown woman and off on her own. It still took some getting used to. The last twelve years seemed to have flown by since the day Kyra became part of their little family. One moment she was a lost little girl in need of protection, the next she was a grown woman off on her own adventures, searching for more beings like herself.

"Where are you?" Alex asked, happy that she called home.

She called at least once a day, something both he and Lucas knew would not last long, so they enjoyed every phone call until that dreaded day that the calls would become less frequent, or worse, stopped all together. Alex refused to dwell on that thought as Lucas leaned against the wall next to him.

"Actually...I'm on the ferry heading to South Baymouth," Kyra answered. She sounded a little hesitant saying that.

Alex's brows rose in surprise. "Why are you going to Manitoulin Island?"

She sighed. "It's a long story. I could have driven over but I needed to clear my head. We'll be launching shortly. I wanted to call before the ferry was out of tower range."

"No, no, that's good," Alex insisted. "I'm just happy you're okay."

"So, what assignment?" Lucas asked, clearly as worried as Alex was.

There was a pause before Kyra answered. "Apparently there's been a bunch of kids going missing on the Island. We...uh...we think they may be hybrids. There could be a hidden temple there or in Lake Huron. Either way, it's been nearly a dozen kids now and while it's not as bad of a situation as down south, it's making people worried."

"What's the plan?"

She hesitated a moment. "Enroll in the new high school in Little Current and try and track down the hybrids from there. The only bridge on and off the island is there so unless they're taking the kids off by boat or plane, I should be able to stop any truck. In theory at least."

Alex nodded. Kyra was very good at sensing others like her, but she was right; it would be near impossible for her to keep up with a boat or plane without such modes of transportation being readily available for her.

"What do you need from us?"

"Anything, sweetheart, money…a place to stay? We can come down there," Lucas assured, ready to pack up and help their daughter at a moment's notice.

Kyra gave a small laugh. "I do need to find an apartment," she admitted. "And paperwork to get registered at the high school. Would you mind filling that out for me and emailing it to the school?"

"Of course!" Lucas answered. "And I'll have an apartment lined up for you before you reach South Baymouth. I'll text you the address."

"Thanks, Papa."

"Are you sure you don't want us to go there?" Alex asked.

It never sat right with him that Kyra was working with Earth Defense Command, a faction of the United Nations that was meant to guard against possible alien attack as well as find and protect the Celestial hybrids that were hidden across the planet. There were a lot more than anyone would have imagined. Many were left alone to be raised by their human parent, not seen as a threat but closely monitored. Those that were a threat…were handled, usually taken to a facility that could help them learn to control their gifts and sedate their hunger. The really dangerous ones…they were put down before anyone else could be harmed. Unfortunately, EDC was not the only agency searching for hybrids. Something much darker was kidnapping them and turning them into weapons. Kyra was doing her best to find them before that

21

happened. She had been a victim herself as a child. A "failed" experiment after the government made sure she could not reproduce. That was how Alex and Lucas met her and later adopted her. Now she did her best to protect others like her. The only thing that Alex feared was she had yet to feed, something both he and Lucas had expected to happen when she began maturing into a young woman. Yet it appeared as if she had no sexual drive, something for which Alex was grateful. He had no clue what he would do if her Celestial side took hold of her. Celestials fed through sex and quite literally eating the heart of their victims. Alex knew that all too well. He had been possessed by one many years ago. It was not an experience someone could ever forget. He didn't want Kyra or anyone else to ever have to go through it.

"I'm okay, Dad. I promise," she answered, drawing him out of his thoughts. "We're pulling away from the dock. I'll call you when I get to Little Current."

"Okay...be careful, baby."

"We love you," Lucas threw in.

"I love you, too," she responded.

A moment later, the phone app turned off. With a sigh, Alex slid it into his back pocket again then wiped at his eyes, unable to help the tears that came whenever he had to say goodbye to his daughter. It was unlikely he would ever get used to her not be home. He missed teaching her about anthropology alongside Lucas and his archeology teachings. Sometimes it felt very lonely without her.

Lucas intertwined his fingers with Alex's. "Let's go home. I promised you lamb and if we want it to marinate long enough, I need to take it out of the freezer now and work on the sauce. After that..." he pressed his forehead against Alex's temple. "I'll remind you of the benefits of having an empty nest."

22

Alex chuckled and leaned against him. "I could use a break."

Kyra stared out over Lake Huron as the ferry moved slowly into the Great Lake. It was the perfect day to travel by ferry. The lake was calm and air warm enough for her to sit out on deck rather than inside with most of the other passengers. The sound of a fiddle playing filled the air as live entertainment played on a low stage. She sighed contently. Two hours on the ferry was much more relaxing than driving the highways all the way to the island. She missed her dads though. The last time she had been on the ferry was with them went they took a family trip to Niagara Falls. They could have flown but Dad said the ferry was an experience everyone needed to have at least once. Kyra fell in love with it. This was her first time taking it by herself but taking the ferry was much better than driving right now, even if it took about the same amount of time.

She needed to think and get herself organized. Almost her entire life had been spent in solitude. The first seven years she had been raised in a lab with no real mom or dad to care for her just lab technicians who were more concerned about her alien half than her being a child. The next twelve were with Alex and Lucas, a gay couple who had done everything in their power to protect her when mercenaries and Shadow demons kidnapped her. They adopted her and together they moved to the Ishpatina Ridge, a remote mountain range north of Sudbury. There she learned to master her gifts and take on a more human like form. Her pale features now had a sense of warmth as she blended Alex's and Lucas's features into her own, as if she were their biological daughter. She had Lucas's height, strong jaw line and nose mixed with Alex's hair colour, eyes, and cheekbones. Her build was slim but not tiny. After all, back home she often hiked all across the mountain side or swam and fished when not studying.

She had never stepped foot in a school before, being completely homeschooled. That worried her. How was she supposed to pretend to be a high school student when she had never been one before? It was going to take some serious research and she did that by observing the teenagers around her. This was not going to be an easy assignment. Finding hybrids were easy enough, convincing them of what they were and trying to keep them away from whomever was kidnapping them was another thing all together. She wasn't sure how to bond with another teenager. Everyone she knew were adults. The hybrids she had saved were either reunited with their parents or taken to a safehouse where humans and rebel Celestials helped them master their abilities before the hunger took hold of them. She rarely even got to learn their names. The difference between this mission and the previous ones was she wasn't there to track down the missing kids but to prevent others from being taken. That didn't mean she wouldn't try to find the others, but she knew how slim the chances were of ever finding them. Those she had rescued so far had been by sheer luck. She couldn't rely on luck to help her find these kids anymore. It was time to go undercover as one of them.

Chapter Three

Another new school. Liam cranked up the volume on his ear buds to cut out the noise of teenagers rushing through the halls to their classes. He had barely been inside the high school for more than a few minutes, but he already hated it. He couldn't understand why his mother loved it so much. It just went in one big circle – or more precisely one big square with a courtyard in the center. There was nothing unique or eye-catching like his old school. There was only one sad looking courtyard that didn't seem quite as welcoming as his old one. Nonetheless, his mother insisted he would come to like it as much as the other one. Liam doubted it. He glanced at the piece of paper the secretary gave him and looked at the numbers on the doors. It might be a square building, but it was confusing. It was bad enough he was the new kid - he had transferred less than a month into the fall semester due to delays in the contract for the building his mother had decided to lease for her bookstore and her reluctance to move until she knew for sure the building was theirs - but he didn't want to draw any more attention than necessary by asking for directions.

He turned a corner certain he had already passed it before and glared at the classroom across from him. Nope, 212B. Which meant 214A should be…

He walked a few doors down then frowned. It should have been the next door, but that lead to an intersection. One way led back to the main office and gym while the other went off into what appeared to be a surprisingly dark and foreboding hallway. It would be just his luck that his homeroom would be down there. He bit back a groan and headed down the hall.

There was a set of doors leading outside. He paused in front of them, debating if he should just make a break for it and forget school all together. But where would he go? This was a new town but it was small, his mother would find out quickly enough. The school would call her and then she would be forced to shut the store down and go look for him which would lead to a lecture and that oh-so-disappointed look she would get when he did something he knew would upset her. Skipping school was something that would upset her, and Liam couldn't bear to see that disappointed look in her eyes, not after how hard she had struggled to get the store up and running. As much as he hated it, he had to make the best of the situation. At least this was only home room. He had computer lab first period. Hopefully, it was as sophisticated as his old school. After computers was another tech class then lunch, Math class followed by English. He could manage that. At least he didn't have French this semester. He would go nuts if he had another teacher butcher the French language like his last one did. Honestly, only French people should teach French classes, or someone who spoke it fluently at the least.

He shook away that stray thought as he finally found the right classroom and slipped inside.

It was much brighter in the classroom. The windows were all open allowing the fresh mid-fall air in and there were plants seated in front of them. It was a vast contrast to the hallway.

"Liam Peters?" a woman in her mid-thirties with dark brown hair and a Korean accent asked.

Liam quickly turned off his music and took out his ear buds. "Yeah, sorry. Hi."

She gave him a pointed look, obviously not happy about the ear buds in the school. "Please turn off your cell phone and put the buds away," she instructed.

He did so quickly without objection which made the woman relax and smile softly at him.

"I'm Ms. Melange." She gestured to an empty desk two roles back and a roll away from the window. "Take a seat next to Kyra. She's also new to our school. Perhaps you two can help each other get acquainted with the layout."

26

He glanced at the girl in question and blinked in surprise. She had fiery red hair tied back in a series of braids that knotted into one thick one that went down her back to just past her waist. Her slim shoulders were tense, and her posture looked as if she was either ready for a fight or to bolt from the room. And he had thought he was having a hard time adjusting.

Taking a deep breath, Liam sat next to her. "At least we have a nice view," he said by way of greeting.

She said nothing in response, her gaze solely on what was happening outside, which was nothing. There was fresh cut grass that was a little patchy, several trees that swayed in the breeze and a path that led up to the street at the top of the small hill. There was nothing remotely interesting happening, not even traffic.

"What are you looking at?" he asked, trying to see what she saw. "Are the pixies playing hopscotch?"

She jerked in surprise at that and turned to stare at him with intense blue eyes. "What did you say?"

He gave her a smile. "It was a joke. My mother owns a bookstore and has a thing for pixies. She asks me that whenever my mind wanders."

She blinked slowly and for a moment her eyes seemed to change and her iris paled, becoming almost non-existent. Liam couldn't help but stare, but it happened so quickly that he doubted he had seen what he thought he had. He stared at her for a moment longer, trying to understand what he had just seen then dismissed it as a trick of the light.

"My name's Liam," he said by way of introduction.

"I know," she answered.

She turned her attention back to the window and whatever had caught her attention outside. It was like a sudden wall went up between them, not visible to the naked eye but certainly felt by Liam.

He frowned and looked toward the front of the class.

"Yeah, it was nice to meet you, too," he grumbled under his breath.

When it was time to go to his first class, he left without waiting for Kyra. He had tried talking to her and she made it obvious she wasn't interested in making friends so he wouldn't push her. That was up to her. He had his own life to worry about. Thankfully, he had spotted the computer lab on his search for homeroom. He headed there, his mood sour. He quickly introduced himself to the teacher and asked for a seat that wasn't already claimed by someone else. The last thing he needed was someone down his neck for taking their favourite computer or some such thing. He just wanted to be left alone.

He felt at home working on a computer. He classified himself as a gamer even though his mother reprimanded him constantly for spending too much time on his electronics and urged him to find a better hobby. He was also a YouTuber and he was slowly working on his own vlog. Most of it was about gaming which meant he bought and tried out some of the newest and hottest games and talked about them on his channel. He filmed himself playing, showed other gamers how to play, and offered tips to pass certain levels. Of course, his mother didn't understand that. She was a bookworm and was a little disappointed that Liam didn't follow in her footsteps. What she didn't know was that all the time Liam spent creating his own videos had also encouraged him to try making his own short films and study computer animation, which just so happened to be one of the things he would be learning in this class. It was basic animation but animation nonetheless and he was surprised that a high school in such a small city had the funding to offer such a course.

Pulling out a thumb drive from his bag, he slipped it into the USB drive and uploaded the files from his old school. The project he had been working on was transferrable and his new school was allowing him to finish it as part of his course. The program both schools used was the same, so the transition was quick and easy. After the teacher gave his lecture about modelling and coding movement – something Liam already knew – he began detailing his model and adding texture. If he wanted to get into the gaming industry, he needed the perfect antagonist for his protagonists to battle. In this case, a dragon. He wanted to avoid the cliché of a dragon guarding a treasure or castle and was almost tempted to try a steampunk take and make the dragon robotic, but it didn't have quite the same feel.

Time flew by as he focused on his creation. He zoomed in, adjusted the eyes, deepened the scales, and elongated the horns, then he would sit back and study it before making more minute changes. He wanted the dragon to appear as realistic as possible given the limited technology he had available. If only he could upgrade his computer and programs at home. He would buy the top of the line if he could. For now, he had to make do with what he had and was available at school while he saved every cent he had to buy an entirely new system. All he needed was half the money and his mother promised to pay the other half. He would need to look for an afterschool job on top of his work at the bookshop if he ever hoped to rake up enough to get the system he wanted. Perhaps there was a job board that he could look at when lunch time rolled around.

Class ended all too soon. Liam saved his work onto the thumb drive and shoved it back in his bag. The rest of the day moved slowly as he was forced to introduce himself to each new teacher. He forgot about looking for a job board and simply focused on not getting lost as he went to the lunchroom then outside to get away from to endless chatter of his fellow classmates. He didn't see the strange redhead from his homeroom for the rest of the day. They obviously had no classes together, and soon enough he forgot about her.

At the end of school, he made the trek downtown. It was only a fifteen-minute walk and Liam took his time. Little Current was a beautiful little town even if it was a in the middle of nowhere, lacked the resources he had become accustomed to, and he didn't know a single soul. The lakes and greenery sort of made up for it but not enough, not just yet. He gazed off over the lake across town toward the old train bridge they had to cross to get onto the island. If he could find people interested, he may be able to pull off a good short horror film. Or maybe his mom would let some of his friends come up for a weekend and they could hike out there and film. The footage could work as a backdrop for just about any film he made. He tilted his head, trying to picture it in his mind. There were a few benefits to living smack dab in the wilderness. He would never have this type of footage back home without having to drive a half hour or more to get away from the city and nearby farmland. But the bridge was narrow, allowing only one vehicle at a time. Getting good shots on it could be tricky. Perhaps he would give it a try on the weekend. All he needed was his smartphone but, in this case, he would prefer his camcorder for better quality and memory space.

The bookstore was situated in an old building on Main Street, not far from shopping or restaurants. There was a steady flow of traffic, both foot and vehicle, but when Liam opened the door, he was surprised to see it was empty. His mother, a middle-aged woman with greying hair, jumped at the sound of the old bell over the door, and stopped setting up books on the shelves to greet him with a smile. There was a moment of disappointment at it not being a customer, but she quickly hid it with a cheerful, "Hey, Liam."

"Hi, Mom," Liam offered.

He returned the smile and gave her a kiss on the cheek then headed to the back where there was a small kitchen with a latte machine and scones. He dropped his bag on the bench next to the stairwell that led up to their apartment.

"How was school?" his mother asked as followed him. "Did you make any new friends?"

"It's the same as any other school. Homework, study, avoid gym."

"Liam…"

He kept the annoyance off his face as he grabbed a mug off the shelf and made a latte. It was his idea to offer custom coffees and treats at the bookstore. Physical books were a dying breed and they needed something else to attract potential customers. He had spent the last few weeks learning how to use the machine and thought himself pretty good at it. Sadly, they had a few competitors against them who had been well established in the community for many years. He still thought their shop offered the best and had a more relaxing setup. Besides, his mom was the hardest working and most creative person he knew.

"It was good, Mom. I got to work on my character for a while. I should be able to animate it soon," he told her as he sat down at one of the tables close to the window. Maybe if he posed as a customer more people would come in. "How about you? Very many people come in today?"

She sighed and sat across of him. "No. But that's okay. I've been dusting and setting up. Perhaps on the weekend we'll have a big open house or something."

He hummed softly to himself. "Next weekend might be better. It gives us time to design posters and get the word out. You know, get a little bit of hype. I can also pass the word around school. Besides, isn't there supposed to be a cruise ship or something coming to town? That's sure to pick up business."

Her face lit up at the suggestion. "You're right. The guy a few doors over mentioned it. Maybe you can design the posters for me?"

She was an artist and could easily do it herself, but she liked it when Liam was involved in her projects. She always let it be his decision and never complained if he was too busy or had other plans. The choice was always his. Nevertheless, he nodded. It might be enough to create some sort of talking point at school. An ice-breaker of sorts. Liam wasn't interested in making a bunch of friends, but it would be nice to have at least one person to talk to. And maybe that person could help him with his film.

He helped her in the shop until nightfall and then it was time for him to do his homework and prepare for school the next day. He gave his mother a kiss on the cheek then headed up to his room. It wasn't completely set up yet. His cousin Jordon had promised to come over on the weekend and help him finish, but it had the essentials: his bed, dresser, and computer system which he turned on and threw his book-bag on his bed. It took a few minutes to boot up. While he waited, he set up his handheld camcorder on its stand and placed it where he thought it would have the best angle. He would likely have to adjust it when his program was up and running, but that was normal. The only thing he was missing was his green screen, but that was still packed away with the rest of his film gear.

"Alright," he announced once everything was ready.

He looked directly at the camera then put on his biggest smile…it promptly fell.

He sighed. "Maybe I shouldn't have done a live feed today," he told the camera and people who may or may not be watching. "Well, this is day one at a new school. Day three in a new city. So far…I'm not overly wowed. Mom loves the store, even if she hasn't had any customers yet. They'll eventually come. Anyone watching this that live in the Little Current, check out the Books & Lattes here on Main Street, she has something for everyone.

"And that was my obligated call out for the shop." He gave a small laugh. "But seriously, I have no idea what to make of this place. It's nice but I miss my friends and home and my studio set-up. The good news, my new room is larger so I may be able to set up a better studio. The downside, my new school sucks. I have yet to meet one interesting person or talk to anyone for more than a few minutes. I mean, where are the creatives in school? Is there a film class? According to my schedule there is but it took ten minutes to find the class only to find out it was cancelled today due to some illness. I did manage to sit in on another computer class, but they are so far behind from my old school that I could have been up front teaching the class. The teacher is nice though.

"And you would think new kids would stick together but no. The only other person in the entire school who was also starting their first day wants nothing to do with me. You'd think my clothes stunk or I had bad breath the way she acted. We talked for all of five seconds before she gave me the cold shoulder and disappeared. Talk about an ice-queen. My fellow men, when a woman treats you like that, avoid at all cost. She's not playing hard to get; she is telling you to stay the heck away. And ma'am, if you're watching this, message received. You don't have to worry about me."

He stretched and gave a small yawn. "So, after that drama of the day, I do have to admit Little Current is actually very picturesque. School is within walking distance and there's not much to see when walking in that direction other than houses and hills but on the way back it's kind of breath-taking with the river and LaCloche Mountains in the distance. Apparently, cruise ships actually come here with tourists, which is one of the reasons mom wanted the store here. Honestly, I think she just wants to jump on one of those ships for a vacation...I can't blame her for that. I haven't seen one yet, but I will be sure to film it when I do."

He glanced around his room as he tried to think of what else to say. Nothing came to mind.

"Well, I guess that's my update for today. Once I'm all set up again, I'll give an update on my film and perhaps take everyone on a tour of the shop. For now, this is Liam signing off."

He reached over and cut the feed to his streaming channel. The video would upload to all his streaming channels if it didn't go live. He didn't often use the live function. He couldn't go back and edit it when he did. But every now and then he liked it, especially when at events and wanting to share with his viewers. It would probably be better if he wrote a script to work from for the next one, at least until he felt a little more at home in the new town. It was better than rambling and complaining about school and some new girl who he didn't know and could be misjudging. Hell, she probably didn't want to be there either and being silent and cold was just her way of coping. He really hoped she wasn't one of his viewers.

Whatever the case, he didn't have time to worry about her. Even though it was his first day of school, he had two homework assignments to do and then help his mom with shutdown. Perhaps he could make a few videos to promote the shop and post on his streaming channels. Free publicity never hurt anyone. Heck, he could use it for his film as well. Maybe when Jordon arrived, they could plan out all the shots together. If his cousin brought his camcorder as well, they could film from different angles at the same time and limit the reshoots. Liam could write the script and Jordon fine tune the dialogue. They could both use the finished project for their final class assignments as long as both their names were on the work. They had done it in the past regardless of always being in different schools. That thought made Liam feel a little better. Things wouldn't be that different in a new school if coordinating with his cousin on film projects remained the same. With any luck, it would give them a high enough grade to be accepted in a film and animation program in college. He couldn't afford to attend one that specialized in it down south, but Sudbury and North Bay had decent enough colleges that offered the program. If he graduated that then maybe he could get a scholarship, or work part time to save up enough money for film school.

He flopped on his bed and stared at the ceiling in thought. He held up his right hand and formed a small plasma ball in it. It sizzled and crackled with energy but got no larger than a softball. It had taken a lot of practise when he first learned of his gifts, but his control over the energy around him had improved to the point that he could create most of the special effects for his films himself. Not that anyone knew.

He hadn't even told his mother. She didn't seem to share his gift; at least he had never seen her conduct energy the way he could, or any other unusual stuff as far as he knew, so he kept his ability a secret. He already felt out of place most days, he didn't need to add to it by letting people know what he could do.

He stared at the ball of energy for several long minutes in consideration. He could make this work. It would take time, but the location could work and once he was done high school, he could always go back to the city for college, but he had to keep his grades up. He needed a scholarship to get into the college he wanted. Even with his school savings, he wouldn't have enough to do the three-year course he wanted, and his mom wouldn't be able to afford to take-on the whole burden. Squashing the ball of energy, he reached for his backpack, pulled out his math textbook and binder, and got to work.

A strange sound caught his attention. He listened for a moment. It was a strange sort of crackling, similar to what his energy ball made, seemed to echo over the water, almost like lightning. It made the hairs on the back of his arms stand on end. Curious, he crossed the room to his window and opened it wide. There was nothing for several long seconds and then another crackling sound. It sounded much closer this time. He squinted his eyes and tried to see over the building across from him. When that didn't work, he turned off his light and tried again. He saw nothing, but the sound seemed even closer. This time he went to his closet and grabbed his telescope. It took a few minutes to set up, but the noise continued. It sounded like an approaching lightning storm, but there wasn't a cloud in the sky. His windows faced North, perhaps the storm was coming from the South. He quickly set the telescope up next to the large window and scanned the area. The streetlights made it hard to focus. Nonetheless, he kept searching until something large shot past his view finder. It appeared to be a ball of energy almost identical to what he had created but much, much larger. It caused the street lights to go out one by one as it passed them, as if absorbing their energy. Liam tracked it for a few moment before it suddenly darted over the bay and disappeared toward the La Cloche Mountain Range.

Surprised, he stepped back from the telescope.

"What in the world…" he murmured to himself.

He went back to the telescope to try finding it again but with no luck. Whatever it was it was gone now. The strange crackling soon ended as well, and the night became deathly quiet. Nevertheless, Liam was determined to figure out what it had been and catch it on video.

Chapter Four

For the first time since hearing they were moving, Liam felt excitement. He was up early the next morning, made sure his smartphone was fully charged, and after a quick bite to eat with his mother, he was out the door. He didn't head immediately to school, instead he wandered around downtown, looking at the tops of buildings for any trace of the creature he had seen the night before. The logical part of him said it had been nothing more than a silly dream, that he had been too tired and made it all up in his head, or that it was a trick of the light. After all there was no chance what he saw could possibly be real. There was no such thing as monsters, regardless of the stories his mother told him as a kid. Whatever he saw had to be caused by light reflecting off water or even a bird flying too close when he looked through the telescope. Nonetheless, he drew in energy from the surrounding area, hoping to find residue from the creature he had seen. Every living thing created a metaphysical footprint, one that could be followed without being seen. He pulled in everything around him, sensing the difference between human and animal and followed anything that seemed strange and unusual.

His excitement began to waver as he crossed the street. Maybe whatever he saw hadn't come into town. Perhaps it was out over the river and closer to the woods and he simply had the wrong eye piece in when he saw it, making it look far closer than he thought. Moving behind the row of businesses, he went to the catwalk and stared out over the water. There was nothing there, just water, the bridge down river, and trees across the river lining the LaCloche Mountain Range. There was nothing to indicate there was anything out of the ordinary. Yet something still felt off. It was as if someone or something was watching him now. It started with a tingling at the back of his head and worked its way down his neck and back. Something was out there, something that didn't want to be seen. His senses couldn't pick up exactly what, as if whatever it was could shield itself from him. He didn't run. He knew better than to show fear. Instead, he pulled out his smartphone and began recording. He kept his energy levels low in order to not effect the device. He moved slowly, making sure to catch the water and far off trees, the bridge and catwalk, until he turned right around and had a full panoramic recording. He was alone but if something was out there his camera was sure to have caught it. Once that was done, he turned off the camcorder part and dialled Jordon. There was something bigger out there than he originally thought. He knew without a doubt he was right.

"Hey," he said when his cousin answered. "When's the next time you're coming to Little Current?"

There was a sleepy yawn on the other side of the line. "Hi to you, too," Jordon mumbled. "What's up?"

"I think I may have found something. Can you come over tonight?"

"I'm studying for tests all week. How about Friday night? I can spend the weekend."

Liam made a noise in the back of his throat but sighing. "Yeah, okay. Do you think you can steal your dad's trail cameras?"

There was silence on the other end before Jordon gave a choked laugh. "You're kidding, right? Are you trying to get me killed?"

Liam rolled his eyes. He should have known asking for that would be too much. His uncle was an avid hunter and photographer. "Never mind, I'll order some online."

"What's going on?"

"I'll tell you when you get here…but it may be our best film project yet."

"Huh-uh…okay. I'll see you this weekend. There better be a cute girl in it."

"Yeah, right," Liam laughed.

He hung up as he approached the school. As if some girl here would ever be interested in one of his projects. So far, they all ignored him. If he was back home that would be different. He had known all the girls in his class since kindergarten and got along with most. Quite a few of them would have gladly helped him with any film project, not to be in it so much as the adventures they all had. Here? Everyone, girls, and guys, seemed to ignore him and for now, he wasn't overly interested in getting to know anyone. Not yet.

He arrived at the school early and headed directly to the library. There were a few other students already at the school. Most were there for sport related activities, but some were at the library finishing home or projects from the day before. Liam found a quiet corner and scrolled through his phone to the video he took. He would have to wait until he got home to run it through his computer and view it closely, but for now he wanted to see if he could spot anything he may have missed earlier.

Kyra stretched as she walked along the hall. It had been a long night and she had found absolutely nothing. The town looked like any other town she had visited over the years, which was the problem; looks were deceiving. Unless she found some sort of evidence of missing hybrids soon, Tyler was likely to try to pull her off the mission, provided she didn't simply walk away from it. Posing as a student was not her strong suit. So far, the Hybrids all seemed safe here. None had gone missing in months. Perhaps it was the time of year, although that didn't seem to matter down south. Of course, Southern Ontario and Northern Ontario were vastly different in both population and weather. There could be any number of reasons for the change in missing people. Personally, she couldn't understand why there were so many hybrids in the South compared to North. Then again it probably did make a lot of sense the more she thought about it. In cities like Toronto or even Ottawa, Celestials could hide in plain sight, find, and take a host with ease, and impregnate more people without suspicion. It could be messy when they fed, but with the number of murders in such large cities, it would be hard to find them. Even if they were captured by the police, the Celestial would simply abandon its host and find another, continuing on its merry way without fear of detection. Such a thing in the North would cause wide-spread panic and towns locking-down to protect their people.

There was a half hour before classes began. She headed to the library and found a dark, quiet corner to rest. It had been a late night.

She must have travelled across the entire island while on patrol. She had seen nothing. It was as if the whole world came to a stop after midnight with only the odd vehicle on the road. It was so much nicer than chasing down transports on a major highway, but the lack of action was also far more tiring than being in the thick of things.

She had just dozed off when a hand grasped her shoulder and gave her a little shake. She awoke with a start. Instinct momentarily took hold of her and it was by sheer willpower that she managed to stop herself from lashing out. Blinking rapidly, she gazed up at the young man standing over her.

The youth was from her homeroom. He was the one who had spoken to her the day before. Now he regarded her with curiosity and a little hesitance as he let go of her and stepped back.

"Sorry," he said.

He didn't seem surprised or upset. Kyra took that as a good sign that she had managed to keep her appearance intact. She opened her mouth to ask what he wanted but he was already talking again.

"The bell just rang," he informed her. "We need to head to class."

She blinked in surprise. So, she had fallen asleep. She must have been more tired than she thought. With a yawn, she nodded and wiped at her tired eyed.

"Yeah, thanks."

"Long night?"

Her entire body felt stiff and it hurt to get up. "You could say that."

"Me too," he said, stepping out of her way.

He fell silent for a moment as she stood and stretched her arms over her head. Kyra paid him no mind. He was nearly a head shorter than her despite being average height for a male his age. Kyra eyed him as she worked out the kinks in her neck. He should have left already but instead he waited for her. He didn't stare at her or anything, he simply rolled his shoulders and looked toward the computer station until she was done stretching and picked up her bag.

"So…uh…did you hear that strange noise last night?" he finally asked as they left together.

Kyra raised a curious brow. "What noise?" she asked, trying to recall if she heard anything out of the ordinary while on patrol.

He shook his head. "Kind of like a storm rolling in. Lightning crackling but no thunder." He rubbed the back of his neck nervously. "It was weird."

"That is weird," she mused, trying to sound genuinely interested.

He shrugged.

She nodded. "It was probably echoing over Lake Huron."

"Yeah, but I checked the weather report. It was clear all night, and there was this…" he fell silent and looked away.

"What?" Kyra prompted.

"You wouldn't believe me."

"Try me."

He merely shook his head and said no more, clearly embarrassed to have brought any of it up.

They were silent as they neared their classroom. Liam seemed to have a habit of picking at his watch as he stared straight ahead, as if afraid he might say something wrong. Kyra had seen others do it around her, a nervous reaction toward her, no doubt caused by the alien aura of power that surrounded her. While most humans could not sense what she was, there were some who were sensitive enough to feel the energy that moved all around her. It seemed Liam was a sensitive.

"So about yesterday," he began. His hand moved from his watch to rub his forearm. "And today…I didn't mean to bother you. I know transferring schools can suck and people aren't always ready to make new friends, so I'll leave you alone if you want."

She blinked in surprise. She hadn't expected that and was taken aback as he hurried ahead of her, not waiting to see if maybe she had had a change of thought. Tilting her head to one side, she watched him enter the class. Was she projecting her distaste of posing as a student too much? Was he sensing it? Or was she simply too standoffish? A sensitive would pick that up instantly.

She kept a closer eye on him during homeroom. Liam was his name, she reminded herself, didn't appear to be a Hybrid. At least he didn't feel like one. He should be safe from whoever was kidnapping Hybrids. Nonetheless, she was curious. Something felt off about him.

She made a note of it and decided to keep an eye on him. If the kid wasn't a hybrid, he could be helping those that were hunting them down, or he could simply be some silly kid that was oversensitive to the world around him. Either way, she needed to watch him.

Unfortunately, that was easier said than done considering they had different classes.

Kyra pushed her wayward thoughts aside as she tracked down those she could sense as hybrids. Few had any clue what they were. That was the sad thing about their kind. Most had single parents, raised by the human parent, were adopted, or foster kids with no clue of what they true were. They often sported unusual feature like unearthly-pale and almost translucent skin, incredibly pale eyes and hair, or gifts that appeared almost magical in nature. Kyra didn't have the heart to tell them otherwise so instead did her best to make friends and get their basic information in order to keep an eye on them. The ones that did know their true heritage were suspicious of her intentions. It was easier to pose as a human when there was no energy around to amplify their own. Which was also why so many of them appeared to be loners, avoiding other people, both of their own kind as well as human.

Very few heeded her warning, but she expected as much. She would protect them as best she could but her true mission was to find out who was behind the kidnappings. Regardless of how each hybrid felt, she let her own energy brush over each one. If someone attempted to capture any of them, she would know immediately.

She was exhausted by the end of school. There were only five hundred students in the school, four of which were hybrids, which was small compared to the high schools in the larger towns. Trying to find and talk to each during the lunch hour as well as pose as a student was not nearly as easy as she originally thought it would be. On top of that, she had homework. She glared at the books in her arms. She was a Hunter not a student. Why did she put herself in such a position? If she had posed as a teacher, it would have made much more sense. Of course, it would have taken longer to get each Hybrid alone without a lot of questions. Strange people didn't just walk into a school and demand to talk to a group of kids without a legitimate reason, regardless if they were a teacher or a police officer. Students mingling together was much easier, except now she had homework that was due the next day. How was she supposed to get all this done plus attend a meeting with Tyler and do patrol that night?

Her gaze shifted as she noticed Liam at his locker further down the hall. It looked like he had homework as well as he shoved a few textbooks in his backpack. She still couldn't understand why she was drawn to him. She watched him carefully, trying to read his aura and make sense of what she kept feeling from him. He seemed nice enough but where she could sense the energy of Hybrids, he was like a black hole, as if drawing in everything around him. She had heard of people like him, not a psychic vampire but a dampener of sorts. It was intriguing. She wasn't sure why she had not noticed this before. There were very few like him. Perhaps it had shielded him from her initial psychic sweep.

Shrugging her own backpack onto one shoulder, she closed and locked her locker then strolled toward him. A small smile lifted her lips as she tried to think of something, anything to talk about.

"Hey," she said in greeting. She brushed back her long mahogany hair and tried not to look threatening.

Liam looked up at her in obvious shock.

"Hi," he answered.

He pulled the zipper closed on his bag before shrugging it onto his back, then closed his locker. He didn't say anything else and instead waited for her to talk. Kyra hummed softly at that. So, she had scared him the last few times they spoke.

"Do you have a lot of homework?" she asked, unsure what to say.

She couldn't straight out ask if he knew he was a "black hole". Not very many people knew such things existed and even less knew when they were one.

He shrugged. "I got most of it done in class. I'm just working on a large project and need a few books. I'd rather be ahead than behind in class."

She nodded. It made sense, especially considering he had just transferred schools.

"What subject?" she asked, trying to sound interested. She was more interested in the way his aura fluctuated with her proximity.

"Computer animation."

42

He bit his lower lip in a way Kyra could only think of as cute, and looked past her down the hall. Her gaze followed his, expecting to find another student watching them, perhaps even a jealous girl who was eyeing Liam as a dating prospect, but all she saw were students hurrying about to gather their stuff for home. As she turned back to him, she caught a glimpse of a ball of energy, too quick for her to follow. It wasn't any of the spirit Guardians. Whatever it was consumed Liam's attention for several moments before he looked back at her.

"I need to go," he said briskly.

He headed for the nearest exit with no other explanation.

Kyra looked back in the direction Liam had been staring moments ago and did a psychic sweep. There as nothing there, not even one of the Hybrids. Whatever Liam had seen or sensed; he was the only one to witness it. Unease filled her. First, Liam had heard a strange crackling sound the night before, now this. There was more to Liam than she originally thought. Perhaps he was a hybrid and had learned to shield himself at an early age.

She decided to follow him. He may not be involved in the kidnappings, but he could be in just as much danger.

Keeping a safe distance, she altered her form to appear older, her red hair less vibrant and closer to a deep brown while her eyes become a deep blue. She followed him from the school downtown. It was quiet, a stark relief from what she had experienced while down south. A warm breeze ruffled her hair, as the smells of fall filled her senses.

One of the many spirits that walked the edge between the living and the dead approached her. A Guardian spirit she often worked with when tracking hybrids. She listened to the Guardian as she walked along the sidewalk. Her gaze stayed firmly on Liam until he rounded the corner on Main Street then she glanced toward the spirit.

"What do you mean he's here already?" she asked the Guardian in a hushed whisper.

She glanced around, hoping no one noticed her talking to thin air before remembering that most people would not think anything of it. What people once would have thought as crazy or the work of witchcraft was generally accepted as technology now. She could talk freely and at a normal volume, and those passing by her would simply think she was talking on a Bluetooth headset to a friend. It was a strange concept and she absently brushed her hand over her smartphone.

She sighed as the spirit spoke, her whispery voice so soft no human could possibly hear it. "Alright, tell him I'll be there shortly. I'm following a lead."

She waved off the being as it insisted she head toward the meeting place immediately. Tyler could wait a little longer.

She rounded the corner, but Liam was gone. Irritation immediately filled her. She had allowed herself to become distracted by the Guardian and lost track of her prey. She sniffed the air. He couldn't have gone far. There were only a handful of stores on either side of the road. It took a moment to catch his scent. It was mixed with all the others: humans, animals, and exhaust fumes from the vehicles traveling slowly along the street. The mixture almost masked the natural smells of the season. Her senses perked when she followed the trail along the sidewalk to a small bookstore. That made sense, he had said he needed to do research for his project. What she wasn't prepared for was the sudden wall of energy she encountered as she reached for the door handle. It caused her to step back in shock. It was raw power, untamed and almost threatening, chaotic in nature. It was not something she expected to find at a store, let alone one that hoped to stay in business long.

Curiosity got the best of Kyra. She pushed open the door and stepped inside. At first glance it appeared like any other indie bookstore. There were shelves of novels along one wall, with the owner's pick proudly displayed on a shelf in front of the window. Related items sat on a counter next to a small digital cash machine along with several gift items. A small café with free Wi-Fi signs and plugins was located across from the books. A few people were seated at the table sipping lattes while reading. It was a nice little setup and would probably do much better if not for the chaotic energy sweeping throughout the store. It would almost be cozy. Kyra was an avid reader and she couldn't help but look over the vast collection of books, her curiosity piqued. She didn't recognize many of the authors but there were quite a few with "signed by the author" stickers and "local author" displays. Two books immediately caught her attention and she couldn't help but smile at them fondly. "Hidden Secrets of the Temples" Volumes 1 and 2 were proudly displayed on two stands on a shelf close to the cashier counter. The gold "signed by the author" sticker stood proudly on each book, next to images of an underground Aztec temple, one she knew intimately. Without thinking, she picked up volume one and turned it over to gaze at the author photos on the back. One the bottom left was an image of Anthropologist Alex Jackson, looking handsome with a tiny grin. The image was of his left side, the side not scarred from a terrible accident that happened when he first discovered one of these temples. Across from him was Archeologist Lucas Griffith, looking dashing as ever with his salt and pepper hair, goatee, and little smirk. Kyra remembered when the pictures were taken and how self-conscious both of them were having their pictures taken. They had all but cut themselves off from civilization, only leaving their mountain home and research centre for vacation. Aunt Elizabeth had taken the photographs, the only person either of them felt comfortable enough with. She was another researcher but worked more as a liaison between them and the government, Earth Defence Command in particular.

"Can I help you find something?" a middle-aged woman with greying hair asked politely.

Kyra looked away from the books to the woman in a mix of surprise and awe, almost forgetting her whole purpose for entering the store.

"Where did you get these?" she asked before she could think better of it.

The woman smiled softly. "I travel and I know some of the authors personally. Is there one you're interested in?"

"No...I was just happy to see these here," Kyra answered. She gave a small laugh and tapped the pictures. "They're my dads."

She almost kicked herself a moment later for revealing that. She could have just endangered them and herself, especially when she felt a sudden flare of energy. Celestial energy. Her gaze fixated on the store owner.

That caused the woman to raise a questioning brow as Kyra studied her. She held Celestial energy, raw and untamed. She should have been able to read who and what Kyra was, yet she seemed unfazed by her presence. It was almost as if she didn't know what Kyra was. Could she be a hybrid? An unknown, someone who had no clue of her origin just like some of the teenagers at the high school. She had no hidden form, no glamour to hide her Celestial heritage. It wasn't unheard of, but to have such power and no one detect it until now was rare and practically unheard of. Kyra may have blown her cover.

Nonetheless, Kyra masked her surprise with a smile. "They would be thrilled to see their books here. They're working on a third volume."

Delight filled the woman's face at the news. "That's great! We're planning a big open house this weekend. Maybe they would like to come. We can host a book signing. I have a few copies in stock, but I can place an order for more. All they can drink lattes!"

"I'll see what I can do," Kyra promised. "It was nice meeting you."

"Marie," the woman said, sticking out her hand.

Kyra hesitated a moment before taking it. She expected a surge of power, but nothing happened. Marie's power may be raw but it seemed she did have a level of control over it.

"Kyra," she returned.

She gave Marie a grin then glanced past her to the back of the shop. She was taken aback when she spotted Liam wearing an apron. He was working with what she guessed was the latte machine. Now it made sense. Liam was Marie's son. No wonder he felt so odd to her. He was a next generation hybrid, his mother the true hybrid. She opened her mouth, about to say something but promptly shut it. If Marie didn't know what she was then Liam certainly had no clue and it wasn't her place to reveal it. She would simply watch them both and keep them safe for as long as possible.

* * * * *

Kyra couldn't stop thinking about Liam and his mother. She was happy her lodgings were downtown, taking up one of the empty apartments over a nearby store. She didn't want to be directly across from them, it would set up too much suspicion, but there was a location on the next street that was elevated by a small hill and gave her a direct view of the rooftops for the line up of stores on the main street. She hadn't thought that to be important until she spotted Liam on the roof of his mother's store setting up a telescope from her perch on the roof of her own building. She hesitated, unsure if she should hide her presence or not. He was looking toward the river and forest beyond and not her direction. It would only take a moment for him to spot her if he turned around. She watched him for a few minutes in fascination as he turned the telescope toward the heavens. It was dark and the stars were shining brightly. So, he wasn't trying to search for the creature he claimed to have heard the night before, he was star gazing. It was the perfect night for it. There wasn't a cloud in the sky, and he could easily see for miles around. Kyra smiled anyway. She couldn't help it; the kid was becoming more and more interesting by the moment. She absently wondered if the night called to him like it did her.

"He's interesting," a soft voice noted.

Kyra gave a small nod. "That he is."

"You're certain he's a second-generation hybrid?"

She was still unsure of that. There was something about Liam, something unique, but it wasn't the same as a hybrid, at least not like any she knew. It was subdued, almost nonexistent. She was certain it was due to his mother. Marie was definitely a hybrid and regardless if she knew it or not, she was shielding herself pretty hard, something most hybrids didn't know how to do.

"Yes," she confirmed.

She glanced toward the Guardian next to her. Normally it would be her Uncle Owen watching over her, but he had stepped back when she declared her independence. After all, she was an adult now. Nonetheless, he would not let her go without someone watching her back. In came Jalyn, a Guardian her age who had been a part of the research team that discovered the underground temple in British Columbia almost eighteen years ago along with Kyra's dad, Alex. She now served as Kyra's eyes and ears when she could not keep on top of her target. The Guardians could best be described as ghosts, the spirits of researchers and rebels who either discovered the temples over the decades, or had fought against the Celestials millennia ago. There were living Guardians, like her Aunt Elizabeth, as well. Earth Defense Command. They were new and worked to help protect the hybrids, teaching them how to live amongst human without feeding from them…or at least feed without killing them, often allowing the hybrids to feed from them instead. This was particularly necessary as the hybrids became sexually active and their hunger almost overpowering. A starving, sexually active hybrid was as dangerous as a Celestial, perhaps more so if they began hunting. Kyra had personally been forced to kill two over the last year and it scarred her in ways she did not want to consider, especially when she almost became the victim of one of them. She didn't want to see the same thing happen to Liam.

In all honesty, she feared what might happen if she ever felt the "hunger". She made it a point not to get involved with anyone and had not felt the desire to do so.

"Keep an eye on him, Jalyn," she said. "I need to meet up with Tyler."

The Guardian gave an annoyed huff. "I don't trust him," she warned.

Jalyn had not been particularly happy when Kyra returned from Toronto to report she had teamed up with someone to find the missing hybrids.

Shaking her head, Kyra left Liam under her friend's watchful eye. Liam should be in bed, not out stargazing at this time in the morning. He had school in a few hours. They both did. And she should be on duty, not meeting up with Tyler at some seedy tavern after hours.

She made a note to change her appearance enough to appear in her mid to late twenties. Last thing she needed was someone thinking she was some kid going to the tavern. That would draw far more attention than she wanted.

Archer's Tavern was across the street from the new apartment which made things much easier. She hurried across, intent on being done with the meeting as quickly as possible in order to do patrol before having to go through another day of school. She had managed a few hours of sleep earlier in the evening but was still extremely tired. She was happy her Pappy was able to find her a place so close to all the amenities and school. Furnished apartments were surprisingly easy to

48

come by when rent was on a week-to-week basis. Lucas had found a studio apartment right downtown. It cost slightly more since it was classified as waterfront, or close to it at least, but Lucas didn't care. He had the funds to cover it.

She slipped into the tavern from the side entrance. It wasn't that late at night, just shortly before midnight, but it was a weekday and it seemed business was slow which meant the tavern was already set to close for the evening. Nevertheless, the tavern was still lit as the staff cleaned up after the now gone night-crowd. Chairs were turned onto tables as the hardwood floor was mopped. Music played from an old-style jukebox, the shiny CDs the only indication it was built within the last thirty years. The bar itself was much older. The floors were made of hardwood stained such a dark mahogany that it was hard to tell if they were the original wood or replaced. She was certain they were made of cedar judging from the matching pillars on either side of the bar. The bar at the far end was also made of wood and polish until it gleamed. The tables and chairs were much newer but still made of wood and stained a sleek black with wine-coloured cushions that matched the two pool tables on the left side of the tavern near to juke box. The building was at least a century old if not older, and Kyra absently wondered if it had always served as the local pub.

The staff gave her curious looks as she headed to the bar, but no one stopped her or told her to leave. She expected to see Tyler seated at a table, but he was nowhere in sight. She took a seat at the bar. Perhaps he was running late or in the men's room.

"Can I get you something to drink?" the bartender asked.

He had a slight Scottish accent, short black hair, and a goatee. His shirt was of a soft material and still looked freshly pressed even after a day of work. He didn't look up from the glass he was drying, seemingly deep in his own thoughts or very particular about smudges on his glasses.

"No, thanks," she told him as she looked around. "I'm waiting for someone."

The man inspected the glass in his hand then put it away and began drying another one. "This is a bar, darling, you need to drink something, or people might ask questions."

She rolled her eyes in annoyance. "Fine, an Irish Coke, hold the Irish, hold the whiskey."

He gave a snort of laughter. "One Coke it is."

He flipped in the glass in his hand in showmanship manner before scooping ice out of a tray and dumping it in, followed by a can of cola. He popped the top and pouring three-quarters of it into the glass. Then he placed it on a printed coaster in front of her.

"Enjoy," he said. He raised the remainder of the can in toast before downing it in one gulp.

Kyra fought back an amused laugh. "Tyler didn't say there would be entertainment."

The man gave a charming smile. "Tyler has a tendency not to completely inform anyone of anything. For instance, he didn't tell me his partner was a beautiful young hybrid."

"I'm sure."

He raised his hands. "Honest. I've known Tyler for ages, he doesn't say a word about who he's working with until we finally meet. Don't take offense to it, that's simply who he is," he explained.

She raised a curious brow. "You're Archer? So, what are you, his informant?"

A small chuckle escaped him as he took a toothpick from container and stuck it between his teeth. "In a manner of speaking, but it turns out I'm supposed to work with you."

Kyra frowned. "I work alone."

"Relax, Kyra," Tyler called as he strolled toward them. "Archer means no harm."

He took a seat next to Kyra and Archer immediately handed him an opened bottle of beer. Kyra gave him a glare, but Tyler paid her little mind. That angered her more. She was not about to let her mission be taken over by either or these two.

"I'm sure you've met already," Tyler continued, unbothered by her sudden anger. "Archer, Kyra. Kyra, Archer." He waved his hand between them.

Archer gave her a curt nod and small smile.

"I have patrol to do. Can we get on with this?" Kyra pointed out. "Do we have back-up or not?"

Tyler shook his head. "No, we're on our own up here. It seems the council is more concerned about the hybrids down south because of the sheer number of them compared to up here." He glanced at Kyra. "You've been here nearly a week. Any leads? Any kidnappings?"

She shook her head. It was oddly quiet on the island.

"We had another twenty over the weekend," Tyler reported. "That's just inside Toronto and that were reported. Lord only knowns how many more were not reported."

"We did have a girl go missing just north of here in Gore Bay," Archer added. "She was reported but I don't think her disappearance was taken seriously. She's fourteen and First Nations. The local police usually dismiss those cases."

"And how did you hear about it?" Kyra asked, surprised.

"Her father was here looking for information. I keep a record of every missing person in the area," Archer explained.

She glanced at Tyler. "And he's supposed to be my informant, yet I only just find out about this?"

"To be fair, I just became your informant," Archer pointed out.

"Do you at least have a picture of this girl? Maybe a description? What she was wearing when she was last seen? Who was she last seen with?" she demanded, growing anxious by the mere thought of another person going missing under her watch. She might be able to track her down, or at least the vehicle she may have been taken in so that she could track it to wherever these kids are being taken. "What's her name?"

"Sara Ingram," Archer answered. He pulled out a small photograph from his breast pocket and handed it to Kyra. "Fourteen, brown hair, brown eyes, five foot-four inches, approximately one hundred and thirty pounds."

"Any distinguishing marks?"

He tapped the image of the girl. "Scar on her lower chin. Anything else you need to know?"

He didn't seem perturbed by this. His face remained calm, almost serene as he continued drying glasses. Kyra frowned at him. He was taking the bartender gig a little too seriously in her opinion. She sipped at her Coke and looked about the bar. The staff were finishing up and slowly leaving. If only she could leave as well. She might be able to find this girl.

"Kyra," Archer said, his voice calm but demanding attention.

She turned back toward him. There was power in his voice. It was warm, like liquid honey and Kyra found herself relaxing and paying attention. He gave her a soft smile.

"I know you're used to working on your own," he continued. His gaze remained steady on hers, refusing to break eye contact. "But I was born and raised here. I know the people and they know me. When something happens here, I'm usually the first to hear about it. I can help you find these kids and get them back. But only if you let me." He patted her hand soothingly. "I'm here to help."

"Archer's right, Kyra," Tyler added.

She blinked and looked toward him. Archer continued to hold her hand. It was a surreal feeling, almost like being in a dream. Kyra didn't like it, but she couldn't pull her hand free. It was like she was trapped yet not.

"He's owned this bar for ages. Everyone comes here. If something happens, he'll hear about it before anyone else," Tyler continued.

He seemed unaware of what was going on, or if he was, he was using Archer's ability to get his point across.

Archer let go of Kyra's hand then patted it once more. As fast as it had happened, the spell broke.

Kyra jerked her hand away.

"Don't you ever do that again," she snapped.

Her hand tingled and residue energy slowly raced up her arm. She got off the stool and held her arm to her chest. She could still feel his hand on hers and she didn't like the psychic link it created. He couldn't enter her mind, her psychic shields were too strong for that, but his calming presence was unnerving.

He didn't seem upset in the least. "I'm guessing posing as a student while trying to patrol the island. You looked stressed out. Now you look a little better."

She stared at him in disbelief for a moment before realizing he was right. She did feel considerably better after whatever he had done to her. Her shoulders fell, the tenseness she had been holding in for so long finally melting away.

"I'm not used to people trying to help me," she told him. She didn't like it either and she certainly didn't like anyone using their powers on her, regardless of how "helpful" they were trying to be.

Archer nodded. "Don't worry about it. I've been there. So, we can work together then?"

She hesitated a moment, a frown still etched on her face. After a deep breath, she nodded. "Yes," she agreed.

She didn't like it, but Tyler was right. Archer knew the island and she needed a second pair of eyes.

Tyler downed the last of his beer and wiped his mouth with the back of his hand. "Why don't you go home and catch up on some sleep? I'll do patrol tonight. I'm supposed to head to Meldrum Bay tomorrow afternoon anyway."

Kyra was hesitant. She was exhausted, both mentally and physically. Sleep sounded like a wonderful idea, but relying on someone else to do her job simply didn't sit right with her. However, if she didn't rest, she'd be no good to anyone. She ran her teeth over her lower lip in thought. Sleep was so tempting.

"You moved into the apartment across the street, didn't you?" Archer asked.

He came around the bar but respectfully kept his distance.

"Yes," she answered.

She took a deep breath. She was already becoming tense again.

"Then if Tyler calls, I'll run over and wake you up. Sound good?"

She hesitated a moment longer before nodding.

"Alright, off with you then."

Kyra opened her mouth to argue but stopped short. She was tired and Tyler was willing to take over for her. Why was she arguing about it? She had been pushing herself endless since taking on this assignment and she was on the verge of burnout. She needed the rest.

Despite being exhausted, Kyra was also on edge. Her body still tingled from Archer's energy and she didn't like it. If anything, it creeped her out and she was happy she hadn't told him or Tyler about Jalyn. Perhaps she'd have her keep an eye on the bartender while she was at school for the next few days. Something just felt off about him. She glanced at the hand he had touched. She could still feel his energy pulsing through it. It made the rest of her body tingle in a strange sort of way, unlike anything she had felt before. Her head tilted to one side in curiosity. Why did it feel good? What had he done to her?

Chapter Five

T he chalet was too quiet without a child running through the house, or even a teenager raiding the fridge and complaining they wanted to go to the city for the day. It had been nearly a year since Kyra left home, but Alex still couldn't get used to her being gone. When they adopted her, he never thought he would get used to a rambunctious child running around or how much he and Lucas would have to go after her to keep her from getting lost in the mountains while exploring, or reminding her not to go swimming alone in the lake down the hill from their home. She had learned as she got older, but now it was hard getting used to her not being home. It gave Alex and Lucas some much needed alone time, but they both missed her dearly.

He sighed. He should be working on his next book – after all, he and Lucas had discovered so many new things since their last book was published, such as the function of the citadels at the top of the temple – but his mind kept slipping back to Kyra and how she helped him write the first two books. She had been good at keeping him from getting sidetracked, often sitting next to him colouring or working on homework. He rarely had to worry about her getting into trouble. Now he had no idea what she was doing. Yes, she was searching for more of her kind to help protect them. And yes, she knew how to protect herself and had military training to back her up, but she didn't have backup. She was working alone. If something happened, no one would know until it was too late.

"I like that picture," Lucas hummed.

He came up behind Alex in the little section of their living room that served as their work station. They didn't have a designated office space. Originally it was going to be the guest room upstairs that overlooked the lake, but it was across from Kyra's and after she left home, Alex simply couldn't bring himself to work up there. He missed her too much and his focus went everywhere but where it should be. He was having that problem now as well, so it really didn't matter where he worked.

Alex tilted his head to one side as he stared at his laptop's background which featured a picture he took of Lucas and Kyra when she was eight. It was a very candid moment. Kyra was sitting cross legged on the wide bathroom counter staring at the oversized mirror in her footie pajamas. Lucas stood behind her with a towel securely around his waist, his hair tied up in a messy man-bun as he focused on brushing her long, glossy white hair. It was before she learned how to hide her true form and hid her beautiful white hair with a darker, auburn shade that was a mix of Alex's and Lucas's. While they both appreciated the sentiment, her natural hair and skin tone was something they had grown to love. She looked ethereal, a perfect blend of Human and Celestial, but she was a grown woman now and her choices were her own. They no longer had a say.

Alex traced a finger over the image. He remembered taking that picture. It had been so unexpected that he couldn't help but catch the moment, and he was glad he had done so. Kyra had run into their bathroom while Lucas was coming out of the shower with her tablet to show off her aunt Elizabeth's new hair style and wanted the same one. Lucas scrambled to cover himself with a towel while reminding her she needed to knock before entering the master bathroom and outright refused to cut her hair, but did promise to style it for her. They spent the next hour brushing and braiding and styling her hair until she was happy with the princess style he created. It had left Lucas exhausted and questioning what he had gotten himself into, but the big happy smile and sloppy kiss to his cheek made it all worth it. That picture remained as the background on Alex's laptop and smartphone ever since.

"It's my favourite," he agreed.

A content sigh left him as Lucas pressed his lips to his neck. The tension he felt in his shoulder slowly subsided as his husband's strong hand kneaded the taut muscles. He needed a good deep tissue massage. They had so much work to do...so much research to get typed up...but at that moment all he wanted was to slip into the hot tub and forget it all.

Except he couldn't.

He grunted softly as a sudden stabbing sensation erupted in his right hand.

"Ow..." he grumbled, glancing toward the palm of his hand.

Lucas pulled away. "What's wrong?"

Alex stared at his hand for a long moment. It had been years since he last felt any pain in his hand. It was scarred, branded with the sigils of the Celestials after holding one of their artifacts that served as a key to the vessels. It usually only bothered him when one of the creatures were near or one of their Shadow-beings. This felt different though. It hurt for only a split second before becoming warm. That warmth spread up his arm and into the rest of him. It wasn't unpleasant. If anything, it felt...good. Real good. Like take Lucas to bed and ravish him good. It was very odd and very troubling. He hadn't felt such intense arousal without foreplay in a very, very long time. Not since he was possessed by a Celestial...and he knew he wasn't possessed this time.

Kyra awoke in a cold sweat. Her breathing was rapid and body tingling in a way she had never felt before, the warmth stilling rolling through her like crashing waves that made her lower half tremble. For a moment, fear and confusion ruled her as she glanced around. She was alone in bed just has she had been when she went to bed but her dream had been so vivid that she should almost swear someone should have been laying next to her. Yet, that side of the bed was undisturbed, the pillow unused and blankets still in one place. She didn't move a lot when she slept and judging by the condition of the bed...she was indeed alone which meant it had all been a dream.

She'd had vivid dreams before, some of which were utterly terrifying, but she had never had a sexual dream before. She had never had the urge to have sex before. When she was a child, her reproductive organs had been removed so she could not reproduce. It had caused issues when she hit puberty. She didn't have a menstrual cycle and had never felt arousal. Her dads told her not to stress over it, that everyone was different, and sex was overrated when forming a meaningful relationship. That coming from two men who had their own sex dungeon that they would hide out in at night when they thought she was asleep. They had a very active sex life, but Kyra had never cared about it. It was simply who they were and they loved each other deeply. She knew the biology of it but had never cared for it, never thought of it, never wanted it, and certainly never dreamed of it until now.

She ran her fingers over her sweat covered stomach, unable to get out of bed just yet. The hand Archer held the night before was still warm and tingling, making the memory of her dream all the more real.

In her dream, there had been a knocking at the door. When she answered, Archer stood there, tall, dark and hungry. His dark gaze roamed over her, not uttering a word as he stepped inside. Normally, she would not let anyone into her apartment, after all, she was only wearing a long t-shirt and nothing under it, but she had stepped back and he followed her, slamming the door shut behind him. The next thing she knew they were kissing, Archer's large hands grasping her hips and shoving her roughly against the kitchen counter, before lifting her up and placing her on it. He broke the kiss to give a sly grin before pulling his t-shirt off, revealing toned abs and thick pecs. Then, not breaking eye contact, he slowly undid his belt and opened his jeans, sliding them down just enough to reveal his long, hard, and impossibly thick cock. She stared at it in awe. She had inadvertently caught her parents nude and in the act on occasion when she was young and knew enough about sex to know what Archer intended, but she had never come face to face with a man's cock on such a personal level. She felt a warm sensation move through her to pool at her neither region.

"Time to break your crown, princess," the man purred.

He pulled her close and entered her smoothly. There should have been pain as it was her first time, but she felt nothing but searing pleasure that caused her to cry out and cling to him, riding that large organ deep inside her. One hand tangled in his hair as the fingers of the other dug into his muscular shoulder. He thrust deep, slamming his entire length into her core, reaching places Kyra never thought possible. Her body and mind were flooded with sensation, so much so she could barely think.

He carried her to the bed and laid her down before climbing on after her. He sat back and patted his lap for her to mount him. She hesitated a moment before doing so, taking his length back into her.

"That's it, baby. You're a queen. Use me," he purred, wrapping an arm about her waist.

She rocked her hips, adjusting to the feel of his length inside her, then bounced, testing it, unsure of herself. It felt good, made her feel powerful and in control. He hummed contently, encouraging her on with pleased sounds as she rotated her hips, rocked, bounced until she found her pace. She leaned back, placed her hands on his knees and ignored all else but the feeling of him inside her, riding him hard until blinding pleasure rocked through her, causing her body to convulse and shake as her very first orgasm slammed into her. She collapsed onto the bed, her legs jerking uncontrollably, but she was alone when she next opened her eyes, Archer never there to begin with.

It was all a dream.

Her legs were weak though, as she did indeed have sex only moments ago. Confused, tried, and body still buzzing, she staggered to the bathroom. She needed a cold shower in order to think. It helped to a point. Washing her body sent ripples of pleasure through her, causing her to shake as a second orgasm rode through her, nearly causing her legs to give out. She did her best to ignore it even as she cursed Archer. The hand he held the night before was warm and tingling. He must have planted the dream in her mind, delayed until she was asleep and defenseless. If so, that was a form of mental rape, something she was not going to take lightly. She'd deal with him after school.

She thumped her head against the tiled bathroom wall. How the hell was she supposed to focus on defending the hybrids like this? Her body was thrumming with energy and as angry as she was with Archer…she wanted to find him, throw him on the ground, and find out if his cock truly was as large as in her dream. The thought made her wet with need.

No…nope. Not happening.

She needed to get herself together, go to school, and focus on her mission. Perhaps she could buy some toys to take care of herself. The last thing she wanted was to trigger her Celestial side and begin feeding on people. Going to a high school with hormonal teenagers was not going to help. Perhaps taking a day off school would be best.

Her body and mind didn't seem to agree with one another. She planned to strip the bed and put new sheets and comforter on it, but that didn't happen. Instead, she went to her closet and pulled out a skirt and blouse, something she normally wouldn't wear and had no idea how they ended up in her closet. She dressed, then headed out, barely acknowledging Jalyn as she headed to the school.

The air smelled fresh and there was the crisp bite of cold in the air. It was not skirt wearing weather, yet it didn't bother her. It felt good against her legs and drew the attention of men and women. Kyra glanced back at them, a strange hunger growing within her as she found herself sizing them up, absently wondering what it would be like to have sex with any one of them. The hunger only grew as she entered the school and she immediately regretted leaving her apartment.

The school smelled of sweat and wild hormones and everything that triggered her Celestial half. Girls and boys flirted with one another, some leaning far too close to the other, their breaths mingling and lips inches apart. Kyra found herself staring at them, wanting to be part of it, her lower stomach twisting in need. She voiced her eyes forward and ignored them as best she could. It was harder as their attention was drawn to her and people began speaking to her, as if just noticing her for the first time. Some were even brave enough to try reaching out to her, but she quickly dodged them and slipped into her homeroom.

She wasn't even projecting but the charisma that came with her Celestial half that wanted to breed and feed were now calling to those around her, wanting her to mate even though she could not reproduce. She forced her mental shields in place, unable to deal with so much attention. It came around her like an invisible wall, cutting off the psychic assault. It was not the fault of those around her. Her Celestial half wanted to reproduce with as many suitors as possible. Kyra had never had to deal with it before but she knew her ancestors' history and it was not a pretty one.

"First time feeling the hunger," a dark-skinned girl asked as she straddled the seat in front of Kyra to face her. She was one of the hybrids who had declined Kyra's offer of protection. Dark brown eyes looked her up and down. "You know fighting it only makes it worse. My advice, find the sleaziest teacher here, let him rail you, and then hold it over him. He won't touch any of the other students and you can use him whenever you need to."

"Ew…" Kyra responded. "You don't seriously do that, do you?"

"Nah…I have a partner who helps me out." She gave Kyra a teasing grin before sticking out her hand. "Kyra, right? I'm Naomi. And to think, we all thought you were this big badass when you got here. That hunger sure takes the wind of your sails, huh?"

"Yeah."

Naomi smiled softly. "Look, it's not so bad. Keep your shields up until you find someone you feel comfortable enough with. If you can find someone like you, all the better." She raised a brow suggestively.

Kyra gave a snort. "Easier said than done. I think coming here was a bad idea. I should go. I'll tell the secretary I'm sick or something."

She reached for her school bag before realizing she had left it at home, along with her phone and everything else she needed. Pressing a hand to her face, she sighed. Whatever was happening to her was making her absentminded. She was no good to anyone like this.

"I'll come with you," Naomi offered.

Kyra shook her head and headed for the door just as Liam came in. Her stomach knotted at the sight of him and the warmth in her groin turned to a pulsing heat. He even smelled good.

She dashed past him before she could even consider doing something awful. If she stayed, Liam would have gotten an education not meant for school.

"Kyra?" he called after her.

She couldn't stay. She pushed through the side door of the high school and all but ran back toward her apartment, fearful of what she might do if anyone tried to stop her. She didn't live far from the school, only a few blocks, but she might as well have been miles away. She could see her building in the distance, but it seemed to get further and further away while Archer's tavern across the street from it seem unbearably close. He did this to her. He awoke her hunger. She needed to deal with him, make him fix this. How could he find and protect hybrids if all she wanted was sex?

"Kyra!" Liam's voice came from behind.

What was he doing following her? He should be in class!

"Stay away!" she shouted back to him.

She was almost there. All she had to do was corner Archer and make him fix this and…

Liam grasped her arm and tried to pull her to a stop. Instinct took hold of Kyra and without thinking, she twisted his hand back and slammed him against the stone wall of the old tavern. They were only feet away from the door but all of a sudden it no longer mattered. She stared at Liam who was only a few inches shorter than her and took in his large, surprised eyes, the scent of his sweat and musk, and the world around them seemed to suddenly disappear.

Her lips met his in a sudden kiss, the dream playing in her mind only now Archer was replaced by Liam. At first, Liam didn't respond, too surprised to do much else than stare at her. Then his lips began to move, kissing her back with just as much passion as he tangled a hand in her long hair. The kiss deepened for several moments before Kyra pulled back, her hands sliding down his chest to his jeans and began fumbling over the closure.

"Whoa," Liam breathed, catching her hands.

Kyra blinked and looked at him questioningly.

"We're in the middle of the street," he explained. He brought her hands to his lips and kissed her knuckles. "And I'm pretty sure this isn't how you normally act. We should talk to my mom. She can help."

"Your mom?" she asked. It took a moment to clear the fog from her mind. "No…I should go home. I need to call my dads and…I can't stay here."

He nodded in understanding. "I get it…but you need help and my mom knows how to deal with these sorts of things. Besides, there's nothing more calming than her bookstore."

She hesitated a moment. "I… Yeah, you're right. I don't know what's wrong with me."

"She will," he insisted.

He kept hold of one hand and led her through the picturesque downtown core to the little bookstore and café. He didn't let go until they were in the back kitchen of the store, away from the few browsing customers, and only shaking his head at the inquisitive look his mother gave him. Once Kyra was seated, he went to speak to his mother in private. When he returned, he placed a cup of tea in front of Kyra before sitting down across from her as his mother told customers she needed to close the store for a short time to deal with a family issue. Kyra wasn't sure how she felt about that, but that energy building within her eased a little. It may have had something to do with the protective sigils placed all over the store, as if to protect it from negative energy. It worked. Slowly, she began to feel better, the warmth in her lower stomach and groin became nothing more than a dull ache.

"How are you feeling?" Marie asked. She handed Kyra a cold cloth before sitting across from her. "The first time the hunger hits is always the hardest. I'm glad Liam was there to help you. He did the right thing bringing you here."

"You knew?" Kyra asked.

She pressed the cloth to her cheek. It felt delightful after the unbearable heat of arousal. She closed her eyes and savour it. If only she could wrap her whole body in a nice cold cloth.

"The moment you first entered the store," Marie confirmed. "It's alright. I've dealt with a lot of young ones over the years. I've managed to shield Liam, but I was also wise enough to prepare him for when it happens to him."

"My dads prepared me as well…I just didn't think it would happen given my…situation."

"What situation?" Liam asked. He sat next to his mother with a mug of coffee. He shrugged when his mother gave him a look, obviously telling him not to pry.

"The hunger comes regardless," Marie explained. "Learning to deal with it is key." She reached over and took Kyra's hand. "I get that this is sudden, but you need to find a partner. How many hybrids do you know personally? Anyone that you're close to?"

Kyra's mind went back to her dream and Archer and for a moment arousal erupted within her again. She pushed it back down, not willing to let her mind wander to him. She did not want him as a partner. Something told her he had a lot of "partners" already.

"No." She took a deep breath through her nose. "I need to get this under control. I can't do my job like this."

"Your job?" Liam asked in surprise.

Her eyes widened. She hadn't meant to say that and had no way to explain it. She could lie, say she worked at the tavern, but the words refused to form on her lips. The sound of bells saved her and she glanced past the kitchen into the store as two men entered. The aura of energy they projected made it clear they were not human.

"Stay here," Marie told Kyra and Liam as she stood.

She gave Liam a pointed look as he stood as well, clearly not trusting these men. Kyra didn't trust them either. Something felt off about them, a familiarity that was not Celestial in nature but something far darker that sent an old fear creeping up Kyra's spine. She watched, transfixed as Marie went into the store to greet the newcomers. The older woman seemed to know them and was more annoyed than afraid.

"I've told you never to come here," Marie said, her voice commanding and unlike the motherly tone from moments earlier.

They glanced at her.

"We're here for the girl," they said in unison.

Marie was unimpressed as she blocked their way. "No. We had an agreement. The children of this island were not to be touched if I came here as their Guardian."

"As you shall remain," they answered, moving further into the store. "Your position does not apply to her. She has become active, therefore she is to be harvested."

Harvested. The word rattle in Kyra's mind. A horrid reminder that even among her kind, she was viewed as less than hybrid, less than human. She could not reproduce therefore her genetic makeup must she studied, her body taken apart like a broken car to see where the problem was, if it could be fixed, or how to prevent it from happening to the next batch of hybrids. It didn't matter that her reproductive organs had been surgically removed when she was a child. The fact that they were gone made her of no use to the Celestials as anything more than a specimen to be studied. They had sent their bloodhounds, Shadow-being possessing human hosts, to collect her.

Kyra stood, energy pulsing into her right hand. As if her day hadn't been stressful enough without these guys.

"Marie," she said in a stern voice.

She didn't want either Maric or Liam to get mixed up her problems, but it sounded as if Marie may have already had her own issues with the Shadows. She raised a hand to stop Liam as he moved around the table, ready to help his mother should these beings attempt to harm her.

"Mom, what's going on?" he asked, worry evident in his voice.

"Just stay there," Marie answered calmly, her focus on the two strangers. "You need to leave. Now."

Instead, she was shoved aside by one of them. "Your services are no longer required. Ya'hym will take them all."

"Mom!" Liam yelled, darting toward his mother.

Kyra grasped his arm, yanking him back. The Shadows weren't just there for her, but him as well. And most likely the other hybrids. They weren't even trying to hide their presence anymore and grab kids off the street at night. They were now attacking a store in broad daylight. She glanced toward the backdoor that led to a small alley way. It was probably already blocked off but it may be their only escape.

"When I tell you to run…go out the back door and get into one of the other shops. Tell them to call 911," she instructed Liam, trying to keep between him and the approaching Shadows.

"I'm not leaving my mother," he snapped, refusing to stay behind her. He grabbed a large knife out of one of the drawers, prepared to defend himself and his mother.

Kyra eyed for a moment, impressed by his bravery, but he had no clue what they were facing.

"Liam, do as she says," Marie ordered. She shoved one of the tables in front of the two men, temporarily stopping them from proceeding into the kitchen. "Go, I'll be fine."

She got onto the other side of the table and held it in place as the Shadows tried to move it, displaying her strength and Celestial heritage. The Shadows were strong but nearly as strong as a hybrid in full control of their gifts. She managed to shove them back, using her full strength and the table to keep them from advancing further.

"This is my store and my home. You will not come in here and take my people," she growled.

Energy wafted off her in waves causing books to lift of shelves and the lights to flicker as the electronics within the store began to go haywire. She continued forcing them back, almost right out the door, but the Shadows were not willing to leave without a fight. One threw a small device into the store toward the kitchen, causing Marie to pause and turn toward it.

It was a small grenade. Smoke leaked out one side and spilled into the room.

"Mom!" Liam cried, managing to break free of Kyra to try get to her.

"Liam no!" both Marie and Kyra cried at the same time.

Marie threw herself toward the device, but it was too late.

The grenade exploded with a blinding light and deafening crack. The force of it sent Kyra and Liam flying across the kitchen, smashing through the back window and into the alley. They slammed the wall of the building behind them before landing in a painful heap on the cement. For a time, the world around them was nothing more than black plumes of smoke, flickering golds, oranges, and deep red, and intense heat threatening to swallow them both.

Chapter Six

Hurt, and with ears ringing from the explosion, Kyra managed to pull herself to her knees and watch in horror as the interior of the store went up in flames. The weapons the Shadows typically used were meant to subdue their targets, not kill them. They said they wanted to harvest her. They usually did such things while the victim was still alive, not blown to bits. Whoever or whatever Ya'hym was, must not have cared anymore as long as they had her DNA. Something had changed.

She expected the Shadows to come strolling out of the flames at any moment to finish what they had begun, but they never emerged. The fire grew, feeding off the books, black smoke billowing out of the blown-out windows.

"Marie?" she called, hoping the store owner survived the blast. "Marie!"

She struggled to her feet, ready to go back in and find her but she was stopped by a large arm wrapping about her waist and pulling her away from the entrance.

"No," a familiar voice said firmly, causing that strange warmness to momentarily re-emerge within her stomach.

She turned in his arms to come face to face with Archer. The man stared at her with concern before glancing past her to the burning store.

"Stay with Liam and Naomi," he instructed before letting her go and entering the building himself.

In the distance the blaring klaxons of fire trucks could be heard racing into the downtown core, but to Kyra it was nothing more than a distant noise as she knelt next to Liam. The reality of what had just happened slowly kicked in as she stared at him. Soot covered his face and burns, and several pieces of shrapnel were lodged in his body. He had been much closer to the grenade than she had been and suffered for it. He lay unconscious but breathing. Naomi was checking him over for further injury but the look on her face was grim when she met Kyra's gaze.

"What are you doing here?" Kyra couldn't help but asked.

"I followed you two," Naomi answered. "Besides, I thought Archer might need a heads up that you're feeling the hunger now. He's good at helping people through it. He helped me."

Kyra opened her mouth to argue the fact and that it was Archer that triggered her hunger but she didn't get an opportunity as the man stumbled back out of the store, coughing from the smoke, and looking even more grim than Naomi. It was clear that no one else had survived the blast.

"We need to move," Archer informed them once he was in the fresh air again.

"We shouldn't move him," Naomi informed him. "He has at least two fractured ribs and head trauma. I would say we have EMS take him to the hospital but…"

"The Shadows would be expecting that," Kyra finished, knowing how the Shadows worked.

The creatures could possess anyone...human at least. They would simply discard their current host and take a new one if they thought it would get them closer to their target.

"We don't have a choice," Archer told them as he knelt next to Liam. "Kyra, brace his neck to keep his head from flopping around. I'll carry him. Ready? One...two..."

Kyra wasn't quite sure what to do. She placed one hand on the back of Liam's head and the other under his chin as Archer carefully took the young man in his arms. It was awkward walking together like that to the tavern, and probably did little to truly help him. None of that mattered though. They needed to get him to safety and all they had at the moment was Archer's tavern and the mysterious man himself. At that moment, dreams and hunger no longer mattered. Helping Liam and staying ahead of the Shadows did.

Archer led them through the back door to the tavern then along a narrow corridor to a staircase. Kyra had to let go of Liam's head in order for Archer to climb the step. They went up to a series of small one room apartments. The were tiny, with just enough room for a bed, kitchenette, and bathroom. Vaguely, Kyra remembered someone telling her that the tavern had once been a hotel. The rooms now served as studio apartments typically housing artists or contract workers for several months at a time. The one Archer took them to appeared to be his. It was simple. Bare really. There was a ruffled Queen-size bed, obviously not made in quite some time, a night stand with a few books, clothing haphazardly piled on an armchair, and a laptop on a small desk. Worse...there were dirty dishes in the sink. Kyra hoped the state of the apartment was only due to Archer being startled awake from the explosion and not an everyday occurrence.

Archer laid Liam on the bed then leaned over him, carefully feeling along his body for injuries.

"His left shoulder is dislocated," he reported after a moment. "And wrist possibly broken, but ...won't know the extent of the damage until he wakes up. We should get him to the hospital. It's only a block from here."

Kyra nervously chewed on her lower lip. Archer was right, Liam needed medical attention. There were pieces of glass and shrapnel lodged in his body. Gods only knew how deep or what internal damage they were causing. He needed help, but the Shadows weren't dumb. They would know that. They would be waiting for them there. It had been a long time since she wished either of her fathers were with her but right now, she desperately wished they both were. They had fought the Shadow being far longer than she had and had first hand experience with the injuries they could inflict.

"Hey, we should look you over, as well," Naomi said. She placed a hand on Kyra's shoulder but Kyra brushed it away.

"I'm fine."

"You have glass embedded in you right cheek," Naomi argued.

Surprised, Kyra touched her cheek and sure enough there was blood on her fingers when she pulled them away. She stared at the red substance for several long moments before allowing Naomi to take her to the bathroom and care for the injuries. As each piece of glass was removed, the laceration sealed itself, leaving barely a mark to hint at an injury. Naomi stared at it in awe but said nothing. It would seem each hybrid had a different gift. For Kyra, he had always been her healing factor. It was one of the reasons she avoided socializing – people tended to freak out if she got hurt, even something as simple as a paper cut, only to heal moments later. It was impossible to explain to anyone not knowing who and what she was. Nonetheless, Naomi pressed a cool wet cloth to Kyra's cheek once she was done. It felt good against her heated skin.

"What the hell happened? I thought you were going to get laid not blown up," Naomi mused. Her dark brown gaze met Kyra's. "Liam's cute and all, but it would have made more sense to take him to your place than his mom's book store. When did explosions become part of foreplay?"

"You're kidding, right?" Kyra asked, unsure how to take Naomi's words. "You saw what happened. We were attacked. His mother may be dead and you're joking about sex?"

The other woman shrugged. "Look, we all deal with stress in our own way. Me...I make bad jokes. I'm not good with this type of stuff, okay?"

Kyra studied her for a moment before sighing. "Yeah, well... keep those type of jokes to yourself." She glanced at herself in the mirror. Despite healing, she was a mess. Her face was greyish, covered in a mix of soot and dirt, as were her clothing. "How does everyone know I'm suddenly sexually active? Am I giving off some pheromone? You realized it the moment I walked into class. Even the other hybrids picked it up. Liam knew...so did Marie. The Shadows tracked me because of it. They've never been able to track me."

Naomi shook her head. "I don't know. It gets better over time. I mean, they've never attacked me and I've been sexually active since I was fourteen."

"What?"

"It's a long story."

Was that how the Shadows were finding the hybrids? The moment they became sexually active? Some of the ones that had been kidnapped were young, far too young for such things. The idea that any of them could be sexual at such tender ages almost made Kyra's stomach churned at the mere thought of what may have led to that.

A loud beeping drew her attention away from those dark thoughts.

"Fuck," Archer snapped in the other room.

"What's wrong?" Naomi called to him.

She handed Kyra the wash cloth then went into the other room. Kyra wiped her face with it then threw it in the sink and followed her. Archer was standing in front of his desk, looking at the screen of his laptop with showed the interior of the tavern below. It was too early in the morning for it to be opened, but it clearly showed two people that were not servers walking through it. Kyra's blood ran cold at the sight of them.

"They're the same people that attacked the bookstore," she told him. She glanced at Liam. There was no way they could move again, not yet at least.

"They may have seen us come here," Naomi said, biting her lower lip.

Archer shook his head. "No, I made sure no one saw us." He stepped back and grabbed a jacket off the arm chair. "Alright, I'll deal with them. You two lock the door and don't let anyone in here. I'll call up when the coast is clear."

Naomi nodded.

Kyra objected. "They're here because of me. I should leave. I can lead them away from town and then you two can get Liam to the hospital. They won't bother any of you once I'm gone."

Archer shrugged on his jacket as he headed toward the door. "No. Stay put and keep the door locked. We'll figure out what to do when I get back. Right now, Liam needs you, both of you. If he wakes up, keep him quiet...and don't say anything about Marie. We don't want him going into shock on top of everything else."

"But..."

He paused at the door and looked back at her. "If something happens to me, then take Naomi and head to the roof. You'll find a ladder on the south side that will take you to the dealership two doors over. Tell Bobby I said to give you the keys to my car and get off the island."

"What about Liam?" Kyra objected.

"They won't hurt him."

She stepped toward him but he hurried out into the hall. A moment later, Naomi locked the door before going around the small space to make sure the curtains were shut and lights off. Then she took the laptop off the desk and sat on the floor next to the bed. Kyra sat next to her, watching the monitor with her stomach tied in a tight knot of fear and worry. She could fight the Shadows on her own, but not when there were so many others that could get hurt. Guilt already filled her for Liam being hurt and Marie potentially killed. She could not allow that to happen to Archer and Naomi as well, but there was nothing she could do. As much as he didn't want to, she had to trust Archer.

There was no audio with the security feed from the tavern. They watched anxiously as the Shadow-beings moved through the tavern. It wasn't long before Archer joined them. The beings went to him, one on either side as if to box him in. He remained calm, seemingly speaking to them in a friendly manner as if they were any other patrons who managed to come in before the tavern was open. He answered their questions, shaking his head and displaying a look of disappointment and then surprise. It didn't last very long. The Shadows looked around a little more, being seeming content and leaving.

"That was quick," Naomi whispered.

Kyra nodded. That was indeed quick. What did he say to them to make them leave so quickly? It wasn't as if the tavern was well lit. There were enough shadows for the creatures to leave their human hosts and search the entire building for them, but they hadn't. They were still within their human forms and had simply left. It seemed too easy.

They both jumped when a knock rapped against the door a moment later.

"It's me," Archer announced before unlocking the door from the other side. He stepped in with one hand raised to show he was unarmed, then locked the door behind him again. "They're gone. I double bolted the doors behind them. Not that that will stop them come nightfall."

"They're stronger at night," Kyra confirmed. "No need for a human host."

She leaned back against the bed. They were sitting ducks here. It didn't matter where they went, night was the Shadows' element. They could move across the planet using darkness as their mode of transportation. There was no place safe for them…at least not here. There was only one place they could go that the Shadows couldn't, but getting there would be tricky.

"We need a plane," she announced, catching Archer by surprise. She stood up and went to the nearest window that looked out toward Spider Bay. "I saw a water plane in the bay. Do you any idea who owns it?"

"No," Archer answered. "I don't know how to pilot one of those."

"You don't need to. I've been flying half my life. We just need to get to it."

"We're not stealing someone's plane," Archer objected.

She sent him a glare. "You're not, I am. Just help me get Liam to it."

He shared a look with Naomi who nodded. "Alright. I'll get you there. Then what? Where will you go?"

"I have a place."

"Then let's get you that plane."

Klaxons wailed throughout the mountainside moments before the ground began to tremble. It wasn't an earthquake, both Lucas and Alex had been through enough of them and explosions to know this was neither of those. It had been years since the last time the alarms sounded, but both knew what it meant as the long forgotten former military base came alive. Twin cannons rose out of the ground, the faux grass that hide the steel trap doors slid under the vineyard between them.

Lucas and Alex watched for a moment, both transfixed by the sheer firepower that was hidden under their home. As impressive as it was, they knew what it meant and snapped into action. Lucas dashed back into the house to where the rarely used radio sat on the island. He flicked it on, and tried to remember the code they were supposed to use when encountering an unknown aircraft. This was a no-fly zone. Any planes that came here sent a special code to the radio tower letting the security network know they were friendly. However, if it was just a private pilot who neglected to follow their flight path – which would have to be reported to Sudbury Air Traffic Control before flying within this region – then Lucas and Alex had to contact them manually and pray they listened enough to alter their route. In the thirteen years they had lived on the old base, they had only had to reroute someone once, and that was within their first year.

"Approaching aircraft, this is a no-fly zone," he said sternly into the radio. He watched through the window as the canons locked on their target. "Identify yourself."

There was static on the other end and for several long seconds, he thought no one would answer. Then a familiar voice came over the radio.

"Pappa, it's me Alpha-Bravo-6-1-2-Echo-Tango-0-0-5," Kyra answered. "I can't log into the system. This isn't my plane."

Lucas typed the code quickly into his laptop, hoping he could override the system before the cannons fired. There was a loud whirling sound outside, indicating they were still powering up. A few more seconds and it would be too late. The whirling stopped and gearing began grinding as the cannons began lowering back into the ground, no longer needed. Lucas sighed in relief as the ground closed above them.

"Baby girl, you nearly gave me a heart attack," he breathed as he sat back.

"I'm sorry," Kyra's responded. "We have a medical emergency. Can you and Dad meet us at the dock?"

"How many are with you?"

"Three. One's in really bad shape."

"Kyra..."

He wanted to reprimand her, to tell her she should have taken the person to a hospital, but he knew his daughter. She would not have brought strangers here without reason. And she certainly would not have stolen a plane. She knew where the family planes were located. There was one less than thirty minutes from Little Current. Whatever had caused her to abandon her mission and steal a plane had to be important.

"I'm on my way, sweetheart," he told her. "Bring the plane to dock two. There's a stretcher in the storage shed at the end. We'll meet you there."

"Okay...love you."

"Love you, too."

He hung up, his hands shaking slightly. What had Kyra brought home with her? What sort of medical emergency was this? The last time she said it was a medical emergency she had found an injured Lynx in the forest and decided to bring it home and care for it. That animal had stayed with her for it's entire life, living well beyond it's seven-year lifespan to nearly ten years old. It was the most spoiled animal a little girl could want, especially considering it was never domesticated. It was as wild as Kyra and only she was able to handle the creature. Lucas prayed this wasn't a similar situation.

"It's Kyra," he called to Alex. "She has people with her. One of them is injured."

He looked toward the sky. A bright yellow water plane was steadily lowering toward the lake. It touched down with ease, gliding over the water toward the docks at the water's edge not far from the A-frame house. He and Alex hurried down the slope to meet it, careful to wait until the engines were turned off and blades came to a full stop before stepping onto the dock. Lucas unlocked the storage shed and pulled out the narrow stretcher. When the planes side door opened, he carefully slid it onto the floor in front of the bench seat where a young woman sat cradling someone's head. Lucas didn't ask who it was. Instead, he climbed into the plane and with Kyra's help, moved the young man from the seat to the stretcher.

"Kyra, go out and help your Dad as we take him out, alright?" he instructed.

"I'll help, too," a male voice offered.

Lucas glanced at man that had been sitting in the co-pilot seat. He was young, late twenties to early thirties and looked oddly familiar. Lucas couldn't place him but gave him a curt nod. The more people working together to get the youth safely off the plane the better. He watched as the two climbed out then strapped the youth to the stretcher to keep him from falling off should the stretcher be tilted the wrong way.

"What can I do?" the girl still sitting on the bench asked.

"What's your name?" he asked. She was scared but he didn't have time to calm her fears.

"Naomi."

"Alright, Naomi. I want you to stay behind me and make sure I don't drop anything. If I do, grab it. Can you do that for me?"

It was a mundane request but it would get her mind off of the situation at hand, even if only for a few minutes. He had no clue what her connection to the boy was. They may have been friends, or boyfriend and girlfriend, or even siblings. It didn't matter. Right now, he needed to get the boy off the plane and he needed her to stay calm. Once they were in the chalet, he would question them and find out what happened.

He and Alex carefully carried the stretcher to their home, Lucas going backwards up the steps. Alex often struggled climbing steps backwards with his prosthetic leg, not feeling when the artificial foot caught against a step until it was too late. They couldn't afford that while carrying an injured person and it was easy to see that this boy was badly hurt.

"Where are we going to put him?" Alex questioned as they entered the living room.

"Floor for now. We can move him to the couch after."

Alex nodded in agreement and together they lowered the stretcher to the hardwood floor. They took a moment to catch their breath before Lucas stood and took in the state of Kyra and her guests. They all looked shellshocked, as if just beginning to realize everything that must have happened to them. Knowing Kyra, it would be a while before she was ready to explain what had happened.

"I'll put the kettle on for tea," he announced, heading toward the kitchen.

"If you have coffee…" the strange man standing uncomfortably next to Kyra began.

"You'll have tea," Kyra all but snapped at him.

The man blinked than looked at Lucas. "I'll have tea," he said, looking surprised.

A small grin lifted one corner of Lucas's mouth as he glanced at Kyra. She took after him. Alex would have made a special pot of coffee just for their guest. He filled the kettle and placed it on the back burner of the stove as Alex went to Kyra and began inspecting her for possible injuries.

"What happened?" her Dad asked, the worry evident in his voice. "Who did this?"

"It's a long story," she answered before hugging him tightly. "I'm just happy we made it here before the Shadows caught up to us."

He frowned and hugged her tighter. "I knew I should have told Caldwell to fuck off rather than let her take you. Those things will never stop hunting us."

"Dad…"

He held her at arms length, ever protective and unwilling to accept the realities of his little girl growing up. "You're home now and the fence will keep the Shadows at bay. We'll figure out the rest after a hot meal and you've had a shower."

A small laugh escaped her as she shook her head. "I've missed you."

"I've missed you, too."

"Alex, it may be smart to put a brace around the boy's neck," Lucas suggested.

He leaned against the island that separated the kitchen from the living room and watched their guests with a careful eye. Something didn't feel right. It was rare for them to have guests in their mountain home. Even the odd hiker that got lost often steered clear of the chalet and surrounding property and it wasn't just because of it being a former base or the no trespassing signs posted around the perimeter. This land was fused with alien energy that tended to cause curious visitors to turn away. Those that did visit, never stayed long.

Alex glanced at him then gave a quick nod. "Kyra, grab the med kit from the master bathroom." He looked to the other woman who was nervously pressed against the strange man's side. "Naomi, right? Can you with her and grab some towels and a damp cloth?"

The girl nodded and hurried after Kyra.

"And you are?" Lucas asked, catching the last of their party with a hard glare.

"Archer," the man asked. "I'm only here because Kyra needed an extra pair of hands to get Liam in the plane and Naomi refused to leave without me."

Lucas raised a curious brow and glanced at Alex, not liking to implication. "And what are you to h…"

"So, what exactly happened?" Alex intervened. He shot Lucas a look that clearly said whatever the man's relationship to Naomi was, it was none of their business. "Shadows rarely attack like this. Not during the day at least when there's possible witnesses."

Archer shrugged. "From what Kyra told me, she and Liam went to talk to his mother then two people came in that she claims were possessed by Shadows and they blew up the place, possibly killing Marie. I searched the wreckage. I never found her body."

"They probably took her," Alex mused.

"Probably. She was a hybrid. Liam is second generation. He's only a quarter Celestial."

"And you know this how?" Lucas questioned.

Archer met his hard glare. "Because Marie was my friend. More than a friend. I helped her keep her hunger in check."

"So, a friend with benefits."

"In a manner of speaking. I help a lot of hybrids curb their more primal urges." He gave a shrug as if it was no big deal.

Lucas looked to Alex, his lips pressed into a thin line. "And how did you become friends with our daughter?"

"I'm not. I'm her informant for Manitoulin Island. I hear things and pass the information to her. Naomi and I just happened to hear the explosion and went to help," Archer answered. "There's nothing between us…"

The word "yet" hung unspoken in the air between them and Lucas felt an urge to tell the other man to stay away from Kyra. It would be unreasonable. Kyra was a grown woman and could be with whomever she chooses. However, fatherly instinct took hold of Lucas. He pushed off the island to tell Archer exactly how he felt about him being an "informant" but was stopped when Kyra and Naomi returned with the requested items. His attention turned back to the injured youth on the ground as he helped Alex place the neck brace on him. Then, together with girls, they lifted him off the cold floor and onto the wide, plush sofa, and bundled him up in a warm blanket.

"We'll keep a close eye on him tonight," Alex told Kyra. "If he doesn't regain consciousness, we'll move him to the sanctuary and spring helps. The healing waters of the spring always helped us when one of us were injured."

"Sanctuary?" Naomi asked, confused.

Kyra shook her head. "I'll explain later."

Lucas turned off the kettle and threw in the metal ball full of tea leaves to steep. He then placed it and five tea cups on a large coaster on the center of the island. Kyra immediately took her favourite cup, put a little honey and milk in it, then filled it to just below the brim.

"You have no idea how much I've missed this," she told Lucas with a content smile.

All the anxiety and fear seemed to melt away from her as she sat on the stool in front of the island and began sipping her tea. Lucas patted the back of her hand, happy that she was home and safe.

"I'll make a big pot of soup. You three look as if you need it. We'll figure out what to do from there," he said softly.

"Yeah." She wiped at her eyes, brushing away the shimmer of tears. "I'll help."

"Alright."

He gave a nod and moved aside as she came into the kitchen to help prepare the soup. It wasn't exactly a plan for dinner but it would help everyone calm down enough to figure out what to do next. Naomi sat at the island and offered to help as well while Archer went outside and sat on the porch. Alex checked Liam one more time before grabbing the satellite phone off the counter and heading to the back of the house to make a call. Lucas didn't need to hear what he was saying to know exactly who he was calling. If the Shadows' attack on Little Current was enough to make Kyra bring people all the way to their home in the Ishpatina Mountain Ridge, then they were facing a serious problem. It had been ages since the Shadows last tried a direct attack on their home, but given the situation, they had to boost their defences and to do that, they needed outside help. There was only one person to call for that.

Chapter Seven

Liam was still unconscious when night fell. If Kyra had her way, she would have slept on the floor next to him to ensure he was safe. Alex ended up shooing her and Naomi up to her room. They were both exhausted, but Alex knew from experience it would take his daughter a long time before she relaxed enough to fall into a deep sleep and would likely be up early in the morning – if she didn't sneak down in the middle of the night.

He glanced out over the porch where Archer as sitting, puffing away at his second or third smoke. There was something "off" about him. He felt familiar but Alex couldn't put his finger on where they may have met before. Lucas didn't like him, that much was obvious. However, Lucas was also overprotective and didn't take kindly to strangers, especially since they moved to the mountains. Though he wasn't usually this defensive.

Stepping outside, he looked over the lake then off toward the woods. The air felt thicker with the taste of electricity sizzling in the breeze despite there not being a cloud in the sky. A sign of the Shadow-beings closing in.

"It's getting late," he told Archer. "We need to lock down."

The man glanced at him with a raised brow before putting out his cigarette. "I don't see how you can stop them. It's night time. They move through the darkness."

"Not here," Alex assured. A bright flash of light in the distance seemed to illustrate his words.

Lucas sighed as he stepped inside. "They're already attacking the fence."

"It'll hold. Reinforcements will be here tomorrow, and the Guardians are already stationed if one of them manages to break through," Alex reminded him.

He waited until they were all inside the chalet before turning on the house's security. Electrified metal storm shutters slid into place over the outside of the windows and doors, effectively turning the building into a small fortress. The lights inside grew a little brighter as the dark spaces under the furniture lit up as well. The taste and smell of static electricity filled the chalet as their last line of security locked into place. Should the Shadows breach the fence, they would not be able pass the chalet's shield. It was a mix of reinforced electrified steel with sensors placed every millimetre specially designed to detect the difference between Shadow-beings, humans, and Celestials. Since both Shadows and Celestials could inhabit human hosts, it took some time to work out all the kinks. Eventually, it all came down to temperature.

The average temperature of a human was thirty-seven degrees Celsius or ninety-eight Fahrenheit. When possessed by a Shadow, their temperature dropped dramatically. A Shadow all but killed their host when possessing them and once their host was no longer useful to them, they discarded it. However, they could possess a host for years. Celestials were the opposite. Their hosts ran hot and their consciousness could survive along with the Celestial inhabiting them.

If the Celestial left them, they often returned to normal. Often being the key word. Unlike Shadows, Celestials could not just inhabit any human for a long time period of time without poisoning both the host and themselves. There was a very sacred bond between a Celestial and their host. Alex assumed that was why they began creating hybrids. There were not enough humans inhabitable that would allow them to take back the planet as they had tens of thousands of years ago. Earth was far too polluted to allow for the ideal host. The few Celestials left were doing everything they could to create enough hybrids to take their place. The Shadows were hunting them down and capturing them. Now they were after Kyra and that frightened Alex. The last time they had gone after her, they attempted to dissect her because she was "defective" after her reproductive organs were removed by government-based scientists. He knew letting her work with Earth Defence Command would only attract more attention to her. This day had been a long time coming.

"So, this building has a shield and there's some sort of big fence in the woods?" Archer asked, taken back by the lockdown procedure.

"The fence runs ten square kilometres," Alex confirmed. He gestured to the stairs that led to the second floor and upstairs bedrooms. The girls were in Kyra's room, hopefully asleep after such a long and trying day. "From the water's edge straight into the mountains."

"But it doesn't bother humans or hybrids?"

"For the most part, no."

"Unless we crank up the juice," Lucas argued. "It doesn't bother *most* hybrids."

Alex shot him a glare. Lucas had been hostile and argumentative toward Archer almost from the moment he stepped off the plane. It wasn't like him. He was normally calm and polite, sometimes laying the British charm just a tad too heavy. This aloof anger was unlike him and it worried Alex, but he wasn't sure who he should be worried about…Lucas or Archer. Did Lucas sense something Alex wasn't?

"This is the guest room," he said, leading Archer to room across from Kyra's. "The bathroom is over there. There are clean linens in the closet if you need them."

Archer nodded, following where Alex pointed. "Thank you."

"And no men in Kyra's room," Lucas suddenly said, his voice stern and leaving no room for argument. "You can talk to the girls in the morning downstairs."

Alex shot him a look but Lucas merely glared at Archer until the younger man answered.

"Yes, sir," Archer said with a small, patronizing salute.

A low growling sound escaped Lucas. He said nothing more, turned on his heel, and headed back downstairs.

Alex inhaled deeply before squaring his shoulders. He and Lucas made it a point to show a united front, regardless of the situation. "We usually have breakfast by 8 am. If you need anything, our room is downstairs." He turned to go back downstairs then paused and looked back at Archer. "If the Shadows manage to breach the fence, an alarm will go off. In that case, immediately come downstairs. We would then move to the bunker."

"Bunker?"

"Yeah." Alex gave a shrug. "It's our last line of defense and a direct route to the Guardians. They'll be patrolling all night…but if worse comes to worse…that's what we'll do."

Archer nodded. "Let's hope it doesn't come to that."

"It won't. Have a good night."

"You, too."

Alex found Lucas in their bedroom when he went back downstairs. He was pacing in front of the bed, unable to go out onto their patio where he preferred to take out his frustrations on the rare occasion there were guests in their home. He looked up the moment Alex stepped in.

"Shut the door," he requested, his voice concealing the anxiety that was evident in the tension filling his body.

"We still have one guest on our couch," Alex reminded him.

Lucas glanced toward into the hallway, sighed, then nodded. "You're right, one of us needs to watch over him through the night. I'll…"

"I'll take the first shift," Alex countered. "Right now, you're too wound up."

His husband opened his mouth to object then promptly shut it. "I'm not wound up," he grumbled.

Alex sat on the edge of the bed and looked up at him. "What is it about Archer that has you so worked up? Honestly, I thought the two of you would be getting along."

Confusion filled Lucas's face. "What?"

A small laugh escaped Alex. "You two are almost identical! I mean, there's a good twenty years between you but he's almost exactly like you were at his age with the exception of him being a bartender and you an archeologist."

"He's nothing like me," Lucas objected, disgust dripping in his words. "Didn't you hear him earlier? He 'takes care of their urges, keeps their hunger in check'? He's a gigolo."

Alex raised a brow. "Okay, so he has a rather…active sex life. In case you forgot, when we first worked together you had two prostitutes fly all the way from England with you in order to help you not take panic attacks on the plane. Two, because one was not enough. And, let's not forget, for the longest time you wanted a polyamorous relationship and even slept with my best friend before finally committing yourself to me."

Lucas raised a finger, about to object again.

"So, it doesn't matter if Archer is sleeping with every hybrid on Manitoulin Island. It's none of our business."

"And what if he's sleeping with Kyra?" Lucas interjected.

That gave Alex pause. He picked at a loose thread on their comforter. "Kyra's a grown woman, Lucas. If she chooses to have sex with him, that's her decision, not ours. All we can hope is that she's react like a human and be fine."

"And if her Celestial side is triggered? If she goes into a feeding frenzy? Alex, you know for a fact how dangerous that can be." There was a moment of silence as Lucas sat next to Alex. "Can we really face her if that happens?"

"She's our daughter. We protect her…even if it's from herself." His left hand intertwined with Lucas's and gave it a gentle squeeze. "We just have to have faith. Besides, I think you're reading too much into this. Kyra's always been asexual. And if she is interested in Archer…it could be because she has Papa issues."

"He's nothing like me!"

Alex laughed merrily. The fact Lucas didn't object to Kyra having Papa issues was funny in itself. She was like his shadow, following him everywhere, more often than she followed Alex. She was always trying to help him and learn from him. An accomplished Archeologist before mastering Anthropology. It was foolish to think she wouldn't fall for someone similar to Lucas. Archer didn't have a British accent but he was certainly rocking the goatee.

"He's at least ten years older than her," Lucas tried.

Alex raised a brow. There was ten years between them.

"You were a grown man when we got together!" Lucas insisted.

"I was only a few years older than she is now," Alex reminded him. He brought Lucas's hand to his lips and kissed the back of it. "And we don't even know if they are doing anything or will be. It's all speculation. You're getting worked-up over nothing."

The older man stared at him for a long time before finally sighing. He flopped back on the bed and stared up at the ceiling. "I hope you're right."

"You know I am."

Alex chuckled, straddled his lap, and leaned over him. He folded his arms and balanced his upper weight on them. Lucas gave a barely audible grunt at the weight on his chest and groin but gave no complaint. Large hands grasped Alex's narrow hips, pulling him even closer as he bucked up, grinding their groins together. Alex groaned softly at the sensation. It was like electricity shooting through them and dispersing from his fingers and toes. After so many years together, a simple touch from Lucas still got him hot and bothered.

"I thought you were worried about older men corrupting young, innocent minds?" he teased as Lucas's hands slipped into the back of his jeans and boxers.

"You? Innocent?" Lucas playfully nipped at his nose. "I don't recall you ever being innocent."

"That's only because I had you and Owen chase away whatever innocence I had within days of meeting you."

A grin of superiority lit Lucas's face as it often did when they reminisced about the old days and how they met – not the horrifying conditions in which that came about but rather the bond they formed before even realizing what it was. Back then, it had been rare for Alex to connect with anyone, let alone consider sleeping with not one but two men, but there had been something unimaginably appealing about Lucas and his brother, Owen. It was like magic. As if a magnet drawing him to them, even when he tried to avoid it. He fell hard for both of them, and even though his relationship with Owen lasted only a few short days, Alex did not regret a moment of their time together with either brother. Owen was no longer in the picture, not exactly. He had died protecting him and Lucas and was now one of the many Guardians that protected the temple below them. He was at peace, and Alex and Lucas had just celebrated their fifteenth wedding anniversary. In a few months, it would be their twentieth anniversary since the fateful day they partnered together to figure out the mystery of the underground temples. They had been together a long time, but it often felt like only days or weeks had gone by, despite having raised a child together.

A small gasp escaped Alex as Lucas rolled them over so that he was now on top. Lucas's grin grew as he gave Alex a predatory look before rolling his hips and pressing his growing bulge against Alex's, his need on full display.

Alex bit his lower lip and pointedly kept his gaze firmly on Lucas's face even as the other man began tugging down the zipper to his jeans.

"We have guests," he whispered. "One of which is injured."

Lucas hummed as he pulled Alex's pants off his legs and tossed them aside. "I guess we'll just have to be quiet. Should I gag you?"

The mere words sent heat shooting straight to his groin, making his cock grow erect. He nodded. The one thing he and Lucas could agree on, he was loud when they had sex. When they were alone it was no big deal, but with Kyra and her friends there it was better to keep quiet. Sitting up, he did away with his t-shirt while Lucas locked the doors then went to their walk-in closet to grab their bag of toys. His erection became impossibly hard as his lover pulled out the ball gag and a length of rope. Gagged and tied up, two of Alex's favourite things. It also meant Lucas was not going to be gentle. He was going to fuck his frustrations out using Alex's tight ass, and Alex couldn't help but lick his lips in anticipation.

Lucas climbed onto the large, King size bed and crawled toward him with a sultry look. Alex sucked in his lower lip as he watched the way his husband's tone body moved and rippled, showcasing his wonderfully broad chest. There were soft spots that came with age and not working out as much as he had in his younger years. A small smile lit Alex's face as Lucas bent over him. Warm lips pressed against his forehead, moving slowly over his face to his jaw then up the left side, peppering a line of kisses to his ear. There Lucas took that ear between his teeth and gave it a playful tug.

"Oh God…" Alex whimpered.

His fingers knotted into Lucas's hair, tugging him down further, wanting more. Lucas obliged and moved downward, kissing behind

96

Alex's hear before nipping along his neck before sucking a mark onto his tanned flesh. His long fingers carded through Alex's thick auburn hair and gave it a hard tug, a silent request to tilt his head so that Lucas could access more of his neck as he sucked another mark into his heated skin.

He bit onto the ball gag as soon as it was placed in his mouth, the only thing that could stop him from making the noises he made when Lucas entered him. It was divine as always. Lucas was long and thick, filling him to the core. Alex wrapped his legs around Lucas's waist, careful not to dig the heel of his prosthetic in his lover's back. It would happen either way. He should remove it but there was no time. Lucas drew back, pulling out until only the tip of his cock remained before his hips pistoned forward. It was hard and a little painful, but it felt oh so good. The first few thrusts continued like that, slow, hard, and deep, rolling his hips before finding his pace. It was hard and fast, the slapping of flesh and Lucas's rumbling growls filled the room. Alex tighten his legs, both thankful his wrists were tied to the bed while simultaneously wishing his hands were free to rake down Lucas's muscular back. His insides felt as if they were on fire, as if his body was primed to explode at any moment.

Lucas came first. His hot juices flooded Alex's insides. It was exquisite. Alex arched beneath, welcoming the heat, and missing it the moment Lucas rolled off him to slump at his side. It took a few moments before Lucas untied him and removed the gag. A moment later, his lips covered Alex's in another deep, passionate kiss.

"I'll take the first shift," Lucas whispered from a breath away. "You rest. I'll wake you up in four hours."

Alex propped himself up on his elbows and stared at him. "Are you sure?"

"Yes." There was a moment of hesitation. "Can you ask Owen to watch over Kyra? I know you're thinking I'm overreacting but..."

"No, you're right. I'll ask him in the morning. Her usual Guardian hasn't returned yet." He paused, worried about the young spirit.

Jalyn was close to Kyra's age. An Archeologist assistant that was killed after discovering a temple in Norway. She and Kyra became close when Kyra was just a child. She was always at Kyra's side. The fact that she was not there and Kyra had yet to mention her, made Alex worry. Could the Shadows kill a Guardian?

Lucas gave a curt nod, not needing to ask why Alex was worried. "Get some sleep. I'm sure she'll be home soon."

Alex caught his hand as he got out of bed and tucked his length back in his pants. Unlike Alex, he had stayed fully clothed in order to take the first watch. He was always thinking ahead.

"Don't forget to wake me up," Alex reminded him.

"I won't," Lucas promised. He placed another kiss on Alex's temple. "Don't forget to take off your prosthetic. The last thing we need is your leg cramping in the morning because you left it on again. Now get some sleep."

With a cheeky grin, Alex saluted his lover, removed his prosthetic leg, then climbed under the covers. Lucas waited until he was settled before turning off the bedroom light and closing the door. Alex snuggled under the heavy, warm covers. It wasn't long before consciousness faded away and sleep took hold of him.

When he awoke, it was morning and sunlight filled the room as the shields slide away from the large windows. Alex groaned and mumbled a curse. Lucas had declined to wake him. He should have known the sneaky bugger would do that. He grumpily sat up and pulled the white cotton sock, then his prosthetic over the stump of what was left of his right leg. The alarm clock on the nightstand read 6:00 am, his normal wake up time. It felt far earlier than that, but he had a job to do and guests in his home. There was food to make, the vineyard to tend to, and a Guardian or two he needed to speak with. And that was before their other guests arrived. First he needed coffee.

He slid on a pair of loose track pants and baggy t-shirt then padded out into the kitchen to start the morning preparation. The scent of freshly brewed coffee greeted him as he entered the living room, as well as the smell of eggs and bacon. The latter sat on a covered warming plate, but he knew they were only a few minutes old. Lucas was nowhere to be seen. Kyra, on the other hand, was sitting on the hardwood blood next to the couch, her focus on the youth still unconscious on the couch.

"Any change?" he asked.

He watched her carefully. Kyra was devoted to people, but he had never seen her take to anyone like she had taken to Liam. He was certain Lucas's fears about Archer were unfounded. Their daughter had always been asexual. Hell, she even walked away from the soldiers that would visit the former base for routine maintenance. More than one, male and female, had flirted with her only for her to show absolutely no interest in them. Some of them had even given Alex pause to admire them. Despite their apparent role, it had also been a test by General Caldwell to test Kyra's Celestial half, to see if she would attempt to feed on one of them. When she hadn't, Caldwell repeated the test with another hybrid. Kyra had no interest in him either. She was safe to assist Earth Defense Command in finding the missing hybrids. Her feelings for Liam could merely be the fact that they were the same and he was hurt or she may have finally found someone that really liked. Her actions were not those of a hungry Celestial needing to mate and feed.

She shook her head. "He hasn't moved. He's breathing but…"

"He'll wake up," Alex assured.

He poured himself a mug of coffee then sat on the small dining room table and glanced out the front window. There was still only one plane docked at the pier. Caldwell would likely not arrive until later in the day. The fence would need to be reinforced but more importantly, Liam needed medical treatment. Moving him again would be an issue. If he wasn't moving, there may be damage to his spine. Moving him will only make it worse.

Kyra let her breath out slowly, her shoulders hunching as she read his thoughts, a gift only they shared. "What if he's paralyzed?"

Her voice shook with the very words. Alex was tempted to go to her, but she was not one that liked to be comforted, not when she so obviously blamed herself. Instead, he got up, refilled his coffee mug then poured her one as well, adding her favourite creamer that he always kept stocked in the house. It was a maple flavour they both enjoyed. He placed both mugs on the table then pulled out a chair for her. Kyra glanced at it, looked back at Liam, then pushed herself to her feet. She took the pro-offered seat with a sigh before wrapping her hands around her mug and inhaling a deep breath of the rich coffee-and-maple aroma.

"We'll help him adjust, just as your Aunt Elizabeth helped me adjust after I lost my leg," Alex told her. He placed his hand over hers and smiled gently. "None of this is your fault." He squeezed her hand when she tried to object. "Tell me what happened. How did you meet these people? Why do you think the attack was your fault? You've always been able to hide what you are."

She shook her head and for a moment there was a shimmer of tears in the corner of her eyes. She wiped them away with a little sniffle then composed herself.

"I met Liam at the high school where I was working undercover," she began. "We didn't quite hit it off. His aura was off but he didn't seem like a hybrid...wrong colours. So, I ignored him at first, but it was like we kept being brought back together. Then HQ decided to change my contact in town. I met Archer at his tavern..."

"Tavern?" Alex gave her a hard look. He didn't like the idea of her drinking, not that he could really say anything. She was an adult after all, and she made that clear by returning his look with one of her own.

"Anyway, Archer knows the island and the people and he had his ear to the ground. If I needed intel, he was the one I was supposed to go to." She shrugged, a rise and fall of her slim shoulders. "I guess I was a little anxious so he thought he was helping me by exchanging calming energy with me...it triggered something in me."

Alex's brows furrowed in worry. "What do you mean 'triggered'?"

She ran a hand through her auburn hair that matched Alex's in his youth. It wasn't her real hair colour, but then few things on Earth could match it.

"I had a dream of him that night. It was...erotic." She swallowed hard and began picking at the edge of her oversized nightshirt. "When I woke up, I felt different. Everything had me thinking of sex. Naomi said to simply sleep with one of the teachers. I thought she was joking, but when Liam came into class I...I had to leave. He followed me...seemed to know what I was going through and took me to see his mother. He managed to help me gain control but then the Shadows attacked the shop. They wanted me. They knew I was there, but Marie...she faced off against them and then..."

Her gaze turned to Liam. "Dad, I remember what they did to the Interpol agents that protected our home in Massey. I know how ruthless they can be. They blew up the shop without caring if the fire spread throughout the block of businesses. They knew I'd survive. If Archer and Naomi didn't show up when they did...the Shadows would have taken us to wherever they've been taking the other hybrids. If Liam wasn't injured, I might have let them take me. If only to find the others."

"No," Alex interrupted. "The last time they took you, they almost killed you. Whatever you do, regardless the reasoning, do not let them take you. We'll find a better way to save the others."

She was silent for a moment then nodded. It didn't mean she agreed with him, just that it wasn't worth arguing over. They sat in silence for several minutes before Alex got up, went back to the kitchen, and dished out breakfast for both of them. He set the plates on the table then sat down and began eating. From the corner of his eye, he watched as his daughter picked at her food, feeling no better after telling her story. That was understandable. He didn't press her for more detail and waited for her to tell him more on her own. A sexual awakening was not an easy thing, regardless of age. For someone like Kyra, who had gone through life believing she was asexual and would not experience such a thing, it must have been shocking. The way it happened had Alex questioning Archer as well. Had he purposely triggered Kyra or was it merely an accident?

"Where's Papa?" he asked, deciding it was time for a new topic.

A small smile tugged at Kyra's lips. "Where else?"

Alex nodded, a smile lighting his face. He finished his breakfast, washed his plate, then kissed Kyra's temple. He took the remainder of his coffee and padded back to his bedroom to retrieve his shoes, then went out the patio doors that led from his and Lucas's room to the backyard. It had the perfect view of the mountain that rose up behind their home. The thick pine trees were a vibrant green. It provided an abundance of shade in the summer but also protection from the harsh winds in the winter. There was a large patch of land nearly an acre large between the forest and chalet that always seemed to get the perfect amount of sun all year long. In the center of it was a small vineyard. The leaves were a rich, bright green and plump red grapes hung from the vines, almost ready for picking. In the midst of them, Alex could make out Lucas's form as his husband moved about, ensuring the long rolls of vines were secure to their root stocks and new vine shoots wrapped around the thick metal wires that ran the length of the vineyard. He was carefully trimming several new shoots to strengthen the main spurs that offered the richest fruit, and likely sampling some of the grapes for richness. In another week or two, it would be time for harvest.

It was always fun watching Lucas tend the vineyard. Originally, it had been Alex's dream to create a vineyard in remembrance of his father. Lucas had expanded it so that they had their own winery. While they had lost both years ago after losing their home in Massey, Lucas had been determined to restore it, even if only half the size. Now they made wine for themselves and had more than enough to do them for the next ten years. They were debating selling some, but had yet to decide how to proceed. They lived in the mountains to protect the temple. Neither of them wanted anyone locating it. They would have to be very careful if they got back into selling it.

"You were supposed to wake me up," he told Lucas as he strolled along the second roll of vines.

Lucas snipped another shoot without looking up. "You needed the sleep."

"And you didn't?"

A frown pulled his lips downward. "I couldn't sleep. My mind was too busy."

"Worrying about Kyra and Archer." It was a statement, not a question. He knew his husband and his obsession with protecting their daughter from every threat possible.

Lucas pressed his lips into a thin line and moved to the next shoot. "Caldwell is supposed to be here by noon. She didn't sound happy."

"Is she ever happy?"

That brought a small smile to Lucas. "No, I suppose not."

He stopped what he was doing to take Alex's mug and take a drink of his coffee. Alex didn't stop him; they often shared drinks and even food. Lucas finished the coffee before taking a deep breath. There were dark circles under his eyes, a sure sign he was more exhausted than he wanted to say. Alex took the shears and cup from him. Lucas gave him a weary look as the younger man took his hand.

"Come on," he encouraged. "You need sleep. Better to get it now before our guests wake up, and before Caldwell shows up. No one wants to deal with her when half asleep."

"I can't argue with you on that."

104

Alex tucked Lucas into bed then went back to the living room. Kyra was back where he originally found her, sitting on the floor next to the couch, watching Liam. Her food was left untouched on the table. He put it in the fridge and cleaned up the kitchen. He hoped the boy recovered. With luck, Caldwell brought a medical team to assist him. There was no telling how Kyra would react if she lost him. They also needed to find his mother and discover what happened to her. If Kyra and Liam survived the explosion, she most likely did as well.

Chapter Eight

It felt odd being home. Not in the bad sense, but in a way that made Kyra almost regret ever leaving in the first place. It was quiet in the mountains. There were no streets, no traffic, no blaring horns or sirens, and very few people. Just the sounds of nature. Kyra hadn't realized how much she missed it until this morning. The cool refreshing water of their lake called to her the moment she stepped outside. She thought about a bathing suit as she strolled toward the beach a few dozen feet to the east of the dock. She often swam in her bra and underwear when by herself. Neither of her fathers gave it much mind. Alex enjoyed swimming but didn't do it often due to missing half his right leg. He often stayed close to shore, his stump and hip bothering him whenever he pushed himself too hard. He preferred fishing off the deck and watching Kyra swim; ready to jump in should she need him. Lucas was the one that taught her to swim. He would swim within arm's distance right up until she was a teenager, always protective, always watchful.

Kyra took her time swimming along the familiar route, following the shore of the lake for a kilometer before diving under, rolling, then heading back. It was calming, the routine helping her clear her head. She kept within the perimeter, knowing where the fence met the water. It wouldn't electrocute her. The design was state of the art and waterproof. It was meant to keep the Shadows from crossing onto their land, regardless of the method they tried to use. All they had to do was get close enough to trigger it and the light would slice through them, destroying them before they could pass through.

She came to a stop and lazily treaded water, keeping her head above as she took a moment to listen to the bird chirping and the slight breeze ruffling the leaves in the distance. The water was crystal clear. She could see the bottom. Looking down, it appeared only inches below her feet when in actuality, it was a few meters between the bottom and her feet.

"So, you do this often?"

Kyra gave a start. She momentarily stopped treading water and went under, going down a foot or two before kicking herself back to the surface. She took a large gulp of air and wiped her hair away from her eyes before turning toward Archer.

The man treaded water several feet away from her with a smug look on his face.

"What are you doing out here?" she demanded. It felt as if he was trespassing in her space.

That stupid smile grew. "Swimming, like you."

She gave a snort, not impressed.

There was silence for a moment as they stared at one another. Then Archer went to move closer. Kyra immediately moved away from him.

"Whoa…okay, okay. I didn't mean to spook you," he said by way of an apology.

"You didn't," Kyra countered, annoyed.

His hands grazed over the surface of the water, slowly back and forth. It was almost mesmerising. Kyra looked past him to the treeline in the distance. There was no way she was going to meet his gaze. Whatever had set off her sudden arousal and need for sex the day before was somehow due to him. She wasn't going to let him cause that again, not when she was finally feeling normal again. She was home. This was her safe place. She was not going to let him take that from her.

Archer seemed to understand and kept his distance. "So, this is where you grew up?"

It was a simple and not intrusive. After all, she had brought him and the others here for their own protection. She puffed out a breath. "Yeah, this is my home."

"Lots of space," he mused, looking around as if seeing mountains and forests and lakes for the first time.

A small laugh escaped Kyra. "Yeah, you could say that," she answered, nodding in bemusement.

"So...you hike and swim and make your own wine?"

"My Dads make the wine, but yes, I hike and swim quite a bit when I'm home." She shrugged. "Even when I'm not home, I guess." She took a deep breath and finally met his gaze. "What did you do to me?"

He genuinely looked confused. "Excuse me?"

"Two nights ago, when we first met, you touched my hand. Since then, my thinking has been...irrational. I haven't been myself. Do you have any idea how hard it was for me just to get us here? Even after the attack, my mind kept going back to..."

She made a frustrated sound. She didn't like thinking about sex. Until recently, she never felt arousal before, not even when she read smutty books. It felt weird, especially considering how active her fathers were. They were usually very private and quiet when they were together, but there were times when she overheard things she wasn't meant to. While the idea of sex was intriguing, it was not something she was interested in…not until yesterday.

"You looked stressed out," he said, as if that explained what he did. "I thought it might help you calm down."

She gave him a confused look.

"Some people find sex to be a stress reliever. Our people tend to be very sexual when anxious."

"Our people? Celestials feed during sex. They *kill* during sex." She shook her head. "I don't want that. I don't want any of it."

"So, you'd rather be a nun?" he countered, thoroughly amused. "Kyra, it's natural. Humans have sex as well and normally…they don't kill each other during it. Hybrids don't usually kill during it. It's why I help people like Marie."

She shook her head. This was not something that was up for debate. "Don't swim out too far. There's a strong current two hundred feet from shore that can drag you under and sweep you away," she warned as she turned back to the beach.

"I didn't think there were any large rivers out here," Archer remarked.

He swam slowly next to her, staying just out of reach. Kyra appreciated that. Perhaps he was finally respecting her boundaries.

"There's one, but it's underground and leads to a waterfall. Go over that and there's no coming back."

He stopped swimming. His eyes were wide as he stared at her with open curiosity. "Have you seen it?"

She stopped as well, the question surprising her. The waterfall came out not far from the underground temple. It helped create the strange ecosystem that allowed vegetation to grow. It also helped circulate the temperature and air quality. According to Lucas, this was the only temple he saw with an actual waterfall and fresh running water. No one was supposed to know about it.

"I've explored most of the caves around here," she explained, giving a half-truth rather than outright lying. "Alex and Lucas are skilled at spelunking. They taught me everything I know about cave climbing, Archeology, and Anthropology. Hell, I could be in university right now if I wanted, but it could never teach me the things they have, just give me a silly paper saying I'm an expert. Why waste four years of my life proving it? Besides, I'm already doing what I love."

"Posing as a teenager and saving hybrids is what you love?"

She blinked in surprise, having nearly forgotten that. Her mind was on where she was at the moment, the investigation of the temple she had been conducting with her fathers before Caldwell recruited her to help find the missing hybrid children.

"Yeah," she lied. "It let's me see the rest of the country."

He studied her for a moment before tilting his head and frowning. "You're a horrible liar. I'm not sure how you managed to pull off being a student."

Her mouth opened in surprise. "I..."

"Kyra!"

She glanced toward the shore where Naomi stood waving her arms. Kyra waved back, relieved for the distraction.

"He's awake!"

Her heart stopped for a moment as she took in Naomi's words. Liam was awake. Excitement and fear filled her. Would he blame her for what happened at the store? For potentially killing his mother? They had no clue if she survived other than Archer saying he found no bodies. They had to hope she survived and managed to escape. For all they knew, she could still be in Little Current searching for Liam. That caused another knot to form in her stomach. Marie may mistake Liam's disappearance as a kidnapping. She would have to contact Jalyn and have her look for Marie, if only to confirm what happened to her.

Archer reached the shore before Kyra. The discomfort of swimming with him grew tenfold when the man stepped out of the water absolutely naked. Kyra adverted her gaze. She had been so intent on not looking at Archer when they spoke that she had not noticed he had no clothing on. It was hard not to look at him now. Water dripped from his hair down his lean back and firm buttocks, down the back of his powerful thighs and strong calves. When he bent done to gather his discarded clothes, his manhood was on full display. Kyra stared in surprise. She may have been raised by two men but she had never seen one naked. Alex and Lucas had always made sure to keep covered or had enough time to pull the covers over them. This was different. This was a man completely nude with not a care in the world who saw him. Comfortable in his own body.

"Hey! Clothing on! Now!" Lucas yelled from the porch.

Kyra quickly looked away and waited for Archer to get his clothing on before coming out of the water. From the corner of her eye, she could see Lucas heading toward the beach with a disapproving frown and a large bath sheet.

Oh great, he had gone into overprotective dad mode.

Embarrassment flooded Kyra as Lucas stood between her and Archer and opened the towel as wide as the length of his arms and gave her an expectant look.

"Papa…" she whined softly, feeling like a little kid again.

He raised a brow and waited, waiting to see if she would challenge him. Instead, Kyra sighed, trudged out of the water, and went to him, letting him wrap her out in the oversized towel. She held it closed as he knelt down to gather her clothing. By then, Archer was fully dressed and looking utterly amused by the whole ordeal. Kyra glared at him. The stupid bastard should have at least worn his briefs.

Lucas wrapped an arm protectively around her as he led the three back to the house. Naomi seemed uncomfortable with what happened, as if she was also in trouble even though all she had done was notify them that Liam was awake. She went inside the chalet ahead of them, kicked off her shoes on the mat, then headed for Alex, who was sitting on the edge of the heavy oak coffee table across from the couch. He was carefully flashing a light in the young man's eyes. Alex was a Doctor of Anthropology, not a medical doctor. There had to be something wrong with Liam's eyes to be conducting an eye exam.

"Is he okay?" Kyra asked. She took a step toward him only for Lucas to stop her.

"Go get some dry clothes on," her Papa directed in a stern voice.

112

"But..."

"Now. He's not going anywhere."

Her lips pressed into a thin line. He was right, but being treated like a child was becoming annoying fast. She was a grown woman. She didn't need him defending her just because Archer had paraded around butt-naked. Her gaze traveled to the bartender. She couldn't read his expression. His face was blank. A mask similar to the one Alex created when he tried to hide his emotions. She hated that look. It always meant trouble.

He caught her gaze and the corners of his mouth lifted in a thin smile. Her dream of them having sex came rushing back, the feel of his body, his thick manhood filling her. It had all been a dream but it felt so real, like an actual memory rather than a dream.

She turned away, heat traveling to her cheeks and pooling in her belly, the image of him nude fresh in her mind. She pursed her lips and headed for the stairs. Maybe a cold shower would help clear her mind.

She pushed her bedroom door open, letting it swing close behind her, and began stripping off her wet bra and panties. She hung them over the laundry basket to dry, not wanting water to pool in the bottom and make the room smell musty. The glamour that concealed her true form faded away, revealing her snowy white hair and alabaster pale flesh. There was a soft shimmer to her skin, like microscopic diamonds laced just under the surface that reflected depending how light landed on her. She should have grabbed a towel from the hall closet before entering her room. With a sigh, she grabbed her housecoat and wrapped it around herself. A shower sounded like a good idea but at the same time, she wanted to get back downstairs to Liam. The poor guy just woke up in a strange house surrounded by strange people with his mother possibly dead. Guilt filled her at the last thought. How was she going to explain that to him? How could she possibly make it right? It was her duty to find and save hybrids and instead she led the Shadows right to Liam and Marie. What happened to them was her fault.

Pulling her hair back, she wringed as much water out of her hair as possible, grimacing at the puddles of water on the hard wood floor. They would stain the wood if she didn't wipe it up immediately.

A knock at her door made her jump.

"I'm changing," she called as he headed to her closet to pull out a clean pair of jeans and hoodie. She wanted to be completely covered when she went back downstairs. She didn't feel comfortable showing skin in front of Archer anymore. If she could hide within her hoodie, she'd feel better...protected. "Give me a minute."

"Whoa..." Naomi's familiar voice said as the other girl stepped into the room, not bothering to wait.

Kyra spun around to face her, immediately defensive with one hand raised to slam the door shut with a burst of psychic energy.

"I said 'give me a minute,'" she snapped.

Naomi stared at her with large brown eyes. It took a moment for Kyra to realize why. She was in her true form, but why would that cause the girl to stare at her with such awe?

"Is this what you really look like?" Naomi asked. "The other you is fake?"

Kyra raised a confused brow. "This is what all hybrids look like..." It came out as more of a question than a statement. The surprise and shock on Naomi's face said otherwise.

"I've never seen one of us that looked like you…and I've met quite a few."

A laugh escaped Kyra. "I've *saved* quite a few and a lot look like this."

Naomi's brows knitted in confusion as she looked Kyra over. "Are you sure? Many of us tend to project the image a person wants to see, especially when scared."

"What are you saying?"

"Those kids you saved…to the Shadows they appeared meek and defenseless. To you…they looked just like you. It's a defensive mechanism used to bond with or deceive people. It's how you blend in with students and I get what I want from men." Naomi took a step toward her and gently caressed Kyra's hair without permission. "You…I've never seen anyone like you. Why do you hide this? You're gorgeous."

No one had said that to her before. Alex and Lucas always told her she was pretty. They hated that she hid her true self but understood it was for her own safety. She took her favourite aspects from both of them to create a more "human" appearance just as Caldwell had taught her. She had always thought that the other hybrids were just like her, disguised as regular humans, but now she wasn't so certain. Could Naomi be right and those she had saved merely appeared the way she wanted them to look?

She closed her eyes as Naomi's soft fingers caressed her cheek. No one had touched her face like this before. It was gentle and loving but not like that of family member or close friend. It was more intimate. Soft lips pressed against hers. This was completely unlike her dreams of Archer. This was real and tender and held an unspoken promise that she didn't understand. It made her knees weak and she had to pull away or risk falling. Naomi followed her, backing her against a wall before delving back in for another kiss. This one was more bold. She held Kyra's head in both hands and pressed firmly against her body. Her tongue slipped into her mouth, wrestling against Kyra's, flicking along the cavity of her mouth. When she broke away it was to nestle the taller woman's neck before sucking a mark onto the pale flesh. Kyra whimpered. She never knew her neck was so sensitive. She grasped Naomi's shoulders and very gently, very reluctantly, pushed her away.

"No...we need to stop," she breathed. She took a deep breath and tried to steady her pounding heart.

Naomi gazed up at her through hooded eyes and wow, was that sexy.

"Do we? Give me five minutes and I promise...you won't regret it." She nipped at Kyra's ear as one hand roamed under her robe. Her fingers slipped between her legs to press against her mound, one finger lazily teasing her clit.

Kyra's breathing hitched as a shock of pleasure rocked through her. She grasped Naomi's wrist and gently pulled her hand away.

"I...I need to get dressed," she mumbled, the words sounding lame after what they had just done.

Naomi hummed. "Pity. You look so hot naked." She licked her lips before heading to the door. "Don't take too long."

Kyra waited until she was gone before sitting on her bed. Her legs could no longer keep her up. She needed to gather her wits before she went downstairs. She was more confused now than she had ever been in her life before. She definitely needed a shower now. Liam would have to wait for a few minutes longer as she tried to calm herself down.

There was a thumping sound in his ears that had nothing to do with the bass of music and everything to do with his racing heart. It had been that way since waking up in this strange place, amongst these strange people, his eyesight gone, and mother missing. Liam barely remembered the explosion. It had all happened so fast. All he remembered was his mother facing-off against the two people who had entered the bookstore…then a flash of light so bright it burned his eyes even as the explosion lifted him off his feet and threw him out the back of the store.

He rubbed his arms, a chill filling his body despite the warm comforter wrapped around him. He was in shock, he knew that, it would take a while to come to terms with what happened. Until then, his hosts Alex and Lucas, took turns comforting him and making sure he was alright. They gave him food and water, making sure he took small bites and ate slowly. They felt like the father figures he had always wanted but never knew.

Liam tried to bury that thought under all the others that were currently consuming him. Instead, he focused on sounds and smells. The shuffling of feet, dishes moved, the rustling of new leaves outside, water lapping the sandy beach, and the delicious scent of food cooking on the barbeque. The front door was open, allowing all those sounds and scents from outside in. Wherever they were, they were far away from any town. There was no traffic, no vehicles, or crowds. It was all wilderness.

He held the glass of ice-cold water in both hands. It kept his hands from shaking and gave him something on which to focus.

People were talking around him, but he gave them little mind. None of what they spoke of concerned him, it was just idle chatter as they waited for Kyra. It almost felt normal, like the chatter at school when kids would ignore him and talk amongst each other. That wasn't what was happening here. Liam was well aware that they were watching him, unsure how to help him or what to say. They felt guilty even if they had nothing to do with what happened to him.

A familiar flicker of energy caught his attention. He turned his head toward it, following the trail as if able to see it. It was different from before, subdued but still powerful, tittering on the precipice of something more. His head tilted to one side as he read the energy as he had the morning before when Kyra had shown up at school in a heightened state of arousal. It was still there but not at the level it had been before. Relief and anxiety filled him.

The comforter fell off his shoulders as he stood.

"Liam?" Alex asked.

He didn't answer. Even without his sight, Liam was able to navigate around the living room to the kitchen, using the energy cast by the others in the living room. It was a strange sensation, not like seeing, not truly, but reading thermal signatures. He was nervous at first, unsure of his footing, but once he realized he didn't need his eyes, he became more steady and intercepted Kyra as she descended the stairs. There was a momentary pause, both surprised by the encounter. Then, without a word, Liam threw his arms around Kyra and drew her into a tight embrace.

"I thought I lost you," he breathed. A small sob escaped him as Kyra hugged him back. "I can't lose you. I can't."

The words shocked him. He should be mad. Should hate her. If it wasn't for her his mother would still be with them. Yet he knew

118

Kyra had nothing to do with the attack. The Shadows had been tracking his family for as long as he could remember. It was why they moved so much when he was young. The bookstore had been his mother's dream and only possible after striking a deal to monitor other hybrids. She tried to keep that secret from him but he knew…he knew what she sacrificed to give them a normal life. It was only a matter of time before the Shadows betrayed them. He was just thankful he and Kyra escaped. He wished he could say the same for his mother.

He held Kyra tighter as his body shook with sobs. His mother was still alive. He could feel her. She existed on the edge of his subconscious, far away from where they were now.

He didn't object when Kyra led him back to the sofa. She sat next to him and kept his hand in hers, her thumb rubbing soothing circles along the back of it.

"I'm so sorry, Liam," she told him, her voice soft and filled with more emotion than he had ever heard from her. "It's my fault. I should never have dragged you into my problems. I should have…I shouldn't have gone to Manitoulin Island. The Shadows followed me and now…" Her voice trailed off and he could almost see her shaking her head. "I'm sorry."

He shook his head and squeezed her hand. "It's not your fault. The Shadows would have caught up with us sooner or later."

"You knew about them?" Kyra asked in surprise.

"We moved a lot when I was a kid. They always found us. They tried kidnapping me when I was little but mom always managed to stop them. She fought them most of her life, too. She's the only one of her siblings born different. We moved back to Northern Ontario to be closer to her family and settle down." He sighed. "Obviously, that was a big mistake."

"Why didn't you tell me?"

"I didn't know you...but I saw the signs when your...eh...hunger started to show. That's why I took you to Mom. She still has those days and well...she found ways to deal with it without...you know...jumping some poor person." He gave a hollow laugh when he heard Alex inhale sharply. "Yeah, it's not always a fun experience. She had a 'friend' that helps her through it."

"Archer?"

He shrugged. "I never bothered to learn his name. They get together...I go the other way."

He heard Alex walk toward them, a distinct limp in his steps. The man sat back down on the coffee table across from him.

"And you? Have you ever had this 'hunger'?" the Anthropologist asked.

Liam shook his head. "No. Don't get me wrong, I like girls. Sure, someday I might want to get together with one, but my focus is my studies. Sex and all that stuff can wait."

"Did you memorize that from some pamphlet?" Another voice teased. It took Liam a moment to place a name to the person.

"Naomi?" he asked. The girl was from homeroom and period two. They had only spoken a handful of times. There were some not so nice rumours about her in the school.

"Yep, I'm here, doofus," she answered, her voice snide as usual. "So, what? You're into that whole chastity until you're married nonsense?"

"No, I just don't have to need to fuck everything that walks," he shot back. "Unlike some, I want a career and life that doesn't consist of what girl I got pregnant and continuing a bloodline that technically shouldn't even exist. Like I want Shadows chasing after my kids or their kids."

"Then wear a condom or better yet, get a vasectomy."

"Trust me, I am." Liam pursed his lips in annoyance. "What exactly are you doing here? Why is she here?"

"She and Archer saved us," Kyra explained. She squeezed his hand. "If it wasn't for them...the Shadows would have taken us."

Anger filled him at that. "They have my mother. Did anyone try to save her?"

"Archer searched for her," Naomi countered. "You know what? I don't need this. Kyra, I'm going outside. When you're done with him, come see me."

"Naomi!" Kyra called out.

She went to stand and Liam was suddenly at war with himself whether he should let go of her hand of not. His fingers didn't seem to work. His arm felt numb as fear ate at him. He couldn't let her go. If he did he may lose her, too. Yet, Kyra didn't pull away or try to break his hold. Instead, she sat back down and patted the back of his hand in a comforting gesture.

"It's alright, Liam," she assured. "How about you tell us everything about you and your mom. We know she's a hybrid and you're a next generation one...which means you both had...have gifts. Can you tell us about them?"

He hesitated. No one knew about his gifts. Not his mother, nor his cousins. He had only ever used them to amuse himself or to create special effects for his films. He wasn't even sure where to begin or how accurate his account would be. The only reference he had were from comic books and movies. He had assumed that since his mother was interested in the occult that perhaps they were magick users and the Shadows chasing after them were demons. His mother hadn't exactly been up-front about what they were…only some of the challenges he would face as he got older and dealt with puberty and such. He only recently learned there were more like them after moving to Little Current and starting the high school. Even though he hated moving, and even though the others like him mostly kept to themselves, he had happy to finally find others like him. He was happy to have met and befriend Kyra. He told her and her father all about himself and his mother, how they moved around, the fact she remained single but worked hard to provide for them, her dream of opening the bookstore and how she had such a love for books. He told them about discovering his gifts and why he felt he needed to keep it secret even from his mother. He told them about how he grew up thinking they were magick users and never considered them to be anything else. Of how the Shadows always seemed to find them and his mother would fight to protect him. His mother was a hero and did what she had to for the sake of her family.

By the time he was done, he was exhausted and hungry. Kyra helped him to the table while Alex brough him a plate of food and glass of juice. A new sound caught him off guard as he lifted the delicious smelling hamburger to his lips. The radio in the kitchen came to life with a woman's voice.

"Water Tower, this is Echo-7-6-5-Niner, requesting clearance. Security 16-5-8-3 pass. Entering air space."

Liam cocked his head to one side in surprise. "Why do they need air clearance?"

"I'll explain shortly," Alex promised as he answered the radio. "Clearance approved. Keep to the left platform. Civilian plane occupying to right pier. Beware of crazy people possibly swimming to the west."

"No crazy people, but I see the plane," the voice answered. "See you soon."

Alex gave an amused chuckle. "Welcome home, Elizabeth."

Liam practically clung to her hand as Kyra led him outside to greet the approaching plane. It was larger than the ones that normally flew to their home, nearly four times the size of the one she had flown the night before. Her stomach churned in anxiety as it circled over the lake. It made its way to the other far end of the lake, almost a kilometer away, then glided along the surface to the pier. A larger plane typically meant the pilot was not alone and in this case meant members of Earth Defence Command were onboard. A part of Kyra resented the idea of soldiers and possibly scientists coming to her childhood home, but at the same time she was grateful. The Shadows were still trying to find a way past the barrier. If they managed to make it through, neither her, nor her fathers could handle them all. They would swarm the compound as they had in the past. The shields would hold, even destroy many of them, but she was not fool enough to believe they would last forever. A part of her hoped Archer and Naomi could help then fight them off, but she had no idea what sort of gifts the other hybrids had. Either way, wouldn't be enough.

The plane pulled up along the pier. The side door slid open and a soldier threw a line to Lucas who in turn, secured it to the dock. As suspected, men and women began exiting the plane, the EDC emblem proudly displayed on the shoulder of the uniforms, soldiers, scientists, and technicians alike.

Kyra frowned at them. They didn't so much as acknowledge her as they went about their work, some heading to the large garage in the distance to retrieve ATVs that were stored away specifically for members of the EDC. The family ones were stored in a separate garage when Kyra was young so she would not get into trouble. It was always weird whenever someone entered the EDC garage but Kyra didn't dare go in, even if she was technically a member now.

"Kyra!" a familiar and friendly voice called to her.

Kyra looked over to see a woman the same age as Alex walk along the pier toward her with a happy smile. Her dark hair was tied back in a thick braid with streaks gray running through it. She wore a brown leather jacket over her dark green jumper, looking every bit like the pilot she had become.

"Aunt Elizabeth!" Kyra cried out.

Relief filled her as the older woman hurried toward her, swaddling her in a big hug, despite being almost six inches shorter. Kyra hugged her back. Elizabeth Monroe was the closest thing she had to a mother. If there was anyone she could talk to regarding her problems, both mental and sexual, without someone being overprotective, it was her Aunt Elizabeth.

Elizabeth pulled away after a moment and held her at arm's length. "Are you alright? Your Daddy told me what happened. Were you hurt?" Her voice dropped a notch. "Have you felt the need to em…feed?"

Kyra shook her head. "No," she assured.

124

Of course, she had only had sex in her dreams, a passionate kiss with Liam, and the moment with Naomi. However, the need to "feed" as associated with the way Celestials fed, had not happened. Not yet at least.

She gently took Liam's hand and stepped back to him. "Auntie, this is Liam. He…"

She fumbled for the right words, unsure how to express who Liam was and what had happened to him. Guilt hit her once more. She could feel the burn of tears building in her eyes. She blinked them away, fighting back the urge to let her emotions consume her, especially when she noticed another woman approach them. She was older, in her early seventies, with an air of authority and a hint of arrogance from centuries of hiding amongst humans. Her dark eyes were fixed on Kyra as they often did whenever they were near one another. Instinctively, Kyra stepped in front of Liam once more, shielding him behind her.

"General Caldwell," she said, her voice low, a hint of a growl rumbling through her words.

"Admiral," the Celestial hidden in a human host corrected as she came to stand next to Elizabeth. Her gray eyes roamed over Kyra before peering behind her to Liam. "And who do we have here?"

"Liam," came the answer as the young man in question placed a hand on Kyra's shoulder before stepping around her. His ghostly white eyes moved toward Caldwell's voice but never focused. "Why are there so many people here?"

"We're here to protect you," Elizabeth answered, her tone much more soothing than Caldwell's. "The technicians will reinforce the shields while the soldiers stand guard. The scientists are also trained doctors. They've been working with hybrids for several years.

They're here to make sure everyone is okay and take blood samples…with your permission."

Liam shrugged. "Can they fix my eyes?"

"I don't know."

A sigh left him. He gave a small sob and took Kyra's hand one more, a move that did not go unnoticed by Caldwell. The elderly woman frowned at the two, opened her mouth to say something but promptly shut it when Kyra leveled a hard glare at her. They had had many arguments over the years but Kyra was not about to let Caldwell say one bad thing about or to Liam. What she did say, felt even worse.

"You and your friends need to stay at the sanctuary," she said, her voice commanding.

"I beg pardon?" Liam answered, confused.

Kyra glanced at him then glared at Caldwell. "No. The sanctuary is for studying. We're as safe here as we would be down there." She glanced at Elizabeth but her aunt had a guilty look on her face. "You agree with her?"

"Sorry, honey. There's been a huge uptick of abducted hybrids. When your dad called…we feared the worst." She took a deep breath and let it out slowly. "We knew this might happen one day. The sanctuary was always meant to be a safe-haven for those like you. Now it has to be. You know better than anyone that the defenses there are ten times better than above ground. The Guardians can handle the Shadows better than any weapon we have."

Kyra stared at her in disbelief. She had spent the first seven years of her life living in an underground bunker, she was not about to hide underground once more. The sanctuary was the underground temple and city hidden beneath her feet. While it was fun to explore and learn about with her fathers, it was not a place she planned to spend more than a few hours in, certainly not hide in. She was tired of hiding. That was why she joined the EDC.

It felt childish but she yelled for both her fathers. Alex was the closest, already on the move to greet his childhood friend, Elizabeth, while Lucas was busy directing the technicians. He and Elizabeth greeted each other with a tight embrace. Caldwell received a mere nod.

"You didn't tell her?" Caldwell accused, making it apparent that they had already spoken of moving the hybrids underground.

"No, I thought your charming disposition would detail the reason much better," he countered, clearly not intimidated by the Celestial.

"You knew?" Kyra accused, not at all happy.

Alex sighed but nodded. He folded his arms across his chest and kicked at the toe of his prosthetic foot against the grass as he tried to form the words he wanted to say. "We spoke about it after you went to bed. It's not just for you. There are hundreds, maybe thousands of hybrids that have gone missing. As much as it pains me to say it, they're safer here than anywhere else. And obviously the house is not big enough to accommodate all of them…and people would question if a city suddenly appeared in the mountains. Heck, even a village would draw too much attention. It would be impossible to keep secret let alone protect. It's not like we can build a dome over it and even a shield will only last so long. If they wander outside it…"

Kyra held up her hand to stop him. "So, your saying that we're going to move them here and what…keep them prisoner?" She looked between them. "And what about their gifts? What if they came of age and need to feed or breed? Then what?"

"Kyra…" Alex tried but his daughter wasn't going to have any of it.

"I'm serious! The Guardians will attack anyone that's a threat. They're sole purpose is to defeat the Celestials and the Shadows. You can't tell me the hybrids will be safe down there. All it takes is one untrained hybrid losing control and they will swarm and kill them. Not even Uncle Owen can control them." She began pacing, swatting away Liam's hand as he tried to stop her. He stumbled when she jerked away a second time and it was the last moment memory that he was blind that made her stop and catch him. "Sorry," she apologized. "And what about Liam? He's blind and you want to send him underground? How is he going to get around?"

Caldwell's brows furrowed. "The same way he has been since losing his eyesight?"

Kyra was about to object but Caldwell had a point. Liam had only been blind less than twenty-four hours. He relied on her to help lead him around. Yet, he also had an uncanny ability to find his way around on his own, using "energy signatures" to maneuver around objects and locate people. He could likely do that regardless of his environment.

"Papa!" she yelled for Lucas. "Can you please tell them they're being unreasonable?"

He looked away from the technician he was working with, gave the man a nod, the jogged over Kyra.

"Whatever it is, no," he jested. He immediately became serious when Kyra turned pleading eyes toward him. "I take it this is about the sanctuary."

Kyra made a gesture that normally would get her in trouble but Lucas immediately understood what was going on.

"I think it's a horrible idea," he answered, siding with Kyra. "As far as we know it's dormant, but these kids could accidentally activate it and unleash an army of Celestials or worse. Wasn't the goal to keep the temple out of Celestial hands? Isn't that why the Guardians died in the first place?"

"Thank you," Kyra responded. She folded her arms under her breasts, a triumphant look lifting her lips. It quickly fell.

"However, it is the safest place...at least for a few nights," Lucas continued. "The technicians are increasing security. They may need to shut down the shield for a short time. They're setting up a back up unit but it doesn't take much for a Shadow to slip through. Until the new system is fully active, it may be safer for you and your friends. We'll discuss the others later. Right now, my – our – primary concern is you." He cupped Kyra's cheek. "Sweetheart, I couldn't live with myself if something happened to you. Please, take your friends and stay in the underground temple until this is all over. Then we'll decide as a family and team whether or not it's the best decision for the other hybrids."

It wasn't the answer Kyra wanted, but it made sense. A few days underground with just their small group wouldn't be so bad. She had spent a few nights there as a kid when they would camp overnight in the temple after a long day of research. She accepted his kiss to the forehead, a fatherly gesture that made her relax and feel safe. It was easy to agree with him when he did it.

"Fine," she murmured, all but melting into his embrace.

Lucas grinned and took a step back. "That's my girl. Go find your friends and tell them what's going on. Liam, can you help me set up lunch. There's more people here than I have food barbequed."

"Lucas, there's no need for that," Caldwell objected.

"Then you don't need to eat. Beth, you want a cold one with your burger?" He gave Elizabeth a wink.

"Damn right. After that flight, I'm more than ready for lunch." Elizabeth wrapped an arm around Liam's shoulders. "And while we're working on that, I'll give you the entire low-down on Kyra. Did you know she collects Troll dolls?"

"Auntie!" Kyra cried.

Elizabeth shot her a grin as she headed back to the house with Liam in tow. Caldwell look slightly put off. She glanced at Kyra, frowned, then followed the others. Alex and Lucas hung back, concern written on both their faces. They waited until the others were out of earshot before speaking. Alex nervously shifted his weight from his foot to his prosthetic, his arms folded across his chest as he worried his lower lip.

"I wouldn't have called them in if this wasn't serious," he explained, looking slightly embarrassed. "The Shadows have never attacked the shields like they are. Something's really riled them up. The technicians aren't only reinforcing the shield but extending it."

Lucas nodded in agreement. "And we don't think it's because of you. Archer and Naomi took off as the plane was landing. The increased Shadow activity could be due to them or it could simply be responding increased emotions and…well, Archer's questionable activities."

Kyra pinched the bridge of her nose. "I get it. Look, I'll find him and Naomi and explain the situation, but please...please don't make us stay down there. It's great for exploration but..."

"It won't be long," Alex promised. "We're going to have Caldwell track down your handler and Dr. White. We'll figure this out and find the missing hybrids."

Lucas nodded. "Hey, we'll be down there with you. Good food, music, maybe a few custom drinks...everyone is of drinking age, right?"

A small laugh escaped Kyra. "What...you're planning to turn this into a sleepover party?"

"Would you like a sleepover party?"

She shook her head, a grin lifting her lips. "I'm going to go find Archer and Naomi. You two...enjoy your party planning."

There was laughter behind her and some comment about finding pajamas for everyone. Knowing them they would. Kyra had never had a pajama party with other kids but her fathers did their best with her Aunt Elizabeth. She usually took control and did girly things with her that Kyra normally never got to do. Elizabeth was the one to teach her about make-up and nail polish. Lucas had spent months watching every video available to learn how to style her hair while Alex was more laid back and let her do her thing. They would make it seem as if they weren't underground surrounded by a spooky abandoned ancient city with an alien temple looming over them. Yeah, they were going to have a great time.

She walked into the woods. If she was Archer or Naomi and wanted to avoid the sudden crowd of EDC agents, she would have taken off into the woods to get away. Neither one of them seemed like the shy type but then again, she really didn't know either of them. She only hoped that they stayed within the perimeter. If the Shadows got either one of them it would be next to impossible to track them down. It was too easy to vanish in the vast mountain range with the millions of trees and dozens of lakes. The Shadows could kill them and dump their bodies anywhere and it would days, even weeks, before they were found. Fear dug a trench in her stomach at the mere thought of something bad happening to them. Yet, she did not yell out for either Archer or Naomi. She wasn't going to let her imagination get the best of her.

The trees were tall and thick, some of the tallest in the region. They towered high above her creating a thick rich canopy of bright green foliage. It blocked out the sun giving an almost twilight illusion. It was the perfect cover for the Shadows if not for the perimeter. That was all that kept them at bay. Right now, it felt like very little protection.

Perhaps her dads were right. Perhaps she was overreacting about the sanctuary. It was secure and equipped not only with overhead light installed by the EDC but also had enough housing to support more than a thousand people with its own eco system. It was better equipped than most bunkers. Not only was there several tons of non-perishable food stored there, but vegetation grew there and were edible thanks to UVB grow lights mixed among the bright LEDs the lit up the entire cavern of the sanctuary. Maybe she was making a fuss over nothing.

She frowned as she reached a tall stake that marked the perimeter. A faint blue see-through wall shimmered on either side of it. Her finger danced over it, barely touching. It always fascinated her how such a thing could keep back the Shadow beings, as well as Celestials. Only Caldwell was able to pass through but that was once because she knew the code to get through. It still hurt her but it would be far worse if she didn't. Small ripples appeared under her fingers and moved along with them. It tingled, electrical shocks racing through her digits and up her arm.

In the distance there was a flash of light. She turned toward it just in time to see a second flash. Was it possible that the Shadows knew the technicians were about to begin working on the fence? Were they waiting for it to go down in order to break through in the microsecond before the new shield went up?

Power pooled in her hands as she moved toward the flashing. She wasn't going to let them come through. She could handle them on her own. They moved on the other side of the shield, flickering in the darkness of the foliage in their true forms, trying to find a weakness in the shield. It was impossible to tell exactly how many there were, possibly thousands moving and coiling amongst one another like insects. Disgust filled Kyra. In essence, that's what they were. Insects waiting to be crushed.

A cry distracted her from the Shadows. She quickly glanced in the direction it came from then back at the Shadows, unsure if it was some sort of trap. Shadows were good at throwing their voice and making one believe in something that was not there. She was willing to ignore it until the cry was followed by grunts and even more cries. They sounded familiar. She gave the Shadows one last sideways glance before following the sounds. The Shadows were secure for now.

The sounds grew lower as she followed the length of the perimeter. Kyra was certain the cries belonged to Naomi but it was hard to tell if they were cries of pain and fear or something else. Why would Naomi come all the way out here? It was too dangerous. If she passed through the shield the Shadows would capture her and lord only knew what they would do to her.

Kyra inhaled sharply in surprise when she found Naomi and Archer in a rather compromising position. Naomi had her hands placed on the trunk of a tree with Archer behind her, on large hand on her hip, the other around her throat. Naomi's underwear were around her knees, her skirt pushed up to her waist. It revealed the curve of her ass as well as her hard dripping cock. Kyra blinked in surprise at the sight of it but her focus was drawn to the much larger and harder length slamming into the other woman. Archer was large and by no means gentle as he rammed into Naomi from behind. For a moment it looked as if he was hurting her but the look on Naomi's face said she was clearly enjoying herself. Her hands grasped Archer's as she pushed back, impaling herself on his long length, whimpering and crying for more.

Kyra was at a lost for words. All she did was watch. She had never seen people have sex before. She knew the sounds, had overheard it, but never had she actually seen two people couple. It made her stomach knot as her own dream of having sex with Archer played through her mind. It wasn't as vivid as this. She could feel the arousal and need wafting off them, could smell their juices mix. She licked her lips, arousal pooling in her groin and watched as one of Archer's hands moved to grasped Naomi's length, pumping it in time with each of his thrusts. The girl whined and thrust into his hand, utterly lost in the sensations.

Archer's eyes opened, a small smile curling his lips as he met Kyra's gaze.

"Come here," he purred, not once stopping his movements.

Kyra glanced up at him but shook her head, unsure what he wanted but unwilling to take part.

His voice was seductive as he rolled hips and groaning in ecstasy. "Come for Daddy, baby."

Naomi whimpered. "Yes, Daddy."

The slapping of flesh was all Kyra could hear as they moved together, neither one caring that Kyra was there to witness their coupling. It wasn't long before Naomi arched her back, coming at nearly the same moment as Archer. Cum came in spurts from Naomi's cock and dripped down her legs as Archer released inside her ass. The man pulled Naomi's head back, still holding her neck with one hand, and kissed her lips.

"Perfect as ever, darling," he murmured before finally letting her go.

"You too," Naomi responded almost dreamily.

She glanced at Kyra in surprise, her cheeks flushing red. Without a word, she righted herself, tucking her length in her panties then fixing her skirt.

"Sorry...I didn't mean to walk in on you...eh...sorry," Kyra apologized, just as embarrassed.

Archer hummed as he tucked his cock back in his jeans and zipped them up. "You could have joined in. More the merrier."

Kyra opened her mouth to respond but instead shook her head. She was not about to explain all the ways that was wrong. "Admiral Caldwell wants us back at the cabin. There's been a change of plans."

"Oh?"

"Yeah, we need to get back before one of the agents happen across you."

Archer chuckled merrily. "Nothing wrong with that."

She glanced at Naomi. The other girl was holding her skirt down, still oddly embarrassed. It seemed odd after the kiss they shared not that long ago. She took Naomi's hand and gave it a little tug.

"Come on, I've got something cool to show you after lunch. I think you'll like it," she told her, leading them back home.

While watching Archer and Naomi may have shocked Kyra, it didn't bother her. Sex was normal, it was nothing to be afraid of. Nonetheless, Kyra could not deny that it aroused her and it left her with questions she'd rather not have answered. The moisture between her legs didn't help. A part of her wished it was her Archer had been pounding into her rather than Naomi. That made the butterflies in her stomach even worse.

Chapter Nine

W hoa..." Naomi breathed as they rode the lift down the old mine shaft to the massive underground cavern.

Kyra couldn't blame her. No matter how many times she had seen it, the temple was always amazing to see. It was one of the wonders of the world, a true marvel to behold. The marble and limestone structure looked almost brand new. It shimmered under the overhead lights. Not far from it was the waterfall she had warned Archer about. It fed a small lagoon that led to a river. The mist from the falls gave the whole sanctuary an ethereal look. The village around it was bustling as EDC agents moved about, double-checking each building, making sure all the electrical components they had installed for security purposes were working. That included the lights, cameras, and security. They weren't the only ones down there. The Guardians, the protectors of the temple, also moved about. They moved around unnoticed by the humans, mere ghosts to the living. Kyra could see them clearly. She smiled gently when she spotted her Uncle Owen watching over the technicians, his large arms folded across his wide chest. He was Lucas's older brother, although he looked considerably younger. He had died nearly twenty years ago protecting Lucas and Alex. As such, he had not aged a day since then. He looked as if he was in his mid thirties, built like a body builder, and with the posture of seasoned soldier. He was a born leader and became the protector of not only the temple, but also all the Guardians under his watch, even those that had existed long before him. It seemed those who died while protecting or investigating the temple became Guardians in order to continue their work. After the destruction of all the other temples, the Guardians moved here, to the last known underground temple.

Thankfully, Kyra wasn't the only one to see the Guardians, which was a relief. Normally only she and Alex could see the spirits. With Kyra being a hybrid, she could see things on other planes of existence as could the Celestials. Alex was bonded to the temples, having been imprinted by one of the "keys" once used to access the Archives hidden within the temples. Turned out the Archives were, in actuality, aliens ships the Celestials used when they first came to Earth. The temples were built over them to hide them. That was what the Guardians were protecting: keeping both Celestials and Shadows from taking control of it or using it to open a portal the to their realm. It proved the Celestials not only existed in their reality, but had the ability both by space ship and portals, to move throughout space and time. It was unnerving, but now Kyra didn't feel as alone as she once did, because it wasn't only her and Alex that saw the Guardians. Naomi and Archer saw them as well, and much to Kyra's surprise, Liam was able to sense them…much as he sensed other energy signatures.

Kyra explained who and what the Guardians were, their entire history and that of the temple. It made her a little giddy to do so. It was almost like when Alex taught her the history of the temples and she enjoyed finally sharing her knowledge with others like her. The best part? They actually listened and asked questions. She was almost able to forget about walking in on Archer and Naomi having sex.

The lift jerked as it came to a stop, causing everyone to stumble a few steps. It was not the best mode of transportation and desperately needed upgrading if EDC were planning on making the sanctuary home to hybrids. It would not handle the volume of people that would be coming through. It was old and rickety and had been in use since the discovery of the sanctuary some seventy years ago.

The gate opened, allowing them passage to the cavern floor. Taking Liam's hand, Kyra led the group into the village. The huts were primitive and like the rest of the sanctuary would need to be upgraded if they were to house people for the long term. There were certain amenities that few people couldn't survive without these days, namely indoor bathrooms, and functional kitchens. Not everyone was into the idea of communal bathing and eating. Kyra certainly wasn't. She liked her privacy as she assumed most people did. Nonetheless, she never expected to ever actually live down here.

"So, you can pick whichever hut you want. They're all the same. Pretty basic. Think of it like camping." She led them into one of the huts that had had some upgrades already done it and showed them through the small space. It was no larger than a typical studio apartment with a large open living space and a smaller space that once served as cold storage but would be upgraded to a bathroom one day. To the left side of the living space was a stone slab with a mattress that was still wrapped in plastic. Next to it was a metal storage locker. "There are new mattresses in about half the huts, and bedding in the storage cabinet. Fresh water comes from the lagoon. It's fed by the waterfall and always moving. It may be small but it's deep. Don't bathe in it. There are heated springs about half a kilometer down river that you can use for that or just to relax."

"How are the springs heated?" Naomi asked, in awe by everything she saw.

"This entire mountain sits over a dormant volcano," she explained. "Thankfully, it hasn't been active for thousands of years. We're safe."

"This is amazing!"

Relief flooded Kyra. She wasn't sure how any of them would react to the sanctuary. Naomi's awe made staying underground a little better.

"Which hut is yours?" Archer asked as he rummaged through the storage locker.

Kyra's stomach dropped at the question. It sounded innocent enough but she wasn't sure if she wanted him to know.

"I haven't decided yet," she answered with a shrug, hoping Archer did ask her to stay with him.

"Why don't we bunk together again?" Naomi asked, grabbing Kyra's free arm and all but hanging from it in excitement.

Kyra hesitated a moment. She worried her lower lip as Naomi gave her big pleading eyes.

"Sure," she conceded.

Sure, they had kissed, but they had already spent one night together without it getting overly weird. Besides, Naomi was obviously in a relationship with Archer. She was overthinking everything. She needed to stay focused and get everyone settled.

"Archer, you can have this hut," she said as she headed toward the door with Liam in tow. "Liam, your hut will be next to ours. I'm going to assign a Guardian to stay with you at night. If you need anything just tell them and they will get me."

"Alright," Liam agreed.

They headed to another hut several doors away from the one assigned to Archer. It was closer to the temple and where the majority of the Guardians clustered. Owen gave Liam a curious look but said nothing, his attention turning toward the hut Archer was in with a small frown. It seemed he did not trust Archer either. Kyra wasn't sure how to take that. The Guardians rarely got the chance to interact with the living. The few people that came to the sanctuary seemed to invade their territory, something the Guardians did not appreciate. Having the offspring of Celestials, their mortal enemies, was not something to which they were going to take too kindly. Kyra gave her uncle a sideways glance and shook her head. Owen was as overprotective as ever.

"Okay, so this is your place," she told Liam as they entered the hut she designated for him.

It was the exact same as Archer's but Kyra took the time to remove the plastic off the mattress then began making it for him. She fluffed the pillows, taking extra time to make sure everything was perfect for him before bundling the excess plastic for disposal. It would have to go in the bin on the edge of the village to be taken topside later to be properly disposed off. Her fathers were obsessive about recycling and composting. Nothing went to waste and those things that could not be composted or recycled had to be taken to a facility in Sudbury.

"I think you'll like Jalyn," she told Liam as she worked. "She's my best friend and has watched over me most of my life."

She paused and looked out the window toward the temple. Where was Jalyn? Normally she was right at her side. Was she still in Little Current? Usually, it didn't matter whether she and Jalyn were together, the Guardian was always able to track her, appearing within moments at the mere thought of her. Something was not right.

"I'll be back in a minute," she said.

She left the hut and crossed the short distance to the temple and Owen as the Guardian paced worriedly in front of it. He stopped the moment he spotted her and waited in place for him. He nervously ran a hand over his head, his dark brown eyes downcast as if he already knew what she was about to ask. She took a seat on the steps and waited for him to join her.

"She hasn't come back, has she?" she asked, not needing to say Jalyn's name.

He sat next to her and hefted a large sigh. "No."

"I'm sorry. Things happened so fast. I assumed she would meet us here."

"It's not your fault, sweetheart. Jalyn is a tough girl. She's probably avoiding the Shadows. If they attacked you in Little Current then there's likely more there. How many hybrids were there?"

Kyra was silent for a moment. "Quite a few. More than I've ever seen in one small town...but then again, they have kids from neighbouring towns also attending. They could be all over the island. Given the number per capita...it's a lot more than anywhere else I've been. Hundreds...maybe thousands."

"What is EDC doing about it?" he asked, his brows furrowed in concern.

She shook her head. "I don't know. I was the only agent there. I was supposed to be. Tyler asked me to. Archer was my informant."

"Hmm...I'm going to send some people to the island to find Jalyn and check on things." He glanced toward Archer's hut once more. "Things aren't adding up. If there's a high concentration of hybrids there, it should be crawling with agents."

"Unless the Shadows got them."

He nodded. "Perhaps." His ghostly hand patted her knee. "Go be with your friends. I'll look into this. Between patrolling and the island, we're going to be busy."

"Don't spread yourself too thin," Kyra warned as she stood. "We need you. Papa needs you."

He smiled tenderly at her before shooing her away. They both had duties to attend to. Kyra watched as he climbed the steep steps of the temple, pausing only to talk to another Guardian. To her they were as real as the men and women of the EDC, but far more valuable. They were her family, the people with whom she had grown up around.

She went back to Liam's hut, where both Archer and Naomi were helping to finish set it up. There wasn't much for them to do. They finished making the bed then Kyra took them on a tour of the cavern. She showed them the large garden that grew fresh produce all year long. A lot of it went into cold storage for use in the cabin while the rest was sold to local grocery stores. The garden had a large variety of fruits and vegetables, some that were not native to Northern Ontario or even Canada itself. The temperature in the cavern was always warm, a comfortable twenty-six degrees Celsius which made it perfect for growing. The irrigation system was fed from the waterfall and set on a timer to mist the garden every hour. Two orchards were behind it, one for apples, another for plums. And of course, there was a vineyard, this one larger than the one aboveground. The cavern was equipped better than any bomb shelter. They could probably host a variety of animals as well which would cover all the food groups if they had to stay underground for a long period of time.

"Can we see inside the temple?" Archer asked as they made their way around the village.

Kyra hesitated then shook her head. "Sorry, I need to clear that with EDC, and Caldwell can be a bit of a bitch when it comes to the temple. She didn't even want me in it when she gave my dads the entire place." She gave a small laugh. "Hell, if they didn't declare that I was their research assistant I would never have been able to step foot inside."

Caldwell's face when Alex told her right out that Kyra was his assistant and would go into the temple with him whether the former general liked it out not had been priceless. The Celestial tried being in command and quickly learned she could not control either Alex or Lucas. They did what they wanted and raised Kyra how they saw fit. It was something Kyra appreciated. It was a huge change from the life she had living in the lab.

"Maybe when things settle down I can show it to you," she conceded.

"Sure," Archer agreed.

He didn't push the subject which was a huge relief to Kyra. Since it was the first time having another hybrid in the sanctuary, she was expecting a little more push-back when it came to the temple.

"Okay," Liam interrupted, causing Kyra to stop and turn toward him. "So, what are we supposed to do down here? I'm guessing there's no television or internet. Are we supposed to garden and read while we're here? I'm not too sure how well I can do either of those things."

Naomi nodded her head. "He's got a point. I mean, I can think of things to do but even I would get bored after a while. No offense," the last part was directed at Archer.

"None taken. Is there a baseball or football field hidden under here amongst all this vegetation?" Archer responded.

Kyra hadn't thought of that. She was usually helping her fathers with their research or planting the garden, orchard, or vineyard. She was always busy when in the sanctuary. "We could have a campfire by the waterfall. Maybe get to know each other better."

Liam tilted his head in thought. "That might work. Maybe you can tell us more about the temple. I mean, I've read your dads' books but how much of that is real?"

"All of it is real," Kyra retorted. She ran a hand through her hair. "Yeah, okay...we could do that. It will also give us a chance to get to know each other better...you know...since we're stuck together."

Naomi rolled her eyes in annoyance. "Oh, that sounds like fun. Are we going to have hot dogs and marshmallows to go with it? Can't go around telling our deep dark secrets without those."

"And alcohol," Archer chimed in. "Lots of alcohol."

Kyra was about to object but decided against it. Given what had happened, a few drinks wouldn't hurt. "I'll see what I can do."

It wouldn't be hard. She knew where the wine cellar was and Lucas would be okay if she took a few bottles. It wasn't as if it was the first time she would be drinking she just didn't do it often.

Archer shrugged. "Alright, let's do it. It's better than sitting around doing nothing. Are there any logs or large roots we can use for seats?"

"Yeah, I'll show you."

There were huge roots that poked out of the soft soil between the rocks that formed the wall of the waterfall. Logs were harder to come by. The tunnel that fed the waterfall was only a meter wide and was underwater which meant very few logs came through. Kyra retrieved axes from a storage shed. She and Archer worked on finding two large, thick roots long enough to be used as seating. They chopped them down, careful of where they fell so that they didn't hit anyone below them or drop in the lagoon where they could potentially float down river. Once that was done, they dragged them to where Naomi was setting up kindling to start the fire. Wood for the fire wasn't hard to come by. With all the renovations being down over the years, there were scrap pieces are wood stored in various locations. They found and gathered them, piling them on the side for continual use throughout the evening. While the others worked on that, Kyra fetched several bottles of wine, making sure not to touch any of Lucas's or Alex's prized Pinot Noir or Rosaria. Food was a little harder. There were no meat products kept underground and they hadn't had hot dogs or marshmallows in a very long time. She was unsure if Naomi actually wanted them or if she was being sarcastic. Instead, she pulled out several bags of military rations. A little water and heat and they would be perfect for dinner.

Not everyone was thrilled with the rations but the wine made up for it. They sat around the fire, poking of their food with wooden forks and passing around a bottle of red wine. It was quiet now, most of the EDC having left for the evening, taking up housing in the empty huts for the evening while others went topside to help patrol the grounds. That left the hybrids alone and able to speak more freely.

"So...we all have different gifts, right?" Liam asked, sounding somewhat timid. He rubbed his right arm nervously, his blind eyes directed toward the fire.

146

"It would seem so," Kyra acknowledged. "Why don't you tell us about yours?"

"Oh…" Obviously, he hadn't been expecting to go first. "Well, you know I can see energy. Even before I lost my sight. And…I can produce energy…manipulate it even." He lifted his left hand and moved his fingers. A moment later a plasma ball appeared, floating above his hand, and crackling with electricity. "I use it for my films. My own special effects without all the cost."

"That's cool," Naomi whispered, impressed.

He looked surprised by her compliment. "Yeah? How about you?"

She blinked in surprise. "Me? Oh…I…eh…I can manipulate minds. You know, make people see or do what I want. It doesn't work on our kind but it's enough to get what I need."

"When you feed," Liam clarified.

Naomi frowned at him. "Yeah, when I feed. I'm not sorry I'm not a virgin. I like sex and I'm not about to apologize for that. Besides, it's easier than approaching people without it."

"What do you mean?" Kyra asked, confused.

"Because of what I am. Not the hybrid part but because…" She took a deep breath, made a face, then sighed. "I was born male."

Kyra guessed as much but stayed quiet and let her talk.

"I knew when I was little I was a girl. My father wasn't happy when I wanted to wear girl's clothing. He…" Naomi shook her head. "Let's just say I left as soon as I could and I haven't looked back. I learned how to manipulate minds in order to find food and shelter until

Archer found me. He took me in, let me be me, and helped me get back into school and gave me a good paying job at his bar. I owe him everything."

Kyra met Archer's gaze, unsure how she felt about that. She was happy that the man had helped Naomi but she wasn't sure how she felt about them also having a relationship. Was it sincere or was it some form of payment for his help?

"What about you?" she asked the bartender.

He shrugged. "I help people tame their hunger."

"That's all?" Liam asked, clearly not buying it.

Archer shrugged. "It's perhaps my most sought-after trait. I can also open portals or teleport, whatever you want to call it."

That had everyone staring at him in awe.

"You can teleport?" Kyra asked, needing him to repeat himself.

"I can teleport," he confirmed with a small laugh.

"Why didn't you just teleport us to a plane?" Naomi demanded. "Hell, why didn't you just teleport us here?"

He poked around his silver ration bag with it fork. "I didn't know where 'here' was. I need to know 'where' I'm going in order to open a portal there." He stuck a fork full of Shepard's Pie in his mouth and chewed thoughtfully as he regarded Kyra. "So, we told you about our gifts, how about you?"

"I have one question first," Kyra began. "Have any of you every changed forms. Not like how Naomi can manipulate minds to see what she wants but really change forms?"

Each one shook their heads.

Kyra sighed in disappointment. "Well, I can." She let her human form melt away to her true form, her skin becoming almost translucent and hair the palest white. Both Liam and Archer murmured in surprise and utter awe. "I can change my appearance, look any age or race. I have increased strength and can sense other hybrids, but that's really about it. I can't manipulate energy or minds or teleport. Most of my skills were gained through intense military training." She felt a little inadequate after learning what the others could do.

"Hey, that's still cool," Naomi assured. "I mean, I've never seen a Celestial before. You're one in human form."

That didn't make Kyra feel any better. In fact, she hated being compared to the Celestials. She wanted nothing to do with them or the Shadow beings. All she wanted was to be normal. To not have to hide from them or people that would use her for their own gain. The only good thing was knowing she wasn't the only one of her kind out there, but then again, this entire exercise proved she wasn't quite like them either.

"You look like a queen," Archer said.

Kyra inhaled sharply and immediately returned to her human form. That's what he called her in her dreams. She stared at him for a moment but there was nothing suggestive in his voice or appearance. Perhaps it was just a off-handed comment with no real meaning. She mumbled a thanks. She certainly didn't feel like a queen.

The rest of the evening was filled with stories and chit chats and even some laughter. Of course, no night would be complete without someone taking a swim in the lagoon. Kyra watched in amusement as Naomi and Archer goofed off in the water as she and Liam sat around the fire. The young man leaned forward, his elbows on his knees as he stared blankly at the fire. There was a shimmer of tears on his cheeks.

"Are you alright?" Kyra asked. It was a stupid question but she wasn't sure what else to say.

Liam shook his head. "No."

"I'm sorry. I wish I had never gotten you or your mother involved."

He was silent for a moment then nodded. "I think I should head to bed. It's been a long day."

She stood with him. They didn't talk as they walked toward his hut. A Guardian was waiting outside of it and gave Kyra a nod as they passed him into the small space. She sat on the edge of the bed with Liam, not yet willing to let him go.

"If she's still alive, we'll find her," she promised. "My Uncle Owen is already sending Guardians to the Island to watch over the other hybrids. They'll find your mother."

He nodded but didn't look convinced. Kyra placed a hand on his arm but immediately withdrew when he tensed up.

"Okay, if you need me just tell Kenneth, he's the Guardian watching over your hut," she told him as he stood. "He'll get me. Have a good night."

"You, too."

If only there was more she could do. Kyra wanted to believe Marie was still alive but in her gut that seemed highly unlikely. She and Liam were lucky to survive the explosion. Even if Archer didn't find her body it didn't mean much. The Shadows could have taken it.

It was impossible to know for certain without going back to Little Current and investigating the remains of the store herself.

Archer was standing outside her hut. He leaned against the stone wall, his ankles and arms crossed as he stared up at the temple. He didn't say anything at first as she approached him, his gaze solely on the ancient structure and Guardians moving about it. Kyra hesitated a moment before standing next to him. His fascination with the temple was understandable. Even after all these years and having explored almost every inch of it, Kyra still looked upon it with wonder.

"Have you ever seen one before?" she asked, leaning against the hut as well.

"Only in those books Marie sold in her store." He glanced at her. "Your fathers have been blessed."

"I don't know about blessed. They've both suffered greatly because of the temples."

"I read that. Doctor Jackson's father and entire team. Griffith's brother."

She nodded. Both her grandfather and uncle were Guardians now, although they had very different jobs. Professor Jackson, Alex's father, was an anthropologist like his son. He tended to bury himself in research even though he was no longer alive. It was rare to see him. Like all Guardians, he was able to transport himself from one temple to another. In death, he was now able to do the research he had never been able to finish in life. Alex missed him dearly but knowing he was following his dream made it hurt less than it would have his father died a normal death.

"I was sort of hoping we could talk in private," Archer said. He turned toward her, his face serious.

"We're alone now," she commented with a raised brow.

He glanced into the hut. "Naomi went to bed but I really don't want her overhearing this."

"This isn't about her being..."

He looked surprised then quickly shook his head. "No, no...this is about the other night."

Her eyes widened. "Oh...sure."

They headed back to the waterfall. Now that they were finally talking about that night, Kyra didn't want to. Just the memory of the dream unnerved her. They sat on the make shift benches around the now dead fire, smoke still wafting off the hot embers. Archer sat close to Kyra, invading her space but not in a threatening way, more in the way she and Liam had been staying close all day. Perhaps he misinterpreted her protective nature over the younger man as something more intimate.

She rubbed her hands together as she waited for him to begin. She really didn't want to be alone with Archer, but curiosity got the better of her.

"I wasn't lying when I said I was trying to help you relax," Archer began as he idly poked at the damp embers in the fire pit. "Relaxing is different for everyone and considering the number of hybrids I've helped, I assumed sex would help you relax as it did them. I'm sorry for overstepping my bounds."

Kyra stared at her hands, unsure what to say. "Thank you."

"If I'm being truthful, seeing how independent you are, it's kind of a turn on," Archer confessed. "I was hoping you would come to me to make the dream come true. You've never had sex, have you?"

Her cheek flushed. It was a very personal question, one she knew she didn't have to answer. Yet after everything they had shared today she found herself confessing. "No. Although I almost jumped Liam. I've never felt like that before. It was frightening. I've never wanted something so bad." She took a deep breath. "Before I was adopted, Alex had been possessed by a Celestial. It turned him into a sex crazed monster. He hunted men and women, seduced them, fucked them, then ripped out their hearts and feasted on them. I was always afraid that if I had sex I would turn into that."

"Is that what they told you?" Archer asked in shock.

She shook her head. "Not exactly. Besides, I never really thought much about sex. I never really cared about it. It's not like I can ever have kids."

"Why can't you have kids?"

She swallowed the lump forming in her throat. "When I was little, I lived in a lab. The scientists their performed experiments on me, trying to figure out what I was. The took blood and tissue and then my uterus and reproductive organs. They didn't want me to have children."

"I'm sorry."

A small shrug of her shoulders was the only response.

"You know, sex isn't only about reproducing. It's about bonding and enjoyment. In fact, a lot of people do it just for the pleasure of it. That's why they created such things as condoms and contraceptives." He reached over and squeezed her knee. "Think about it. Your dads obviously have sex. And Naomi, she loves it. Given the chance, she'd be eating you out right now."

Heat filled Kyra's cheeks, making her blush brightly. She had been thinking of that earlier, curious of what it would be like having sex with another woman.

"Myself...I would be honoured if you let me do it in her place," Archer purred, leaning in so that his lips were an inch away from her left ear.

She turned to him, her eyes wide with surprise. "I..."

His lips pressed against hers. It was warm and sweet, not demanding, or forceful. It lasted only a brief moment then Archer pulled away, an apology already on his lips. Kyra didn't give him a chance to mutter it before pressing back, returning the kiss. Archer hummed softly against her lips before pulling away.

"Do you want to get out of here?" he asked, his voice soft and alluring.

"Where would we go? We were told to stay down here. And my fathers should be coming down as soon as they're done with Caldwell." Considering how long they were taking, it could be another hour or two before that happened. Caldwell had a tendency to drone on and on about how she thought things should be run which often led to all sorts of arguments from Lucas and Alex.

"Do you always do everything your daddies tell you?" Archer teased. "Is that why you're such a good girl?"

She studied him for a long moment. "Maybe I'm not so good."

His lips turned upward into a pleased grin. "Then let's blow this joint."

He dove in for another kiss as he opened a portal. A moment of light-headedness assaulted Kyra as it wrapped around them, moving them through time and space to a new location. When they reappeared, it was in the forest high above the lake. It was dark now, the sun fully set and stars shining high above. It took Kyra a moment to orient herself. They were just below the shield, still safe from the Shadows but in an area that was unlikely to have any EDC patrols. Guardians perhaps, but Kyra didn't see or sense any.

"It's time to stop being afraid, Kyra," Archer purred. He stood behind her, his large hands on her upper arms. "You've spent your life in hiding, doing what everyone else tells you to. Why? You are so much more than they let you believe. You're still learning about your gifts. Gifts they've locked away because they're afraid of you."

"You're wrong," she whispered.

Or was he? She barely remembered everything that happened to her as a child. She was able to change her form, psychically speak with Alex, and see the Guardians, but she had no offensive power like Naomi and Liam. Were those skills locked away from her? She closed her eyes as Archer's lips brushed across the side of her neck. It sent a tingling sensation throughout her body as heat pooled in her groin. She closed her eyes and tilted her head to one side, allowing him better access. It was such a new sensation and she couldn't get enough. Her knees felt weak but she didn't fall. Archer held her up, one arm around her waist, the other holding her chin, keep her head tilted as he sucked a mark into her flesh. She reached above and behind her, her fingers knotting in his hair, holding him in place. Her free hand covered his over her belly and followed it as he slipped his hand into her shorts and panties. One large finger rubbed against her clit, making her gasp in surprise and pleasure.

"You're already wet," he purred in her ear.

A moan left her as one of his large fingers rubbed between her folds, back and forth slowly before pushing inside.

"Oh gods!" she cried.

Her hips bucked forward, wanting more. Between that and what he was doing to her neck, Kyra thought she might lose all control. She whimpered, feeling moisture pooling in her neither region. A second finger pushed inside her and her stomach pulsed, as if butterflies fluttered within it. Pleasure filled every inch of her being all centered around her neck and core. If he kept this up, she was going to come and he hadn't even been inside her yet. His glorious fingers didn't count.

When he removed his fingers, she turned in his arms to kiss him. "Will it hurt?"

He gave a small nod. "At first, but I promise you, it'll be worth it." He gave her another quick peck to her lips. "Can I make love to the real you? As much as I adore this form, I want to see the real you in all your glory."

Her gaze searched his, looking for any hint of a lie, then let her glamour fall, once more revealing her alabaster flesh and ghostly white hair. He ran his fingers through her long locks then cupped her cheeks. "Why do you hide? You are a goddess given human form. You could command the hearts of men and women with barely a glance." His thumb wiped at stray tears that rolled down her cheeks at his words. "I have never seen one so beautiful in all the people I have ever lain with."

"Are you trying to scare me away?" Kyra laughed. "So many men and women before me."

"None of which are like you," he assured. "Would you feel better if I wore a condom?"

She hadn't thought about it. Giving what they were about to do, even if she could not have children, a condom was still preferred for their safety. She nodded and watched with wide eyes as Archer unbuckled his belt then pulled down his zipper and released his thick, long length that was already hard. It was just as Kyra remembered from her dream and seemed much larger than it had been when he was fucking Naomi. Her mind had to be playing games. No man should be so large. She fumbled for words as Archer ripped the corner of a silver wrapper between his teeth. He removed a translucent blue condom and rolled it over his hard length.

"Is it supposed to be so big?" she wondered out loud.

He smirked as he pumped his cock. "Don't worry, babe. We'll make it fit."

He pushed her against a large oak tree then reached for her waist. He began undoing her shorts, quickly pushing them down as he fell to his knees before her. She didn't have a chance to ask what he was doing before his mouth latched onto her mound, his tongue running over her folds. If his fingers felt good before, it was nothing compared to his mouth and tongue. It licked and flicked and dove into her, alternating between licking and suckling. His teeth ran over her mound, nipping at her clit. She pressed a curled fist against her mouth, biting on her knuckles to keep from crying out. Her other hand gripped his hair, threatening to pull out chunks as she pressed his head harder against her as she rocked her hips, as if riding his mouth. She wanted more, needed it. Needed something more than just his tongue inside her neither lips. Every nerve in her body felt on fire, as if she might explode. It was sweet and painful all at once and she wept with the new sensation. She threw her head back, on the crisp of coming, a tidal wave of sensation and unimaginable pleasure so close to breaking every sensibility she thought she had. Then, just as the pleasure was about to crest, Archer withdrew and stood up.

"No…" she whimpered, trying to force him back down.

He caught her hands and held them tightly in one of his large ones. "It's about to get much better, darling," he purred, rubbed the tip if his hard length against her dripping folds. Then, without warning, he pushed into her.

Her eyes widened at the sudden sharp pain that all but chased away the pleasure. For a moment they stood still, Archer's hard length deep inside Kyra, filling her to the core.

"So tight," he mused, rocking his hips gently. "It's like your insides are sucking me in."

She stared at him, fear and pain warring with the pleasurable sensation of being full. More than full. Overflowing. A moment passed and then he pressed further, something that should not have been even remotely possible. She was not sure if a normal human could take something so huge inside them but she instinctively knew Archer was now inside her right to the root. She leaned her head against the trunk of the tree and panted, unsure what to expect next.

"Look at me," Archer instructed, catching her chin. She did as he said. "Wrap your arms around my neck. Good girl. Now your legs." He released her chin to grasp her ass with both hands, then held her up as she wrapped her legs around his waist. "That's my girl. Now hold on tight."

He pressed her against the oak and pulled out until only the tip remained within her then pushed back in, slowly at first then faster. His hips rocked and rotated with each thrust so that his cock didn't hit the same place twice. The friction was both painful and sweet, confusing Kyra to no end. How could something hurt and feel good at the same time?

She clung to Archer has continued delving into her body, his muscles rippling under her fingers. His own hands tangled in her long hair, tugging it, forcing her head back as he rammed every inch of his length into her. The tugging brought it's own strange mix of pleasure and pain until she found herself moving with him, countering each of his thrusts with her own. Pushing down as upward thrust, she met him half way, impaling that huge cock impossible deep inside until it felt as if it might tear through her stomach.

"This is what you're entitled to, Kyra," Archer's voice rumbled in her ear. "To a man who would adore you, to pleasure you, to make you Queen." He groaned, his pace increasing, going harder and deeper until it was hard for Kyra to think. All she could do was listen. "To show you what you truly are and unlock your true potential."

The pounding of her heart and wet sound of slapping flesh filled the space between his words. She had so many questions but words refused to form on her lips. All she could do was moan and whimper until it felt as if her insides turned to liquid as the fire within built and built with every piston of Archers hips until fire and pleasure consumed her. Her world turned a blinding white as her core swelled within her, pulsing in time with the beating of her heart.

They clung to each other as the aftershocks rode through them. Sleepiness filled Kyra but she was able to open her eyes long enough to notice they were no longer in the forest. Instead, they were in a stone chamber unlike any she had seen before. Archer lie her on a bed made of fur before curling protectively around her, his deep voice rumbling sweet nothings in her ear.

Chapter Ten

It was late by the time Caldwell called the meeting to an end. It seemed the situation with the hybrids was far more delicate than they originally thought with thousands in Ontario alone having been abducted. Now it wasn't only as matter of saving those that had been taken but protecting those that haven't. EDC agents were stretched to their limit.

"We need a safe place for them," Elizabeth concluded after presenting her report.

Lucas nodded. "I agree, but the sanctuary can only support a few hundred at best. If there's as many as you say then we're looking at a few hundred thousand hybrids, and that may be Ontario alone. Where do we take them? We would quite literally would have to build a city to house them all. That's not including basic necessities."

"And what about their families? If we start taking kids, even if for their own good, we're no better than the Shadows," Alex chimed in. He leaned his elbows on the table and met Elizabeth's gaze. "You're asking us to take these kids from their parents and put them in a bubble. Is that really protecting them?"

She sighed. "It's not the best solution, but I don't know what else to do. It's next to impossible to track the hybrids. Kyra can sense them, you might be able to as well. If we can find them, we may be able to stop the Shadows." She fidgeted with her mug of coffee as she spoke, clearly not happy with her plan either. "Six kids went missing in Little Current after Kyra fled with the others. Six kids we could have saved had we known about them. We need to find them and the others."

"We'll bring those we can here for now then find or build another sanctuary," Caldwell said. "Our first concern is to stop the Shadows and find the hybrids they kidnapped. Once the Shadows are back in their dimension then everyone will be safer."

Alex shifted in his seat. "Why are there so many? Why didn't they leave with the Celestials? I always thought they served them. Wouldn't that mean they serve the hybrids?"

Caldwell pursed her lips. "They serve an alpha, the ruling class of the Celestials. Right now, there is none so they have gone rogue."

"You make it sound as if they were prisoners," Lucas observed.

She nodded. "In essence, they were. Just like the Guardians were victims killed protecting the temples, the Shadows were also victims of the Celestials. People who had been sacrificed to them and forced into eternal servitude. Without a ruler, they would lash out and attack those they see as a potential threat, something that could become as powerful or even more powerful than the Celestials could ever be, Human-Celestial hybrids."

"That doesn't make sense," Alex objected. "When Kyra was kidnapped they claimed she was a failed experiment. They were going to dissect her and harvest her organs. If they were afraid of her why do that? What would they have to gain?"

Caldwell was silent, only answering with a shake of her head. It infuriated Alex to no end. Every time he tried to get more answers about that night, when Shadows possessed an entire black ops squadron, attacked their vineyard in Massey, killed the MI6 and Royal Canadian Mounted Police teams protecting the house, Caldwell fell silent. If it were not for her and team, they may not have gotten Kyra back, but why she was taken was still a mystery, just like why the other hybrids were being taken.

The Admiral pushed her chair back and stood. "Let's go check on the kids," she suggested. "I want to make sure the security is up to par."

"Isn't that why the technicians were there?" Lucas asked.

Caldwell glanced at him, her mouth slightly open. Instead of answering, she left the cabin. Lucas and Alex shared a look, both concerned by what Caldwell wasn't telling them. With a frustrated frown, Alex looked to Elizabeth. She would know better than anyone what was going on in the Celestial's mind, but she only shrugged. Annoyed, Alex stood and followed Caldwell. His right leg was irritating him, the stump rubbing against the prosthetic. The weather was changing, a storm brewing in the distance again. It would be hours before it hit but Alex could already feel its affects. It was going to be a bad one. Hopefully the new power grid for the shield would hold up against it.

They caught up with Caldwell near the edge of the woods. She was fast given her advanced age, the Celestial given her human host added strength and agility. She still gave her youngers a run for their money. Lucas caught up to her, huffing and puffing as he began walking next to her. It took Alex an extra few seconds.

"What about Kyra's handler, Tyler? Has anyone heard from him?" Lucas asked once he caught his breath.

Caldwell was silent for a moment. "Dead." She sighed and stopped walking. "His body was found three days ago near Centre Island."

"Dead?" Alex repeated in shock. "What about Archer?"

"Archer?" Elizabeth asked which was echoed by Caldwell.

Lucas stopped and stared at the two women in confusion. "Archer, the bartender…about my height."

"Looks like a younger version of Lucas," Alex added. "He's Kyra's informant. He was at lunch with us today. Stuck close to Kyra and Naomi."

"You mean the blind boy?" Caldwell asked, confused.

Alex looked to Lucas in confusion. "No, the older man. Late twenties…early thirties."

Caldwell shook her head and even Elizabeth seemed to have no idea who they were speaking of. "There were only two people with Kyra, the dark-skinned girl, and the blind boy. No one else was there." She paused, looking back and forth between Alex and Lucas. "Unless…we need to get to Kyra. Now."

She turned on her heel and hurried into the woods, heading in the direction of the old mine that hide the entrance to the sanctuary. The other hurried to catch up. It would have been faster if they had the ATVs but the patrol was using all of them, including the family ones. They were left to walking, or rather running, the urgency evident in Caldwell's movements. They followed the path, ignoring the soldiers they passed, needing to get to Kyra as quickly as possible.

"I thought Shadows and Celestials couldn't possess hybrids," Elizabeth panted as she struggled to keep up with Lucas and Caldwell while keeping close to Alex.

"They can't," Caldwell answered.

Which meant Archer was either a Shadow or a Celestial possessing a human. Or he was a much more powerful hybrid than they had dealt with before and was able to hide in plain sight. The mere thought of that was frightening. Was he helping the Shadows? There were so many questions Alex had that he had no time to voice. All he knew was that he needed to get to his baby girl before something bad happened. Lucas was right to not trust Archer.

Elizabeth radioed the EDC agents and ordered every available one that wasn't already in the sanctuary to head there. Without knowing for certain what Archer was, it was best not to take any chances.

Kyra's entire body tingled, from her head to her toes, when she awoke. She felt rested but sore, her groin stinging slightly from the friction of what seemed like hours of endless sex. It had been unlike anything she felt before and her mind grappled for a way to explain it. I had been like a river of orgasms, one crashing after another as Archer brought her to new heights of pleasure. It had been so intense that she had passed out on more than out occasion only to awaken as another wave of immense pleasure washed over her, leaving her in a euphoric haze before happening all over again. Each time it felt as if Archer filled every inch of her. She lay on her belly, a feather pillow clenched in her arms under her head and let herself drift in and out of sleep. She felt content, a feeling she had not felt since leaving home to work with the EDC. Her body was relaxed, limps almost as light as air even though she did not want to move them. She wanted this moment to last forever. No rules, no responsibility, just utter pleasure and contentment and the hand that was lazily tracing patterns along her back.

There was a soft whispering beside her, Archer's deep rumbling voice speaking words in a language she only vaguely remembered from sometime in her childhood – before Alex and Lucas came into her life. It was like a lullaby, comforting as a mother's touch, something she had forgotten about over the years.

"What is that?" she mumbled with a small hum.

"An old chant to help younglings unlock their power," Archer answered. "To help you reach your full potential."

She laughed softly and turned her head to the side to gaze up at him. He was naked and what a sight that was. His skin, darker than hers, had a certain glow about it, giving him an ethereal look. She admired his toned pecs and abs, her vantage point only allowing her to see half of his gorgeous body.

"Is this how you help the others?" she inquired, resting her head back on the pillow.

His large hands moved down her spine slowly, his fingers tracing over each dimple. "Sometimes. Ah…there it is." He pressed hard midway down her spine then rotated his thumb causing an audible pop.

Kyra grunted. It didn't hurt, far from it. It was as if he released a valve and the pressure in her lower back suddenly released. She sunk deeper into the mattress, her body sagging. "What did you do?"

"Releasing the pressure in your body. You're always so tense, that may be why you haven't been able to reach your true potential. Just let the stress go," he explained as he repeated the process several more times until finally she lay utterly limp, her body feeling as if it was floating. When he was done, Archer lie next to her, a small, pleased smile adorning his lips. "How does that feel?"

"Amazing," she breathed, returning his smile.

She closed her eyes, on the edge of dozing off. If only they could remain like this forever. Perhaps in a better setting. A tropical one, faraway from all their worries, with no Shadows to bother them.

"Something's wrong."

"Hm?" she murmured, happily dozing off.

"I didn't say anything," Archer answered, pausing his chant.

Perhaps she had been hearing things but then it happened again, another voice whispering in her ear. Then another and another. More and more voices talking all at once. She winced as the voices piled on top of one another until she could barely make out individual words.

"Stop…stop!" she whimpered.

Her body curled away from Archer, and covered her ears. It did nothing to help. She'd heard voices before, normally Alex's, but nothing like this. There were so many. Most were as frightened as she was, as if they suddenly heard each other and had no idea how or why, just like Kyra. Others were in pain or despair, trapped and hurt. It brought tears to Kyra's eyes as their despair rode over her. It took all her strength to erect her mental shields in an effort to block out the voices, but all it did was muffle them a little not stop them. It was enough to let her think, if only for a few moments.

"What did you do?" she demanded.

She turned to glare at Archer but he was gone. Not even his clothing remained. He must have slipped out as she struggled with the voices. Anger filled her at that but the voices were already getting louder again, as if even more were joining the others. It wouldn't be long before they consumed her again. She needed to get to her dad and figure this out. She didn't think she would be able to think properly if her shields fell, there were just too many voices.

Taking a deep breath, she focused on what she needed to do and pulled on her discarded clothing. Just one step at a time. Once her shoes were on, she glanced around the room she was in. It was one of the two small temples on top of the pyramid, often known as the Queen's chamber. How the heck did they end up there. With a groan, she rubbed her face as she descended the steps. The voices were pushing against her shields. Why were there so many.

"Kyra, stop!" Owen's voice suddenly yelled out to her.

She blinked in surprise and looked toward him. There was a lot of fear on his face, something she was not accustomed to with him. "What's wrong?"

"Just stay right there," he said, approaching her slowly with one hand raised as if approaching a wild animal.

Kyra's eyes widened as she noted other Guardians moving toward her. The Ancients, the first Guardians, had weapons drawn, something they had never done in all the time she knew them. Those weapons were aimed at her and Owen was moving to get between her and them. Kyra took a step back in shock.

"What's going on?" she demanded.

"I don't know, honey, but you need to stay perfectly still," Owen insisted.

Pain sliced through Kyra's head as the voices began pushing past her shields, flooding her mind once more. She gave a small cry of surprise and fell to one knee. The sudden noise wasn't only deafening but almost blinding in intensity. She placed her left hand against her head. She had to reinforce the shield but she could barely think. Her gaze caught sight of her bare arm. She was still in her true form but instead of alabaster white flesh, there were batches of crystals forming over skin, blue and pulsating with energy. She drew it away from her eyes, her eyes impossibly wide. What was happening to her?

"Celestial!" one of the Ancients cursed.

She glanced toward him. "No...I'm not..."

Her words didn't seem to matter, they rushed toward her even as Owen stepped protectively in front of her. That caused the Ancients to turn against Owen, who had been, up until then, the Guardians' leader. Now he seemed to be viewed as their enemy for protecting Kyra. It made no sense. What had happened to turn them against her? Between the voices and the sudden changes to her body, Kyra was beyond confused. She was terrified. Energy was riding through her body just as powerful as the voices, searching for an outlet.

One would not think spirits could hurt one another, let alone the living, but they could. Owen cried out as he was attacked.

Kyra watched in horror. Could Guardians kill other Guardians? Was it even possible to for spirits to die.

"Stop!" she yelled. She forced herself back to her feet. The pain in her head was unbearable. Her arms were tingling, the energy and crystal taking over them and her legs, filling her entire body. She flung out one arm toward the Guardians. *"Stop!"*

That energy rushed through her to the palm of her hand then out in a wave of plasma far more powerful than any light attack she had produced before. Light attacks were more like flashes used to repel the Shadows beings. This was something far more deadly that did not encompass her entire being. It was like a gun shot, expelling from one location but expanding to consume all in its path. It overtook the Guardians, tearing them apart, erasing them from this realm and with them...Owen.

Kyra stumbled back in shock. She stared at where they were just moments ago, shock and confusion filling her. The voices in her head calmed down, not gone but momentarily muted.

"Owen?" she called. She looked around but he was gone just like the Guardians who attacked them. "Owen!"

He was gone.

Terrified, she hurried down the temple steps to the village. Liam and Naomi were at the bottom, looking just as fearful as she felt. EDC agents were there as well, more hurrying to join them. Many with their weapons drawn just as the Guardians had been.

"What's going on?" Liam demanded, clearly sensing something was wrong.

"I don't know," Kyra answered. She looked at the agents. They seemed confused, unsure where to aim their weapons. "Where's Archer?"

Naomi shook her head. "I thought he was with you."

"That's what I want to know as well," Caldwell's voice interrupted as she pushed her way through the EDC agents. "And why no one seems to have seen this man except your group." She paused a moment and looked around. "Where are the Guardians?"

Fear filled Kyra's face. How was she supposed to explain what happened to them when she herself didn't understand? It must have read on her face because Caldwell's face paled as if she understood. Or more precisely, read her mind. Kyra could feel her in her head, her thoughts mixing with the other voices. She could also "hear" Liam and Naomi's thoughts.

Are they dead?

Did you kill them?

What have you done?

"It was an accident," Kyra pleaded. The voices were going louder again. She covered her ears with her hands. "Stop! I need to get out of here."

"Kyra, what's going on?" Lucas asked.

He, Alex, and Elizabeth stood a short distance from Kyra. Alex leaned against him, looking just as pained as Kyra, as if he too heard the voices. Lucas was holding him up, his focus on both his husband and daughter. Elizabeth stood slightly in front of them, a hand on her sidearm.

Kyra looked from Lucas to Alex, her fear growing. Whatever was happening to her was happening to him as well. Their bond shared their pain. "Dad? Papa?"

"Kyra, you need to stand down," Caldwell told her. The Admiral took a step toward her, one hand raised much as Owen had, fear filling her pale grey eyes. "You need to come with me. Something's very wrong."

She wants to lock you up again, Archer's voice whispered above all the others. *She's afraid of you. She's been lying to you, they all have.*

"Stop it," Kyra told him as she took a step back.

Ask her. Ask her what you truly are.

She turned her focus to Caldwell once more, silently asking what Archer was talking about. Surely, the woman could hear him as clearly as she could. All Caldwell did was shake her head, her eyes wide with terror.

She murdered your parents...both your parents, Archer continued. *She stole you. Locked you away because she thought she could control you...use you for your power. You're not a hybrid, Kyra. You're a Celestial born in a human form. Both your parents were Celestials who possessed humans. You are so much more than a hybrid or Celestial, but she made certain you could not reproduce. You were born to be our Queen.*

Kyra's eyes grew impossible wide at the revelation. "No...that can't be true."

"Kyra..." Caldwell breathed but it wasn't that single word that verified what Archer said, it was the fear and guilt that came from her mind.

Kyra stared at her in disbelief. "Is it true? Did you murder my parents? Did you experiment on me because you were afraid I would become Queen?"

Caldwell raised both hands. "I can explain." *I'm sorry.*

"No, you can't." Kyra moved toward her, her arms changing into the blue crystal form as they had when the Guardians attacked her.

"You took them from me, stole my ability to have children of my own, locked me away, and trained me to be your lap dog. You don't get to say, 'I'm sorry'."

Weapons were drawn on her, the EDC agents, and soldiers ready to fire on her at a moment's notice. Lucas and Elizabeth were yelling at them to stow the rifles but no one was listening.

"Why?" Kyra demanded.

Caldwell met her gaze, the fear hardening to anger. "Because you are the single greatest threat to this world since the Celestials first came here." She made a hand gesture and a moment later the EDC opened fire.

"No!" screamed Alex, Lucas, and Elizabeth. Agents that weren't shooting at Kyra grabbed them, holding them back so that they did not get caught in the crossfire.

The gunfire should have killed Kyra. It should have wounded her but no bullet made contact. Instead, it was as if a shield formed around her, catching, absorbing, and sending them back to very people who shot them. Many fell, killed upon impact while others were seriously injured. Not satisfied, Kyra channeled the energy flowing through her, directing it at her assailants as she had inadvertently done to the Guardians. And just like the Guardians, they were torn apart, ripped to shreds and away from reality without even a chance to scream. She turned that power on Caldwell but before she could completely destroy her something interfered, another voice. Her Dad.

Kyra, no, his voice whispered in her mind as calming energy washed over her. *This isn't you. Stop, sweety. Stop. I love you.*

She gasped, realization of what had just done hitting Kyra like a punch in the gut. She turned to her fathers, her mouth open. Caldwell lay at their feet, her Aunt Elizabeth knelt next to her while Naomi and Liam cowered close by. The remaining EDC had dropped their weapons in surrender.

"Kyra?" Lucas asked cautiously when he met her gaze.

She swallowed thickly. "Papa? Dad?" She looked between them, horrified by the fear she saw in their eyes.

A hand caught her elbow. "We need to go," Archer told her.

She spun around, surprised to see him. Behind him was a portal, swirling in silver and gray. She glanced at it, relief feeling her. She didn't want to be here anymore. She needed to run. The voices were telling her to run.

"Naomi, Liam?" Archer offered as he led Kyra to the edge of the portal.

Naomi moved to join them but Liam didn't. He stayed next to Alex, as if feeling safer with the Anthropologist than he did with Kyra. She couldn't blame him. She was afraid of herself but knew she could not stay without endangering those she loved. With Naomi at her side, Kyra followed Archer into the portal, leaving the sanctuary to the surviving EDC.

Chapter Eleven

Elizabeth held Caldwell as the surviving EDC agents searched the temple for Kyra and the other hybrids. Alex knelt next to them, his stomach twisted into series of knots. He could still hear the voices, so many voices, echoing in his mind. Hybrids, he assumed, but not just the ones that had been within the sanctuary. There were more. Thousands. Perhaps hundreds of thousands. It took all his concentration to sort through them, to search for Kyra but there was something or someone blocking him. All he could feel was her fear and confusion and anger. All were justified but he could not reach his daughter, could not soothe her and it pained him to know he could not help her.

"Is it true?" Lucas demanded. He stood over Caldwell, rage written on his face. "Did you murder her parents? Was this whole thing orchestrated to turn her into your own personal weapon?"

Caldwell grunted, a hand over her ribs. She met Lucas's gaze with pain filled grey eyes. "Yes," she answered simply. "But I had no choice. Her parents wanted to populate the world with hybrids...to erase the human race entirely. With Kyra they would have succeeded. I had to stop them." She groaned as she tried to shift to a more comfortable position.

"We need to get her medical attention," Elizabeth told them. She shot Lucas a glare. "You can interrogate her after."

Caldwell placed a hand on her arm. "No… This is my fault. I should have killed her when she was still a baby but I couldn't…she was so small and harmless. She was an innocent. It wasn't her fault." She drew in a shaky breath. "Celestials came to Earth thousands of years ago, made humans worship them…enslaved them even in death and made them into Shadows. They bred with their slaves, creating an army of hybrids. When the rebellion happened and Celestials were forced underground, the humans hunted and slaughtered every hybrid they found." Her eyes closed for a moment as her strength began to drain from her. "When the first Celestials were awoken five decades ago, they began the program all over again. We tried to stop them but they were smarter this time. They didn't merely impregnant random humans, they found the perfect matches. Descendants of the original hybrids. They possessed them and mated on another. Our culture doesn't have kings and queens as you know them, but Kyra's parents were as close to royalty as they come. I hunted them down. I killed them, and I removed Kyra from her mother's womb. I had her reproductive organs removed because if she bore children they would be powerful enough to wipe out every living creature on this planet."

"How can you be so certain?" Alex asked, bewildered by what she was saying but knowing it was true.

Caldwell's gaze shifted to him. Her eyes were glassy now, a thin film covering them. "Because it has happened before. On other planets. Entire civilizations wiped out in the Celestials' quest to dominate the universe."

Elizabeth shushed her. "Admiral, you need to possess another body. This one won't last much longer," she advised. She brushed the older woman's hair aside. "You can inhabit mine until we find you a suitable host."

A small laugh escaped the Celestial. Her hand shook as she reached up and cupped Elizabeth's cheek. "No, my dear. I have lived countless lives. Let me die. You have much more important things to worry about. You must find Kyra. Stop her. This Archer, I don't know who he is but he is not what he seems. Whatever he wants from her will only endanger humans and hybrids. Our two peoples will never live in peace unless he is stopped." She reached out and grasped Alex's hand. "Find Kyra. Stop her...no matter what you have to do."

Alex stared at her, unable to believe what she was asking.

"We'll find her," Lucas confirmed.

Caldwell nodded. "Go."

She closed her eyes, her breathing growing shallow. It wasn't long before she was no longer breathing at all. Elizabeth gently laid her body on the ground then stood. Liam, all but forgotten, stepped closer to Alex. Alex tried to sense his thoughts but they were jumbled with the rest of the hybrids, almost like a hive mind. It was unsettling, not that Alex normally reached out to sense anyone other than Kyra.

"Are you really going to kill Kyra?" Liam asked. He clenched and unclenched his fists. "Those things killed my mother...don't let them take Kyra, too."

"No one's killing Kyra," Alex assured.

"We have to find her first," Lucas said. He picked up one of the discarded rifles off the ground. "And I'm guessing, since you're now part of this hive mind, that you're our key to finding her. So, let's get to the planes and go after our girl."

Alex hesitated a moment, uncertain by the guarded look on Lucas's face.

"Go," Elizabeth told them. "I'll gather the surviving EDC and meet up with you. Alex, I'm sure there's some remaining Guardians. Find them and take them with you. If there's any chance of saving Kyra, we need every single one of them."

"And then some," Alex threw in.

With luck, the Guardians that had been patrolling above ground had survived Kyra's blast. There wouldn't be very many of them left. Not from this sanctuary at least. He needed to find out what triggered it and how. That would be the key to saving her. Lucas was right not to trust Archer. Whatever was happening to Kyra was somehow because of him, and he was going to pay for manipulating his child.

He took Lucas's offered hand and let his husband pull him to his feet. "Finding her isn't going to be easy. There's a lot of chatter. Everyone is frightened. Most have never been part of the hive before, they don't know how to shut each other out. Neither does Kyra. Her thoughts and theirs are overlapping."

Lucas didn't seem concerned by that at all. "If anyone can weed through their thoughts it's you. You've had almost twenty years experience dealing with Celestials and the Guardians' thoughts invading your own. You know how to shield yourself from them and how to navigate through them. You'll find her and then…we'll bring her home."

Alex searched his eyes. There were still dark, as if hiding something, but he couldn't place his finger on what. He wanted to dismiss it as mere concern over their daughter, but he couldn't. There was anger, likely directed toward Archer and Caldwell for keeping yet another secret of Kyra's origins from them. He gave his husband a small nod and squeezed his hand reassuringly. Lucas was right. He could track her down. They'll find her and stop her before she unintentionally hurts anyone else…and before anyone could hurt her.

Nausea filled Kyra as the portal opened and dumped them in what appeared to be a large white room. The above lights were horridly bright, making her feel sicker. The voices were louder here, more desperate, screaming for help. She fought to create a psychic shield. Anything that might muffle the voices if only for a few minutes. It took all her remaining energy to form the shield. It left her disoriented and dizzy. Without a word, she hurried to a corner and vomited the contents of her stomach, the reality of what she had done hitting her like a ton of bricks to the gut. She threw up until her stomach was empty and there was nothing left but painful, dry heaves. Placing a hand on the wall, she took a deep breath before leaning against it and sliding down to sit on the floor. She pulled her knees to her chest, feeling small and uncertain; wanting nothing more than her dads to hold her and tell it was going to be okay. It wasn't going to be this time. She had murdered the Guardians – killed her Uncle Owen and dozens of EDC agents. She had become everything she had fought against. The mere thought almost made her throw up again.

"Kyra?" Naomi asked in concern. She sat down next to Kyra, wrapped an arm around her shoulders, and let her rest her head against her shoulder. "Are you okay? Bad question, you're obviously not. Do you need water? I'm sure we can find some."

Kyra shook her head and simply leaned into the other woman.

Archer stood by the door. He looked up and down the hall, his shoulders tense and jaw set. "Kyra, I know this is all a little much for you, but I need you to pull yourself together. We're not going to make it out of here without you."

She glanced at him. Anger filled her but she was too exhausted to yell or lash out at him just yet.

"Where exactly are we?" she asked. She pushed herself to her feet, ignoring the nausea and dizziness that threated to consume her once more. "Where did you bring us?"

"You wouldn't believe me if I told you," he answered.

Kyra frowned. She didn't trust him, not after what had happened. "Try me."

He looked toward her, a scowl tugging at the corner of his lips. "Do you really think you're the only hybrid they experimented on?"

Her blood ran cold at the very thought. "What are you talking about?"

"This is a government research facility. The Shadows have been working with certain factions of the government to find and capture our kind and bring them here," he continued. He turned toward her, his face almost unrecognizable as it twisted in anger. "Caldwell and the EDC have been lying to you. They don't see us as hybrids. They see us as Celestials, Aliens to be dissected and experimented on then discarded. Do you want to know why so many of us have been disappearing? It's because they're taking us, Kyra. And those they don't kill they turn into weapons…against our very creators. They want to use us against the Celestials!" He took a deep breath and slowly calmed down. "But you already knew that. After all, they made you a living weapon. The only difference is, Caldwell kept your true potential from you, like a dog on a leash."

Kyra sneered at the comparison. Her hands balled into fists, ready to show him just how powerful she was. "And what exactly are you? Their Pitbull?"

His eyes narrowed. "Perhaps…but I broke my chains."

They glared at one another. Whatever attraction Kyra felt toward him was gone now. He was not the same person she had spent the night with, nor was he the one she had fantasized in her dreams. He was something far more twisted. Someone broken from whatever had happened to him in his youth.

"Why are we here?" she demanded, even though she was already sure she knew.

His lips pressed into a thin line, as if he wanted to continue arguing. Slowly, he relaxed. "To free the others."

She gave a curt nod. That had been her mission with the EDC. Find missing Hybrids and free them. Regardless where they were, that was her duty. Nonetheless, this felt wrong. There were hybrids there. She could feel them all around her. She could also sense the Shadows. She could feel them before but not like this. She could almost hear their thoughts, like the hybrids, and the Guardians. She could almost reach out and touch them. Twist them and make them serve her as they once did the Celestials. She withdrew her mind from theirs. Even that brief moment left her ice cold. If those creatures were here, even in human hosts, they had limited time to save the hybrids. Whoever they were working with had no clue what they were dealing with.

She crossed the room to what appeared to be cabinets and began searching them one at a time.

"Do yourselves a favour, find lab coats or maintenance clothing, and nametags. Let's try blending in before they figure out we're here," she instructed. She found a blue jumpsuit. It looked like a custodian jumper. "The last thing we need is to draw attention to ourselves. It won't buy us a lot of time, but at least enough to figure out where the others are being kept."

"We don't have time to play dress up," Archer sneered. "I know where they are. Let's go."

Kyra opened her mouth to argue but he was already on the move. She and Naomi hurried after him. "If you knew where they were, why do you need me? Why not tell me at the bar?"

He kept moving, not bothering to look at her as he answered. "Because I didn't know if I could trust you."

He paused when a man and woman exited a room to the right. "Naomi," he said, a silent command.

She moved forward, catching the attention of the two newcomers. They looked at her in surprise as she caught their gazes. No words were exchanged, but a moment later they walked away, as if never seeing them.

"We're invisible to them, and everyone else here," Naomi explained as she took the lead. "Just stay close."

She and Archer moved through the building as if they knew their way around. It was obvious they had both been there before. Naomi looked nervous, even a little scared, but her face was one of determination. Everyone they passed walked by them as if blind to the trio.

"They captured you, didn't they?" Kyra asked as Archer pushed open a large set of beige double doors. "You escaped."

Naomi nodded. "We were in a lab. They were going to kill Archer and dissect me. They couldn't understand why I had male organs if I was female. They thought something was wrong with me and wanted to fix me." She hugged herself as she passed through the doors. "I wasn't lying when I said Archer saved me. He took me with him when he broke free."

That explained Archer's attitude. He had been one of their victims, and so had Naomi. They knew first-hand what was likely happening to the others, and yet, rather than outright killing everyone they passed, they were letting them go. Did they know the difference between those that hurt them and those that simply worked there?

That thought fled from her as she entered what appeared to be a large prison, four stories high and nearly a hundred feet long. This was the source of the hybrid voices. Not all of them but well over a hundred, perhaps more. It took all Kyra's strength to block them out and stay focused. She slowly followed Archer and Naomi, pausing momentarily as she gazed into each cell and the frightened hybrid inside. There was one per cell, as if the Shadows were afraid to have them together. Perhaps it made it easier for their human companions to experiment on them one at a time. Some were very young, only a few years old. Others were older, in their fifties or sixties. Far older than Kyra suspected a hybrid to be, but confirming Caldwell's theories that hybrids have existed far longer than anyone expected, meaning second and third generation hybrids must also exist. Some were likely here as well. She took her time, reading each name and known gift labeled on the cell door.

"Kyra?" a familiar voice called to her from across the vast room.

Surprised, Kyra looked across the wide opening between platforms. There, standing in a cell, was Marie. She held the bars and looked wide-eyed at Kyra, her hair disheveled and face bruised. Her clothing was torn and covered in soot from the explosion in her store. Relief filled Kyra. She hurried around the platform to get to the other woman.

"You're alive!" she cried. She grasped the bars next to Marie's hands. "Thank god! Liam has been so worried about you. He's safe. He's with my dads."

Marie sighed, her shoulders sagging as if the fear she must have felt the past two days finally melted away. "Thank you," she breathed. Her eyes closed for a moment as she slowly began to relax. "What are you doing here? What did you do to your hair? Never mind...you need to leave before they find you."

"I will," Kyra promised. "We're all leaving."

The locks were digital, requiring a password or specialized key card. They wouldn't be easy to hack into. Kyra was good with computers – when they didn't fry on her – but she wasn't nearly as accomplished as her Aunt Elizabeth at hacking into systems. She pursed her lips, trying to think of how to deal with the situation when it came to her. It was so simple, making a problem she normally had with electronics the answer. Wrapping her hand around the device, she let the energy she usually fought to control flow freely through her and into it. It took only a moment before they smelt a small electrical fire and heard the pop of the lock disengaging. Kyra slid the door open and let Marie out before hugging her. Klaxons blared all around them, alerting the guards to their presence and Marie's escape.

"How did you do that?" Marie asked as she pulled away. She winced at the sound of the alarms.

Kyra shrugged. "Electronics don't like me."

"That could prove useful," Archer remarked as he came up to them. He took Kyra's arm. "Come, I need your help."

She yanked her arm free. "After I free everyone on this level."

"Once we free my friends, they can help us free everyone else. These ones are priorities. They are set to be executed."

Her face paled. Why would they going to be executed? Was that the fate of each hybrid after being experimented on? Her stomach churned at the memory of almost being harvested. Had Lucas not found her she would have died long ago. She could not allow that to happen to anyone else.

"Go," Marie told her. "I'll free the others." She glanced toward Naomi who presently had three guards under her control and barricading the doors. "She's going to need help."

Kyra nodded then turned to Archer. "Okay, let's find your friends then get everyone out of here. I assume you have a plan?"

His lips were pressed in a thin line as he regarded her. "I do, but I need you to trust me."

Her brows rose questioningly. "Let's find your friends. We'll discuss trust after."

"Works for me."

Kyra paused before following him and turned back to Marie. "Anyone who can help Naomi, send to her right-away. The others help you protect the children. I'll be back shortly."

"Be careful," Marie said in a motherly tone.

Kyra gave another nod then hurried after Archer. They had to run up two flights of stairs to reach the level Archer's friends were on. By then, guards were already filling the level from doors on either end. Archer rushed them, a bestial snarl rumbling through him. His finger elongated, finger nails lengthening and turning into claws. He looked most beast than man. Almost like a werewolf minus the fur. He tore into the men and women as if they were nothing more than paper, flinging their bodies over the rails as a warning to those below. Kyra pushed the imagery from her mind as resorted to her military training to take down those that attacked her. Rather than kill them, she disarmed them and knocked them out, trying her best to avoid using the new power that was still roiling through her. She didn't want to kill. She never did, and regretted her actions in the sanctuary, but she needed to free the hybrids. If she had no other choice, she would kill these guards as well. She just hoped she didn't have to.

"This one!" Archer ordered, pointing to a cell as he tore into another man.

Kyra glanced into the cell. The person inside was a man, larger than Archer, built like a professional wrestler. He glared at her with bright, unearthly green eyes. They reminded her of acid and were far from friendly. Nonetheless, she grabbed the panel to the cell door controls and fried them as she had Marie's. The man pulled open the door and towered over her, almost seven feet tall. She gazed up at him but felt nothing more than annoyance toward him. He left her to help Archer.

"That one!" Archer yelled, pointing at another cell.

She frowned at him. He was completely skipping over cells to get to the people he wanted and forgetting the others. She only hoped that the people they were freeing would try to help save the rest. A moment later, that cell's lock was also fried. This was another man, a twin to the first. He regarded her with open interest, his gaze sizing her up as something more than his saviour. It made Kyra's skin crawl. There were two more cells Archer wanted opened. Two more big burly men who had lingering gazes for Kyra.

"Right, let's go," Archer said once everyone he wanted was free.

"Not without the others," Kyra snapped. She returned to the cells Archer had skipped over.

"We don't have time," the man snapped.

He grabbed her wrist and tried to pull her along but Kyra was not going to put up with it. She didn't let him pull her away and instead yanked him toward her. That surprised him and knocked him off balance, freeing her wrist. She didn't give him a chance to recover and instead punched him square in the jaw.

"I agreed to help you free *everyone*, not just the people you want," she sneered at him. "Now, help me open these doors and get them out."

"And go where?" Archer countered. He nursed his jaw. "There are hundreds of hybrids here. You expect to be able to walk out the front door? Maybe have someone fly them all home?"

"You can open a portal," she pointed out.

"I can't teleport that many people! And again, where would they go? Your sanctuary? It's crawling with EDC agents. You'll just be handing them back to them." He inhaled deeply. "Kyra, you can't save everyone, but we can stop the Shadows from harming anyone else. All you need to do is help these guys unlock their powers."

"What?"

"We'll be discreet," one of the men said. He approached her, a dark, hungry look in his green eyes. "Pretty thing like you can probably handle two of us at a time. Make it fast and sweet."

"Excuse me?"

"Kyra, you're our Queen. You have the power to unlock our true potential," Archer explained. "I could not shift forms until this morning. You can do the same for them. Unlock their powers and we can end the Shadows and their companions once and for all."

She took a step back, unable to believe what she was hearing. Archer had been using her all this time? It wasn't just about sex but power as well? It made her sick to her stomach. There was no way she was having sex with any of these men.

"No," she told him, her voice stern and leaving no room for argument. Of course, these men were not about to take no for an answer.

The largest – Jeb, if she remembered the name on the cell correctly – grabbed her by the throat and slammed her into the wall next to cell. Her head banged painfully against the wall. His large fingers put enough pressure against her throat to make it hard to draw breath.

"No one's asking, sweetheart," he growled. "You may be Queen but you're also power and we need that. You can either be a good girl and open those pretty legs or have them opened for you. Either way, I'm stuffing you full of cock and filling you with my seed until you're choking on it."

Kyra struggled, her nails digging into his thick arm. Her shields fell in the struggling, allowing the thoughts and minds of all those around her to invade her thoughts. Jeb's stood out the loudest. Perhaps it was due to the fact they were touching. She could see what he had planned, what he imagined would happen as they had sex. He would be in front, his large, thick length buried to the hilt in her cunt, ramming into her with hard, measured thrusts that were meant to bring him pleasure and show her who was boss. Behind her was another man, one of the other three she had freed. His length, just as long and thick, would be in her ass, his pace matching Jeb's as the two raped her. She could almost feel them inside her now, the friction both pleasurable and painful all at once. While they tore into her body, the remaining two men would jeer and touch her, biting and suckling her breasts and neck until she was begging for them to stop only for them to go harder and make it terribly worse.

"*No!*" she screamed.

The energy within her lashed out with such force and heat that Jeb had no time to process what was going on or avoid it. The power engulfed him, tearing him limb from limb until he was no more. He turned to dust before all their eyes with not so much as a scream.

"Kyra, stop!" Archer ordered. She turned that power on the next man who dared to attack her. "Go!" he yelled at the remaining two before Kyra could turn her focus on them.

They ran like cowards. Kyra watched them, her entire body glowing with power. Anger and rage at what they had intended filled her. She would find them later and finish this but for now, she had more important things to concern herself with. She slammed her fist through the metal wall she had been pinned to moments before and channeled her power through it, short circuiting all the cell locks at once rather than doing it one at a time. When she removed her hand, the blue crystal texture had returned, only now it encased her entire arm. It looked almost like armor yet flexible, allowing her to move her arm naturally. It didn't just cover her arm, it was slowly moving across her body, under her clothing. She could feel it, as if her body was turning to crystal…or perhaps a diamond. Her white hair shimmered against it, looking even more ethereal than usual.

A gun shot startled her from her musing. A bullet slammed into her chest, but rather than harm her, it crushed upon impact. She turned toward them, her eyes narrowed as they fired upon her again only for that bullet to be crushed as well. Once the guards realized their weapons had no affect on Kyra, they backed away and radioed for help. She grabbed the nearest one and for the first time dove into a human's mind. She blocked out the fear he felt and instead used his memories as a map to find the quickest and safest way to get all the hybrids out of the facility. It wasn't as hard as she feared it would be. Navigating the human mind was surprisingly easier than the many hybrid voices that had overwhelmed her in the past hour or so.

She released the man once she had the information she wanted.

"Leave," she ordered, the command meant for all the guards. "*Now!*"

She waited until they exited the prison before turning to the freed hybrids.

"We don't have much time," she told them. "Stick together. Naomi…Naomi?"

"She took off after Archer," Marie reported. She led the freed hybrids from the lower levels to Kyra. "How do we get out of here?"

Kyra's gaze moved over them, silently counting the endless sea of hybrids. She never imagined there would be so many. And these were only the ones that had been caught and brought to this place. How many facilities like this were there? There could be dozens in each province. If it wasn't for the guard, she wouldn't even know which city they were in.

"Follow me," she instructed.

They were all leaving, one way or another.

Chapter Twelve

The two water planes landed within minutes of each other just outside Trenton less than an hour later, the morning sky still dark and sunrise still hours away. There were so many voices in Alex's head now that he could barely make out which one was Kyra's. She was there, her voice loud but it wasn't hers at the same time. He tried reaching out to her. There appeared to be a wall between them, as if she was trying to shield him from what she was seeing and hearing. Kyra was strong, he knew that, but this new psychic wall that she had built…was it truly to block him or was it to keep out the voices of the other hybrids? She had managed to block him out before, when she was younger and they was still new to each other, but now he was her father he protected her he did everything he could to make sure no harm befell her. Despite what had happened at the temple she should trust him. She should know that he would do anything for her, and yet it was as if she was now pushing him away. Perhaps it was for his own safety or something more is going on that she had yet to tell him. What had Archer told her? What had he done to her? It didn't matter. He was her father he would find her. He would save her if he had to, and he would do whatever he needed to in order to protect her.

His plane was the first to touch down on the Bay of Quinte, not far from the Trenton Air Base. The larger one piloted by Elizabeth landed several minutes later. Soldiers were already waiting for them not far from the shore. They have been informed already of the situation. They rushed Alex, Lucas, and Liam into one Jeep and headed straight towards the base while Elizabeth instructed a second group to take the injured to the triage where a medical team was waiting to care for them. There was nothing they could do for the dead. Their bodies would be recovered by another team which had already been assembled and sent to the temple.

No one asked any questions, and for that Alex was grateful. He was exhausted and his head hurt. He tried blocking out the voices, in order to hear Kyra's thoughts better, but nothing he did worked. He rested his head against the back of his seat and closed his eyes, hoping to get a few moments of rest before he had to explain the situation, yet again, to the generals and commanders who would likely lead the search for Kyra and the other hybrids.

Lucas patted his knee, a silent reminder that he was not alone. In fact, Lucas had been unusually silent the entire flight. Alex knew he was mad, not at him, or even at Kyra. No, it was the situation. Alex is still unsure if Archer was the problem or if there was something more sinister behind what had happened. Caldwell had lied to them. She had kept Kyra's origins a secret. Even now Alex wasn't quite sure if he should believe her last words. He knew Kyra was powerful, perhaps even more powerful than the Celestials themselves. The question was how powerful, and if she can control that power. If she couldn't, she might be more dangerous then the Celestials ever were.

The Trenton air base was a large boxy building not far from the museum. The Jeep pulled-up in front of the main doors and Alex couldn't help but think it wasn't so many years ago when he and Lucas went to Wing 22 in North Bay. That has been when they first met Kyra. She had been so small and frightened. He had fallen in love with her, as only a parent could, the moment they met. She may have been small but she was not helpless. She was fierce, ready to fight, and only hid to escape the Shadows. Since then, she had begun hunting them, but it would seem after all these years they may have outsmarted her.

"I'm glad you're here," said Commander Scott as they walked into the building. The man was a few years younger than Alex with sandy blonde hair and bright blue eyes. He held the door open waiting until Lucas was inside before shutting it behind him. They walked towards the command centre, the commander visibly nervous, despite his cool demeanor. "It's been quiet so far. None of our bases or research facilities have reported any problems. However, a research facility in Ottawa recently had alarms go off. Which is strange because it's a pharmaceutical plant."

"Pharmaceutical?" Lucas asked. He raised a curious row. "Why would that matter?"

The commander nodded. "We don't normally get reports on these sort of things, but they sent us some footage and…your girl appears to be involved."

Alex and Lucas exchanged a look of surprise. Why would Kyra attack a pharmaceutical lab? However, the fact that it was a lab made Alex worry about the hybrids. After all, Kyra had once been kidnapped and taken to a lab. It had nothing to do with pharmaceuticals at the time however this could be a disguise for something more sinister. It wouldn't surprise Alex if the Shadows had possessed the lab technicians. They had done it before. In fact, the Shadows had possessed almost an entire base of soldiers once. Not to mention the scientists that had been on site. So, it wasn't that far fetched for the Shadows to have taken control of a lab in Canada's capital. The problem was getting there and finding Kyra before the Shadows did. If Kyra was even there still. Depending on how long ago the alarm went off, she may already be gone. She was several hours ahead of them.

"I don't understand," Liam said. He stayed close to Alex, unsure of himself without his eyesight and everything that had happened in such a short period of time.

"Where is this facility?" asked Lucas.

The commander fidgeted. "I was told to wait for General Monroe," He said nervously.

Alex frowned. It seemed odd that they had to wait for Elizabeth before learning where their daughter was. If she was in charge, then they had no choice but to wait. At least for now. He respected Elizabeth as his best friend and as a general, but Kyra was his little girl and he would only wait for so long.

Lucas had even less patience then him and once he was in the command centre he took charge, choosing not to wait. "I want a map of Ottawa and where this lab is located," he told the men and women in the room.

"Sir?" Scott asked, clearly taken back by the order.

"Do as he says," Elizabeth commanded as she strolled into the command centre, two EDC agents flanking her. "That's my niece out there, and none of you are prepared to handle her. So, unless you want an entire city locked down and in a panic, you'll get that map and everything you have about that lab. I want to know what company runs it, the CEO, and every other person connected to it…I don't care if it's the Prime Minister."

Scott hesitated a moment before nodding. "Yes, Ma'am. Do it," he told the others.

Alex gave Elizabeth a grateful smile then turned back to watch them. His arms folded across his chest to keep from picking at the mark on his right palm. Between it burning and pulsing – normally a sign of a temple or Celestial close by – and the voices echoing through his mind, he was in agony. All that kept him from collapsing into a miserable heap, was his fear for Kyra and sheer determination. Once she was home safe, he would let the pain consume him. For now, he couldn't.

He stiffened when he felt Lucas wrap his arms around him from behind. He didn't mean to. He was on edge. It took several moments for the tension to melt away so he could relax in his husband's warm embrace. He sighed softly and leaned into Lucas. Exhaustion filled him. It was nice to simply be held for a few minutes.

"How are you holding up?" Lucas asked softly, so only Alex heard him. He pressed his cheek against the back of Alex's head and sighed softly.

"It's been a long night."

He took a deep breath but kept his emotions from taking over. It wasn't three in the morning yet but it felt like an entire day had passed since what transpired at the Sanctuary. He'd had no sleep. He couldn't sleep no matter how much his body wanted to.

"We'll find her, babe," Lucas promised. "She's a smart girl. She'll figure out Archer is using her."

"And what if she doesn't?" Alex countered. "What if she loses control of this power? She took out the Guardians and half the EDC. What if that power goes rogue in the middle of Ottawa? She could kill thousands without even realizing it."

Lucas hugged him a little tighter. "We won't let that happen. Besides, it's still early in the morning. There are less people on the streets right now. We'll go to the lab, with luck she's still there. If not…we'll find her. You managed to track her this far. You can track her anywhere."

Alex wished he was as confident. That shield separating his mind from Kyra's came up mid-flight. Ottawa was the last location he had. Due to their involvement with EDC and their plane being designed for water, Elizabeth had instructed them to go to Trenton. From there, they were supposed to go together by helicopter to Ottawa, an additional forty-five-minute ride provided the weather was with them.

A map of Ottawa is displayed on a large table in the centre of the room. It wasn't a normal table but rather a large computer screen that projected the map in 3D, giving a detailed image of the city. It hovered several inches above the table, showing every building, house, and factory within the city in bright neon green. The lab that Kyra allegedly attacked was lit up in red. This distinguished it from all the other buildings. Alex inspected the map as he tried to figure out where Kyra might go after the lab. There were a few options but he highly doubted that his daughter would be fool enough to be on the street. Especially if she had a number of hybrids with her. She would have to find another way out, something less conspicuous, and easy to hide numerous other hybrids with her. That's the reason why she was doing this, to find and protect other hybrids. Her outburst at the sanctuary displayed her concern and fear for others like her. There was no telling how many others may have been experimented on as well. And despite being a loner, Kyra did worry about others and would do anything to keep them safe.

"The lab is owned by an international pharmaceutical group called *Veteres Renascentis*," a female pilot read from a tablet.

"Ancients Reborn," Elizabeth translated.

She glanced at Lucas as he inspected the lab. He nodded. He had translated it as well, his skill with ancient languages just as good as Alex's and Elizabeth's.

"Caldwell said the Shadows were rebelling against the Celestials, but this sounds more like they're trying to bring them back," Alex noted. He rubbed the palm of his right hand, his anxiety making the mark burn even hotter.

"It wouldn't be the first time she lied," Lucas responded. "Or perhaps they're being more ambitious and trying to find a way to harness the hybrids' gifts to make their own."

The pilot, Captain Ranger, hummed softly. "You may be right. It seems that *Veteres Renascentis* has their hands in all sorts of stuff, and was investigated for their involvement in the creation of bio weapons. The investigation is ongoing at their Vancouver office. As well as in Texas...both include possible human trafficking." She swiped the screen and continued to read. "No owner is listed and surprisingly, no charges have been filed. Either nothing conclusive has been found yet or someone has been protecting them. Considering the company is one of the oldest in North America, I wouldn't be surprised. They apparently have contracts with every major company on the planet."

"Something that old has to have massive influence in the government in order to not be shut down amongst these allegations," Alex mused. "Why have I never heard of them before?"

"Anonymity," Lucas responded. "They use multiple aliases for their products and brand." He gave a small shrug at Alex's surprise. "I've seen it before. How many products are sold today under a specific brand or label but the parent company is either not marked or in such fine print that even with our glasses, we struggle to make it out?"

"Good point."

Lucas turned to Ranger. "Can you pull up a blueprint of the building?"

She shook her head. "I'm running a search but...I can't find one. It should be in the Ontario Property Records but all I have is an address." She paused for a moment as she swiped the screen several more times. "We did an initial scan when the alarms went off. From what we can tell, there appears to be a void of some sort here." He pointed up the upper floors of the sky scraper. "I can send drones back and have them conduct another thermal sweep. If they've been keeping hybrids there, then we should be able to pick up their heat signature, as well as the number of Shadows and possessed individuals." Her gazed flicked toward Lucas. "And Celestials."

"Kyra will be long gone by then," Lucas told her. He placed his hands on the table and leaned forward, his gaze never leaving the building. "What about underground? Underground parking, sewers, subway system...anything that passes close to or may connect to it?"

The hologram rose higher above the table as the underground maze of subway tunnels and sewer, underground parking lots, maintenance tunnels appeared under it. Alex stepped closer to the map. His brows furrowed as he tried to make sense of the complex network under the city.

"Can we zoom in and focus on the area around and under the lab?" he asked.

He pressed his lips into a thin line. There were at least four levels beneath the lab but his gut told him there were more. Perhaps even another temple. Every time the Shadows and Celestials were involved, or even some crazy foreign entity from another country, there was often a temple hidden close by. Yet there didn't appear to be one under the lab or even close to it. The tunnels were too close together for something so large to have gone unnoticed for so long. He tried listening to the voices in order to get an idea of their location, even a visual, but all he got was panic and fear and more questions than answers.

"They could be anywhere," Elizabeth sighed. She rubbed her face, obviously tired as well.

Lucas gave her shoulder a squeeze. "They may not even know where they are or what direction they're going in. Right now, they're going to be laying low. Who sent the video footage? I can't imagine a company that's kept so many secrets letting something like that slip. Whoever took these kids wouldn't want anyone knowing they were running loose."

Ranger bit her lower lip while Scott shifted his weight from one foot to the other.

"Well, the footage was rather unusual," Scott said.

He directed their attention to a large monitor on the far wall then played the security footage they were sent. It opened on what appeared to be the interior of a prison but it was unlike any prison Alex had seen before. It was a pristine glossy white and appeared to have multiple levels. Even the bars of the cell doors appeared to be new reinforced steel with high tech locks. Amongst it all was Kyra. It didn't look like her at first. Her body was different, as if she wore skin tight crystal armour under her clothing. She was no longer hiding her true form. Her long white hair flowed freely, a striking contrast to the blue crystal that covered her arms and parts of her face. She fought against guards, using her years of combat skills, mixed with her new powers. Alex's heart almost stopped when someone shot at her, but it bounced uselessly off her, unable to crack her armour. He caught a glance of her eyes. They glowed brightly as she fought, but her power didn't lash out as it did in the Sanctuary. She appeared to have more control of her new-found power and spared the guards. They retreated as what Alex could only guess were captured hybrids, joined Kyra.

"Where's Archer and Naomi?" Alex asked, curious that they were not in any of the footage.

Lucas gave a snort. "Want to place a bet on who sent the footage?"

Scott rubbed the back of his neck. "I have no clue but...we're not the only ones to get it. The Ottawa Police Department got it before us. They've sent an Emergency Task Force and called in the Armed Forces. EDC got it shortly after and since we're the nearest affiliated base, we got it. We're not equipped for something like this!" He waved at the video still playing on the screen that clearly showed where Kyra had punched a hole through a brick and steel wall. "They shot at her and it did nothing, not even a scratch!"

"Kyra is not a threat. She's on our side," Liam all but yelled at him. "You said it yourself, this company...or whatever it is...is being investigated for human trafficking. They're trafficking us...people like us. Kyra's just doing her job."

Lucas gave a huffed. "It's all about optics." He sighed softly. "Archer made sure to send the worse possible image of Kyra to make her into the bad guy. He wants them chasing after her, not him."

"Why?" Scott asked, confused.

"I'm not sure. To escape?"

Alex shook his head. It didn't make sense. Why bring Kyra to Ottawa then leave her as a scape-goat? There had to be more going on. Something that they were missing. It didn't make sense for Archer and Naomi to abandon Kyra.

"We need to get there. Now," he told Scott. "There's a lot of landing pads on those skyscrapers. Get us to one and we'll find Kyra."

He had no clue what they would do with all the hybrids. It would take time to get each one home. Making sure they weren't taken again was another matter. Especially if *Veteres Renascentis* was controlled by the Shadows or Celestials. They would have to find a way to stop them. They would deal with Archer once they find him.

"Let's focus on the service tunnels, if Kyra has gone underground, that's where she would go," Elizabeth interjected. "She'll use them to find a way out of the city."

"Should we send EDC there?" Scott asked, clearly not liking the idea of possible underground combat.

Lucas shook his head. "No, she already has a head start and can be going in any direction. Our best bet is to lock down the city. We also need to figure out where Archer is and what he's up to. This break-out seems a little to convenient. Why bring Kyra here then take off with a dozen or more hybrids and leave her with the rest? He didn't do it to save them."

Alex sighed. All he wanted was to get their daughter home safely, but Lucas was right. Kyra wasn't their only concern. Whatever Archer was planning was likely to make things worse for hybrids and humans. Ottawa was the Canadian capital. He could do some serious damage if he and his followers attacked any government facility in the city. He could cause a war between their kinds that would endanger everyone.

Alex placed his hands on the table, causing the map to fizzle before righting itself. "Get us over there," he told the pilots. "We need a pilot and a helicopter."

"And drop you where?" Scott countered. He gestured toward Lucas. "He just said she's likely long gone."

"Maybe, but if that lab was holding hybrids then it needs investigating. I want to know who Archer took with him and why. Kyra's not going to go far without finding that out herself. So, let's help her."

"Help her?" Scott choked.

Lucas nodded. "Yes, help her. Archer used her. Don't think for a moment she's going to take that lightly. Whoever he took with him is likely to be bad news for everyone. Let's find who they are and stop them."

Scott opened his mouth to object then stopped and nodded.

"Prep a helicopter," Elizabeth ordered. "I'll fly it myself. And patch me in with the head of the Armed Forces and Police Chief. We need to call them off before someone gets hurt...namely one of them."

Relief filled Alex. He gave a curt nod before Scott and his team led them back outside. As much as he wanted to find Kyra, he knew she could take care of herself. They needed to intercept the agencies likely to go after her. Not just that but the only way to stop the hybrids from being kidnapped again was to figure out who was behind the lab and stop them. Hopefully, it would also help them stop Archer from doing whatever he had planned.

"Liam, I want you to stay here," he told the young man. "It'll be safer for you."

He had almost forgotten about Liam. The youth had remained quiet throughout most of the briefing.

Liam stared ahead, blind to that around him. "No," he answered simply. "These people likely took my mom. I'm going to find her."

Alex glanced at Lucas, but his husband nodded. "Alright, but stay close to us. We have no idea what we're up against."

He hoped he was wrong about that. He and Lucas had faced off against the Shadows before, as well as their hosts. However, they were evolving and that made them unpredictable.

Chapter Thirteen

Although the building they found was almost completed and still under construction, it served as a place to rest after hours of trekking through the service tunnels that ran under the city. With well over a hundred hybrids in her care, some as young as two years old, Kyra had to find a way to move them to safety without losing any of them. She had sent Marie to the front, along with several of the older and stronger hybrids to keep them moving forward while Kyra took the strongest fighters to defend the rear. If any Shadows or their hosts appeared, they would not be taken by surprise or corralled into a corner. Those able to manipulate electricity like her, kept the tunnels brightly lit, dispelling as much darkness as possible. Of course, small children walking for so long so early in the morning made it hard. The older hybrids carried those they could until finally Kyra decided it was time to move above ground. Now the children slept while the adults watched over them, plotting their next move and how to leave the city undetected. It wouldn't be easy with so many of them. It would be even harder to return all the children home, especially the younger ones who had no idea where they were or how to find their families. Letting anyone go on their own only risked them being caught faster. They had to stick together.

She leaned back against the cement pillar and closed her eyes. Exhaustion tugged at her mind and the urge to simply fall asleep filled her, but she only had a few minutes to rest. She still needed to figure out where they were and how to transport everyone to a safe haven. Ottawa was a large city, much larger than Sudbury, especially when Gatineau was factored in. The twin city sat on the Quebec side of the provincial boarder. For all Kyra knew, they could be on either side of the border or in some far-off country. There was no way to be certain. Archer could have lied. Everything he ever said to her could have been a lie. After all, the security guards with whom she had faced-off with were not EDC agents. She wasn't sure who they were, but they were trained mercenaries just like the ones that had kidnapped her as a child. The memory sent chills down her spine as her gaze swept over the sleeping children. What were the Shadows going to do to them? Why had Archer taken a select few and where were they now? She was still angry that he expected her to simply let them fuck her. What had that been about? She had thought she had made it clear that sex really didn't mean anything to her…of course, having sex with him probably hadn't helped. What was she thinking? She had never cared about sex before until whatever Archer had done to her in the Tavern. Now that she had done it, she really didn't care if she ever did it again. It was honestly nothing to write about, despite the momentary euphoria she had felt. She could get the same sensation from sky-diving.

"Hey, how are you doing?" Marie asked as she sat next to Kyra.

"Tired," Kyra answered honestly. She wiped the sleep from her eyes and forced herself to sit up straight. "So, where exactly as we?"

Marie sighed. "Ottawa," she confirmed. "I woke up in my cell but the guards talk. Some of had no clue why we were there. One day they'd ask questions, the next…"

"They were quiet and distant," Kyra finished for her, the memory of her past invading her thoughts.

"Yeah."

Possessed by a Shadow, Kyra surmised. She tapped her fingers on one knee. "Okay, we know where we are, now we need to find a way to get all of us out of here."

She sorely wished they had come out closer to the airport. At least then she could call her fathers and have them come for them...if they would after all she had done. Could they even forgive her for destroying the Guardians? She had killed Owen. She had killed the Ancients. There was no bringing them back. She couldn't even sense them anymore.

"Kyra?" Marie asked gently.

Blinking away the rogue tears that threatened to fall, Kyra shook her head. "I'm fine." She took a deep, calming breath. "Can you handle everyone? I'm going to try and find us some transportation...a school bus or something."

"Of course."

She pushed herself to her feet, changing her appearance as she did so. Her white hair turned black, her skin tone a dark beige, and eyes a vibrant green, giving her an almost Eastern European appearance. She left through the opening for the underground parking lot and into the crisp morning air. The sky was hints of pink and purple, the morning sun not yet risen. It was dangerous for her to be outside. The Shadows were able to hunt freely until the sun rose above the tall buildings. She had no choice though. She needed to find a something... anything...to get the kids to safety, even if that meant stealing a plane.

It turned out a plane wasn't necessary. Two blocks from where they were hidden was a bus station with coaches preparing to take passengers to cities all across Canada. She silently watched the people moving in and out of the terminal for several long moments before making up her mind. It wasn't the ideal solution, and no doubt someone may even have the foresight to think she may attempt it, but it was better than nothing. She walked into the building, her head held high as if purchasing a bus ticket was something she did quite often, but rather than head to the ticket booth, she searched for the drivers until she caught the eye of one.

Something in her stirred when they made eye contact. It wasn't like before, there was arousal but something else, something darker, almost animal like. It frightened her. Her body suddenly wanted sex again while her mind felt disgust at the mere thought. Alex had told her stories of the "Beast" – what he called the Celestial that had possessed him years ago, and how it fed off sex and flesh. She almost walked away, determined to find another way to get the hybrids out of the city, but the driver had fallen for whatever spell her Celestial-half had cast and was making his way toward her. The beast within roared to life, wanting its pound of flesh. Her body and mind seemed to shift into automatic, no longer completely under her control. She gave him a coy smile, added an exaggerated sway to her hips as she walked, and led him to the men's bathroom.

All she needed was access to a bus, she kept telling herself as he pulled her into an empty stall. Her heart raced with anxiety, her breathing becoming rapid. He mistook that as excitement and pressed her against the stall door, his erection felt through his black slacks and pressing against her thigh. She tried not to make eye contact as his large hands slipped under her top to feel her breasts. Fuck him and steal his keys. It should have been easy. She didn't need to think, just let her Celestial-side take over. She grimaced at each kiss, her skin practically crawling at every touch. The hunger she felt quickly disappeared as logic returned to her. This was wrong. The driver either didn't notice or care about her sudden change of heart as he wrestled to get his belt off while trying to feel her up at the same time.

Despite her trepidation, she didn't stop him. She watched, her mind seemingly detached from her body as he shoved his pants to his knees and grabbed his manhood, stroking it like some beloved pet until it stood erect.

"You want to ride the Beast?" he said with a suggestive grin as he sat on the toilet, clearly wanting her to straddle him.

A smirk curled one side of Kyra's mouth. "You've never seen a Beast," she purred, letting the creature within peak out.

"Kyra, you don't need to do this," a voice whispered in her mind as she stared at the man.

Her breath hitched as she glanced behind her. There was nothing but the stall door.

"Uncle Owen?" she breathed in surprised. She could feel his warmth, as she had many times throughout her life even when she could not see him. He was there now, surrounding her, protecting her just as he always had.

The driver laughed. "Uncle Owen? Sure...I can be your Uncle Owen. Have you been a naughty girl? Should I give you a good spanking before we shag?"

"Ew," she muttered to herself.

"You're made of energy, Kyra. All living things are," Owen continued to whisper in her mind. "Access the energy within his mind. Take the information you need. Don't let your Celestial-half take control of you or you'll be lost."

"Hey, are we doing this or not?" the driver said angrily.

He grabbed Kyra's hand and tried to drag her down to him but she didn't budge. Instead, she was as still as a statue as she contemplated Owen's words. Disgust filled her as she felt the man stand and press his body against hers once more, his hand fumbling to get her shorts off. She watched him for a moment before shoving him back down on the toilet and finally straddling his lap.

"Sorry handsome, but you're not getting lucky this morning," she purred sweetly. He gave her a confused look as she placed her hands over either temple. "But you'll feel as if you did."

She had never delved into another person's mind before, not like this at least. She could read Alex's thoughts to a point and sense Lucas's emotions, but fishing through someone's mind...if felt like swimming through sludge and invaded her senses, or perhaps that was merely the scent of the man himself. She could feel his excitement pressed firmly against her rear. It was hard not to notice, especially since sex was forefront on his mind. She manipulated his thoughts, let him believe they were actually fornicating. In his mind she was absolutely naked on his lap, taking his thick length deep inside her. In his mind he was much larger than he was in real life. The imaginary her moaned and whimpered, begging him for more, telling him how good he was – the best she ever had. She rifled through his thoughts, searching for a way to get her hands on a bus without being detected. It took a surprising amount of strength to push past his sexual fantasy and find what she needed. It came in the form of images; a massive garage and parking lot with busses lined up, some in the midst of repairs and maintenance, others being prepped for long drives across country. Inside the garage was a large metal cabinet that housed dozens of keys, each clearly labeled to which bus they belonged. There were security guards and an office where drivers went to sign in before being assigned their bus and route. Many drivers had established routes and assigned busses that they used most often. Through the driver's mind,

Kyra could see a list of drivers and their assigned busses and it wasn't long before she found one that would suit her need. Best of all, the driver was a new woman driver who had yet to sign in, at least according to the man's current memory from twenty minutes ago. With luck, she still hadn't signed in. If she had then Kyra had to find her and take her place.

Something warm and wet spread across her upper thighs, startling her as she exited the driver's mind.

"Ew…" she groaned, realizing the man had ejaculated while she was straddling him. "Seriously?"

He sat back, a happy little grin on his face, completely oblivious to the fact they had not actually had sex and still living in the fantasy. Disgusted, Kyra cleaned herself off.

"At least one of us enjoyed ourselves," she grumbled as she threw the used toilet paper at the driver.

She left the stall and went to the nearest sink to wash off the hideous white splatter off her shorts. When she was satisfied it was no longer noticeable, she finally exiting the bathroom. No one took notice of her, her form blending in with people waiting for the coach that would take them to their destination. She paused long enough to swipe a bottle of water from a kiosk as she passed it, all but invisible to those around her, then left the station and began the long trek to the garage several blocks away.

She touched her left ear as she walked, as if adjusting a Bluetooth ear piece. "Uncle Owen, are you there?"

She couldn't see him but the hope that she had not imagined his presence and he had survived the energy blast filled her. Perhaps the other Guardians were still alive as well. He didn't answer, not in words at least, but that familiar warmth surrounded her like a cozy blanket. With it came a much-needed boost of confidence. He was still with her and would stay by her side like a Guardian Angel as he had her entire childhood. They would find and defeat Archer together.

The garage wasn't far from the station, only a few blocks over, but it took precious time away from the hybrids. Time in which the Shadows could find and recapture them. Even if she secured a bus, it may be too late by the time she got back to them. The sun was finally rising, painting the city in hues of purple and orange. If she was visiting Ottawa as she used to as a child, she would watch it as it highlighted the Parliament building. It was always a sight to behold, but not today.

She altered her form as she neared the garage, taking on the form of a seasoned bus driver. She didn't have the uniform but perhaps that didn't matter and the new driver had yet to receive one, in which case she would get it once she signed in. Anxiety ate at her as she approached the garage. So far things had seemed easy, but she knew from experience that wouldn't last long. There was no way the Shadows would have given up on the hybrids. It was only a matter of time before they reappeared.

The garage was busy with drivers picking up or dropping off their busses. Men and women signed-in and checked-out in quick succession. Kyra joined the line of drivers checking in. It wasn't long before she reached the front. Luck was still on her side as her gaze fell upon the name of the new driver and her bus. The driver had yet to sign in.

"Christina Carmichael," she told the garage manager.

"ID," the man said, not looking up.

Kyra hesitated. She had no ID on her. Everything was at home. It was the first time since childhood she left such important documents behind. Given the situation, it was just as well. If something happened to her, Alex and Lucas wouldn't be tied to it.

Her gaze shifted to the business cards on the corner of the desk. She took one and turned it over to present to the manager. Her fingers brushed against his and she planted the image of a driver's license in his mind. He glanced at it then nodded.

"Route 501. You're heading to Timmins," he told her. He handed her a print-out of the route she was to take and a key. "Your uniform is in your locker. The one with your name on it."

"Thank you," she said before a thought hit her. The big problem was she simply couldn't take the bus. There would be passengers waiting and if it didn't show up at the station the police would be notified. However, with over a hundred hybrids, there was no room for anyone else. It was already going to be a tight fit. "There's a second bus to Timmins. I will come for it shortly."

He looked up, slightly startled by her words. She held his gaze, forcing her will upon him until he nodded in agreement.

"Yes, the second bus will be waiting for you."

That handled the driver situation. The real Christina Carmichael will still have her bus and a missing bus would not be reported, at least not for quite some time.

The manger waved her off, as if no longer interested in her now that she had her route and uniform and the other bus was scheduled. Kyra frowned at him. He was certainly unpleasant. Not as bad as the driver she had not had sex with, thankfully. Nonetheless, she was running out of time. She went to the locker and grabbed the uniform, but instead of putting it on, she carried it to the bus she had been assigned. There was bound to be confusion when the real Christina Carmichael arrived and she did not want to be here when that happened.

The one good thing about being in the male driver's mind was that she had quite literally downloaded all his knowledge of driving such as large bus as a coach. She threw the uniform onto the front row of seats then slid into the driver's seat. Her hands moved automatically, adjusting the seat and controls before finally starting up the bus. It roared to life, the entire vehicle vibrating beneath her. It felt almost like starting up a plane before taking off, that same power and energy coursing through the vehicle. It was fully gassed up and ready to go.

"Alright then, Uncle Owen," she mused as she set the bus into gear. "Let's see how well this goes."

Flying planes, and driving cars and motorcycles was nothing compared to trying to steer such a large vehicle as a bus through city streets. There were far too many one-way streets and it took longer than Kyra wanted to reach the building she had left Marie with the hybrids. Worst, it was too large to drive safely into the underground parking. Instead, she had to park next to the club and run instead to retrieve them.

They were just as she had left them, huddled in groups trying to care for one another. Marie looked up from the set of toddlers she was caring for as Kyra hurried toward them.

"Have you ever driven a bus?" Kyra asked as she gathered everyone together.

Marie lifted a curious brow. "No, I've driven a few moving trucks over the years."

Kyra shrugged. "Close enough. Everyone head outside and get on the bus."

"You found a school bus? That's not going to be big enough."

"Nope, we have a coach and I need you to drive it. I'll give you the coordinates to take it, but once you get there you'll need to hike the rest of the way. It's a few kilometers off the highway." Kyra took a deep breath as she took one of the smaller children in her arms. "I'm going to try and get my dads to meet you there...or at least someone who can help."

"Where exactly are you sending us?"

Kyra bit her lower lips, feeling suddenly unsure. "The Sanctuary...the underground temple my fathers have been studying. It's the safest place I know. The Shadows can't get to you there. After that...I'll figure it out."

Marie studied her for a long moment. "And what about you? You're not coming with us?"

"No," Kyra answered with a shake of her head. "I need to find Archer. He didn't bring me here to save you, which means he's up to something and I have to stop him." She handed the child to one of the teenagers entering the bus, then pulled out the route that had been printed for her. She traced out the highway between Sudbury and Timmins then marked a turn off into the mountains. "Just get them to the Sanctuary. I'll meet you there. I might even make it there before you."

Marie nodded. Then, much to Kyra's surprise, the older woman drew her into a tight embrace. "Be careful."

"I will," Kyra promised as she stepped back.

Marie paused before entering the bus. "If you find Liam…please bring him home."

"What?"

She looked off into the distance, concern marring her features. "He's close…but not captured. Whoever he's with, he feels safe but worried…about you."

Kyra's brows rose in surprise. The only thing she could think of was that he must have come with her dads to find her. She didn't remark about that, instead she promised to protect Liam once they found each other. She waited until Marie changed into the coach driver uniform before stepping back and watched as the bus pulled away. The dark tinted windows hid the hybrids and she was content in knowing that the older hybrids would do their best to protect the younger ones. With them safely on their way to the Sanctuary she could focus on finding and stopping Archer. She could sense him, just as she could all the hybrids now. He wasn't far, only a few kilometers away. There were more with him, far more than the group that had escaped with him and Naomi. Perhaps a two dozen men and women. She lowered her mental shields just enough to sense their thoughts and get a feel for where they were and what they were up to. What she discovered made her blood run cold.

"Ancients help us," she breathed, unsure if she was talking to herself or Owen's unseen spirit.

She looked to the east, toward the Parliament buildings. Earth Defense Command's main office was housed in a series of buildings across the plaza from Parliament. There were agents from all around the world there, many of which were housed in the adjoining dorms. Canada was the leading country that headed the EDC, that was why it was so close. Any of the country's decisions affected the EDC and vice-versa. If Archer managed to cripple one organization, he could very well destroy Canada's entire infrastructure, and then each country one by one. That was how tightly intertwined EDC was with each and every country around the world.

It was still early in the morning. Rush hour traffic had yet to fill the streets. If she moved quickly, she may be able to head-off many of the officials before they went to their offices in the buildings surrounding EDC and Parliament. Perhaps she could stop Archer before it was too late.

She turned around and glanced down the street, searching for an approaching taxi she could flag down. There was bound to be one soon, but she couldn't stand around and wait for one. She had to hurry. She was a fast running but Parliament was still quite a distance. She had no choice, she needed to make a run for it and pray she wasn't too late.

The sound of the propeller blades of the helicopter was oddly soothing despite the intense noise. The noise canceling headphones helped in that respect, however, he could still feel them vibrate through the vehicle. He kept his eyes closed despite his inability to see. His lost sight wouldn't help him right now anyway. He was searching for Kyra's energy signature much as Alex was using his connection to her. He had listened carefully to General Monroe's report and continued to do so as he and Lucas discussed where Kyra could have gone. Alex was struggling to locate her, claiming she had put a wall between them. No such wall existed between Liam and Kyra. She was his queen now and where she went he followed. It was a strange sensation, one with which he was not accustomed. He knew the moment she found his mother and the other hybrids. He knew when she was about to feast on a human yet turned away from that primal instinct, he knew when she sent the hybrids away. And he knew now that she was hunting for Archer. She managed to stifle the need to feed and replaced it with the need to stop Archer. The Celestial within her would still feast before nightfall, but the offering would be vastly different than originally intended.

He tracked her with his mind, following her in her hunt. There was something or someone else with her, like echoes in the dark. Whispering to her, encouraging her, keeping her other half at bay. Keeping the Beast in check.

His mind finally connected with her. Only for a brief moment, but it told him everything he needed to know.

"Where is EDC's main headquarters?" he asked through the mic of his headphones.

Lucas turned in his seat up front to face him, the movement felt throughout the helicopter. "Why?"

Liam tilted his head, curiosity filling him. "Because that's where she's going. That's where Archer is."

"Oh fuck," Monroe cursed. "Are you serious?"

"Why would they be going there?" Alex asked. He shifted in his seat next to Liam to face the youth. "EDC has headquarters all across Canada and the US. The one on Parliament Hill has a skeleton crew and primarily run by MI6. It connects with the offices in Europe. Even if they took control of it, it would have no affect on the others."

"Perhaps…but many of the Members of Parliament and the leaders of the various parties do work closely with EDC. An attack on either building will practically shut down the country," Lucas pointed out.

The general cursed again. "Not to mention the fact that all the MPs are in Ottawa to vote on the Hybrid Protection Initiative today. Damn it! Why didn't I see it? The increased disappearances, the strange attacks, Archer tricking Kyra into bringing him to the temple then transporting her here? All those hybrids captured…it all has something to do with today's vote."

Liam's brows furrowed in confusion. "What vote?"

Alex let out a frustrated sigh. "Most people don't know about hybrids – it's a National Security Secret. In essence, the vote is to recognise them as human and give them the same rights as any other human which means protection. If the Nos win, then anyone discovered to be a hybrid will be treated as sub-human, no rights, no protection, no anything. It would mean they could be taken into custody and studied…which as we've discovered, is already happening, only EDC won't be able to do anything about it."

"It means that the lab may not be run by the Shadows but someone with government connections who would benefit from the hybrids being stripped of all rights," Lucas added.

"Why would Archer interfere with the vote? Wouldn't he want more protection for us?" Liam asked. Anxiety filled him. If Lucas was right then everything that had happened the last few days suddenly made sense. The question was, was Archer and his followers there to ensure the vote was passed or to stop it? What was their end game and how did Kyra factor into it?

Kyra altered course to Parliament Hill while Lucas got on the radio with EDC, hoping to warn them before Archer attacked. It was a no-fly zone, but with any luck, they would be able to land there or close enough to reach Kyra before all hell broke loose.

Chapter Fourteen

Kyra stumbled to a surprised stop as she neared the Parliament buildings. Security was on high alert and were escorting people out of the various buildings and behind blocked roads as a mix of police, RCMP, and soldiers secured one building at a time. The people they evacuated were lower office workers, not the MPs that would hold meetings and vote on decisions for the betterment of the country. They would be evacuated separately to a secure location for their protection. Kyra watched from behind the barricades, trying to spot Archer or anyone that remotely felt like a hybrid. She could feel them, but that may very well have been Archer and his goons. There were at least one or two and it was surprising to Kyra to see that they were among the soldiers moving in to secure the safety of those who were in the buildings. EDC agents, she realized with a sigh of relief.

The relief quickly turned to panic. They could be there searching for her. What if they knew about what happened in the temple and thought she had something to do with what was happening now? As much as she wanted to go to them, she chose not to. She had to do this on her own, at least until she figured out exactly what she had done, and if it could be reversed. Owen was still with her, whispering in the back of his mind. She hoped he would be able to guide her through the battle she was about to face.

She glanced around the plaza, searching for another way to the EDC headquarters. Every entrance into the building was blocked. It looked as if the RCMP, dressed in tactical gear, were preparing to ram the main entrance open. There were automatic rifles strapped to their backs or in their hands at the ready. They were expecting to face-off against a deadly opposing force and kill them if necessary. Kyra's chest tightened at the thought that Naomi may have been killed in cold blood. What had happened in the short hours between the time they were separated until now? What had Archer done to warrant such a response from the government?

Surprise caught her off guard when she noticed the EDC agents break away from the rest of the armed contingent and began heading toward her. None of them were looking at her directly but into the growing crowd with a mixture of awe and confusion. Kyra stepped back to escape the crowd, but they seemed to move along with her, as if attracted to her presence. One agent finally noticed her and seemed to zero-in on Kyra. Rather than shout for the others, she went directly to Kyra, relief brightening her features.

Relief filled Kyra as well.

"Katie," she breathed. The other woman took her by the arm and escorted her out of the crowd and to a small alley way. They had trained together in one of Caldwell's crash courses to the EDC. Not quite a military academy but a special facility for hybrids wanting to join the EDC. The other agents took positions just inside the entrance, as if protecting her.

"Kyra, what is going on?" Katie demanded, her voice just above a whisper. "They said you attacked a lab and are now leading a revolt...they say you've captured and taken control of EDC HQ?"

Kyra's eyes widened. "What? No! That lab...or whatever it was...had hybrids locked in cells and they were experimenting on them. It was run by people possessed by Shadows. And I obviously didn't take control of headquarters! Do you think I'd be standing here if I had?"

"No," Katie answered. Annoyance filled her voice as she glanced back at the rest of her team. "What happened at the lab?"

"Some jackass took me there," Kyra answered with a sigh. She shook her head. "I freed the hybrids and..." She wasn't sure how much to say. She trusted Katie. They had worked together many times in the past, but right now she had no clue who was on her side. "Let's just say they're safe. That jackass...he and his followers took off and came here...I presume to cripple the EDC. He said they were the ones behind the lab."

"Not as far as I know," The older woman seemed perplexed and stared at Kyra intently, as if she held all the answers. "What aren't you telling me? What happened to you? We got reports that something happened at the temple. A power surge. People were killed...by you. And now you're here and you feel...different. Like one of them..."

"Them?"

"A Celestial. Like you fed but not a normal feeding. More powerful..."

Her voice trailed off as she examined Kyra. There was fear in her eyes, real fear, and something else. Something almost like an attraction. Not necessarily of a sexual nature but close to it.

Kyra pulled away, unsure what was happening. When she looked toward the other hybrid EDC agents, they had the same look. It was not a look normally directed toward Kyra but had now appeared on numerous hybrids she had encountered since the incident in the temple. No...since Archer first touched her, triggering her own hunger. It had only grown since then. She briefly wondered why the hybrids she had saved were not affected. She supposed that the fear and adrenaline of escape may have kept that at bay, if only temporarily. That may change when she regrouped with them at the temple. It was not something she wanted to think about.

"It's a long story," she told Katie. "For another time. Right now, I need to get inside HQ and stop Archer from whatever the hell he thinks he's doing. The MPs have been evacuated?"

Katie nodded. "Safely moved to the bunker and sealed in. We even did a UV and light sweep before and after. They're safe."

Kyra nodded. Precautions were in place to avoid anyone in the government from being possessed by a Shadow. "Good. Help me get inside HQ. A distraction so I can sneak past the blockade."

Silence met her request as Katie glanced toward her comrades for support. Kyra inhaled slowly, prepared for them to turn against her, reject her request, and hand her to the authorities. Instead, Katie began removing her armored vest, then her boots, and soon stripped off her entire uniform without so much as an objection or inquiry from the others. She stood before Kyra in only her bra and panties, holding out her uniform in offering to Kyra.

"It'll be easier for you to get in if they think you're me," Katie explained.

They were the same build. Both tall and slim with Kyra having slightly more muscle mass due to growing up in the mountains and having more labor-intensive work. Nonetheless, she had not expected Katie to switch places with her. The armour was bulky enough to hide the differences in their build and it took little to no effort to change her facial appearance to match Katie's. It simply did not feel right. She had very few other options. Taking the uniform, she stripped out of her t-shirt and shorts and changed. The boots were tight and pinched uncomfortably at her toes. She had no choice but to give them back to the other woman and continue to wear her sneakers. Someone was sure to notice, but with luck, it would be too late for anyone to say or do anything about it.

Katie gestured to the other hybrids. "They'll escort you to the far side of the building. It's surrounded but you should be able to enter from the side entrance. It's barricaded from the inside but there's an escape ladder close to it. You may be able to get in through a window but keep low. There are snipers on every roof. If they figure out who you are…"

Kyra nodded in understanding. They would shoot her on sight. She tied her hair back in a tight ponytail like Katie as her features shifted to match the other woman, then slung the rifle across her back. Nervousness ate at her gut. She had spent most of her life preparing to fight the Celestials and Shadows, now she had to battle her own kind, people she had sworn to protect. Regardless of what Archer had done, he was a hybrid. So was Naomi. She should be protecting them. Yet it was them that abandoned the others. It was Archer who wanted her to have sex with two of the brutes he freed. It was Archer that unleashed her power and caused the Ancients to turn on her. Everything that had happened was because of him. She wouldn't be surprised if the attack in Little Current was tied to him as well.

"Alright," Kyra began once she was ready. The EDC agents gathered around her. "I'm going to try and flush them to the north wing. I need a contingent there. High priority capture. I want to avoid casualties. If Archer thought he suffered in that lab before, he's seen nothing yet. I'm personally taking him down."

"We've got you covered," a male agent, Richards, told her.

"Thank you."

For the first time since the attack in Little Current, Kyra finally felt in control. This was her element. She was a warrior at heart, and while she didn't want to fight her own kind, she would do so to protect most of the hybrids. She moved with the agents toward the building while Katie stayed behind. They moved as one, acknowledging the Armed Forces and police along the way.

They couldn't reach the ladder Katie had indicated on the North side. RCMP already had it under guard, as if expecting Archer and his followers to use it as an escape route. Archer was too smart for that. He likely already had an escape plan figured out. He seemed to be two steps ahead of all of them. How else could he have taken control of the EDC headquarters so quickly. They were trained for such things, always prepared for a Celestial or Shadow attack. It likely never occurred to them that the very people they were supposed to protect would be the ones to take control. Kyra couldn't let those thoughts cloud her mind. Her mission was to stop Archer and save the agents inside before things got any worse. She'll find a nice icy cell for him when this is done. One filled with blinding light, so he never has to worry about Shadows and too cold for him to summon whatever twisted powers he had.

She was led to another door on the west side, one that would not have been easily noticeable. The door had been forgotten over the years, rarely used after the many renovations the building had endured throughout the decades and seemed to be masked with some form of glamour. Only a Celestial or powerful hybrid could do that. She glanced at the agents with her and let her mental shields drop just enough to read their thoughts. They seemed just as confused as her, as if they were led there by instinct alone…or perhaps by something much more sinister.

"I've got it from here," she told them as she overrode the mechanical lock. She paused a moment, half expecting alarms to sound. All was quiet on the other side. She didn't trust it.

"My Queen, we cannot let you go in there alone," Richards remarked. He placed a hand on her wrist, stopping her from pushing the door open. She stared at him in shock. He spoke formally now compared to mere minutes ago. His gaze fixed on her, like a loyal guard ready to defend her.

"What did you call me?" she asked.

Only Archer had called her that. Was Richards and the others working for him as well? She shook her hand free, her mind racing with endless questions that she had no time to find answers for. Without waiting, she pushed the door open and hurried inside. The agents followed her in, no longer objecting nor trying to stop her. They flanked her with Richards attempting to take the lead. She ordered him back as understanding slowly seeped in. Before they had acted like soldiers, at least for the most part, but had been able to sense her. They should have turned her in, it was standard procedure, even if she wasn't involved in what was going on. She was an agent, and right now, seen as a traitor if they were associating her with Archer. They hadn't. In fact, Katie had swapped clothing with her, let her take her armour and weapons. The others did not question or stop it as they should have. Now they were following her orders and trying to protect her, not as their comrade or even their commanding officer but as their queen. It had been the same when she rescued the other hybrids. No one questioned her, they simply did as she said, no questions asked. They didn't treat her as their savior but as their queen.

Owen, what happened to me? What did Archer unleash, she asked the spirit of her uncle. He was still with her, like a silent ghost staying by her side.

Kyra...Owen's voice whispered in her mind. *Now may not be the best time.*

He was right, of course, but she had so many questions. Why was everyone treating her so strangely? What did Archer have to do with it? Surely having sex with him had nothing to do with it. Sure, he claimed to help people unlock their full potential, but Kyra was certain that was just a pickup line he used to get people in bed with him. And she had been one of those fools to fall for him and his lies.

The agents with her were a well-adjusted team. Despite Kyra being in the lead, Richards still directed the others as they moved cautiously through the main hall, pausing to check offices and rooms along the way. Most were empty, the staff likely corralled into one place, others fleeing the building, while some were killed where they stood as was discovered in several offices. They weren't simple gunshot wounds to the head or chest. They were brutal; entire hearts ripped from the body, necks snapped, or heads decapitated. And more than one had been sexually assaulted, raped before fed upon. It was like a feeding frenzy gone horribly wrong. Archer was letting his followers feed on the men and women of the EDC. This painted a horrible image of what hybrids could do if their Celestial side took control. It would make people fear them and paint a target on every hybrid's back. Surely Archer knew this. He had fought to escape the lab, to escape imprisonment. This would only send him back...or worse...have him hunted and killed. What was his end goal?

They encountered the first real resistance in the control room. It was the command center that connected every EDC building and agent throughout the world, with a global map that showed exactly where every agent was. Every country had their own headquarters, but Canada led the effort to protect the planet from alien invasions, detect new temples, and track any Celestials that may still be on planet. Two guards, large burly men like the ones that tried to force themselves on her at the lab, blocked the entrance to the command centre. They weren't armed, at least not in the traditional sense. Neither carried a firearm or weapon of any sort, not that they needed any. They were huge, towering over Kyra despite her impressive height. The guards stared them down, daring them to open fire. That was unusual. Hybrids could be killed. A bullet would kill a hybrid as much as it would a human unless…

Understanding dawned on her as she met their glares with one of her own. They had a high healing factor. They could be taken down, but only for a few moments at best. Few hybrids had such a gift, normally it was humans who were possessed by a Celestial. Her own dad, Alex, had developed an uncanny ability to heal quickly after he had been possessed. If that was so, then these two would be near impossible to defeat.

"McIntyre, go to the basement," she breathed to the agent to her left. "There's a climate control system. Drop the temperature as low as possible."

"Why?" the young man whispered back in confusion.

"Just do it," Kyra ordered, her patience razor thin. "Then get out of here."

She glanced at him, a warning in her gaze to do as she ordered without further question.

"What would that do?" Roberts questioned as the younger agent dashed down the hall.

The two guards glanced toward him but held little interest in where he was going or why. They moved as one, their gazes fixating on Kyra.

"My Queen, we request you come with us," they said in unison.

Kyra raised a curious brow. So, being called "Queen" was going to become the new normal? She wanted to object and sneer at them. What was more surprising was the fact neither of the remaining agents with her so much as questioned the new title. She glanced at them but there was no confusion written on either of their faces. They looked to her for guidance, as if they would follow her wherever she led them. That sort of responsibility was frightening, but Kyra could not refuse the guards. She needed to make sure the remaining EDC agents were alive and safe...or as safe as they could be given the situation.

She took a deep breath, squared her shoulders, and gave a curt nod. "Take me to Archer," she said sternly.

Remarkably, they did as she commanded without question. Archer was likely who they were going to take her to either way. Nonetheless, the command gave Kyra a small sense of control of the situation. If they were willing to follow her orders perhaps, she could use them against Archer, have them follow her instead of him. It was impossible to say how loyal they were to him or what he may mean to them. If she was Queen, then what was Archer? Certainly not a King...was he? That could complicate matters further. What was the hierarchy amongst the Celestials? Did it affect the hybrids the same way?

Archer was waiting for her as she was led into the command center. He stood before a series of monitors that covered the far wall, his arms folded behind his back and hands clasped. He looked nothing like the bartender she had met only days before. Physically he appeared the same as when she last saw him only hours ago, but his posture and the energy he was projecting felt completely different. This was the real Archer. The one she met before had been nothing more than a mask.

The EDC agents, or more precisely, the human EDC agents lay scattered along the ground. Dead, every last one, their bodies brutalized and used. That sickly sweet scent of the freshly dead filled the room. It made Kyra want to gag but she held it back. The hybrid agents sat docilely on the floor to one side, seemingly lost and confused by what was going on.

"Are you insane?" Kyra demanded, unable to believe what she was seeing. "Are you trying to turn the humans against us? They'll think we're terrorists!"

"Yes," Archer agreed, not so much as looking at her. "They'll will see we are the real power."

"They will hunt us down…throw us in more labs like the last!" she argued. "Archer…why are you doing this?" It felt cliché to ask such a thing but none of what had happened made any sense and she needed it to make sense.

"They'll try," Archer began. "He turned to face her. "But ultimately they will fail." His gaze met her eyes. "This world was always meant for us. That was their goal…to merge our two species, to create a superior race. We are that race, Kyra."

Her brows furrowed. She took a step back as he approached her. "If that's so then why abandon the others, hmm? They're hybrids like us."

The look he gave her was so alien compared to before. They were no longer warm brown but a cold, coal black. If she didn't know better, she would have thought he was possessed by one of the Celestials. It would have made better sense than what she was witnessing now. Hybrids couldn't be possessed though.

228

"They're not like us, my dear," Archer purred. His gaze searched hers before he tutted in disappointment. "You really don't know, do you?" His lips lifted in a twisted smile. "We're not hybrids, you, and I, we're pure bloods. As pure as a Celestial could be in a human form."

Kyra said nothing. She wasn't sure how to respond. Calling him a liar seemed childish. What he was claiming seemed utterly insane. No one around them questioned Archers claim either, they took it as if it were gospel…even the EDC agents.

Archer watched her, waiting for her reaction and almost looked disappointed when she gave none. He waited a moment more before shrugging and turning away from her to continue his monologue. "The only two pure breeds on the entire planet. Can you imagine?"

"So what? We're siblings?" Kyra asked. She folded her arms across her chest and cocked one hip. "That's twisted…I mean we had sex. It was okay but it explains why I felt nothing."

His shoulders tensed. She had hit a nerve. A small smile tugged at her lips. It was better than the disgust twisting in her gut. She watched him carefully, wishing him to make a wrong move.

"Celestials don't view familial bonds as humans do," Archer explained. He turned back toward her. "We were meant to be, Kyra. We were created to be the perfect match, to create the next generation of Celestials, and rule this planet."

The air conditioning kicked on. Kyra carefully listened as it whirled. It was barely audible, but she knew what to listen for. She could feel the slight breeze as the cool air blew through the overhead vents. It slowly grew colder. She glanced around the room at the numerous hybrids who sat or stood, watching them as if captivated, without will of their own. Their eyes were blank, like no one was home. These weren't followers, they were trapped within their own bodies, enslaved by Archer's will. That included the two guards, and now the two agents that were with Kyra. Her gaze traveled over each of the hybrids until it landed on Naomi in the far corner. She wasn't under Archer's control but obviously not in on his plans. She looked scared and confused and tried to hide amongst the other hybrids, as if afraid Kyra may take her wrath out on her. Kyra shifted her gaze back to Archer, not wanting to draw his attention to the girl. Despite what had happened at the lab, she still liked Naomi…at least for now. She didn't feel the same level of betrayal as she felt with Archer.

"So, let me get this straight…we're supposed to be this perfect match, yet you wanted some of your followers to fuck me in public with or without my consent?" She pursed her lips and nodded slowly in thought. "That makes perfect sense. What, am I supposed to 'unlock their true potential' like you supposedly did to me?" Her eyes narrowed. "You caused me to kill the Ancients, destroy the Guardians, and numerous EDC agents."

He wasn't interested.

"Alright," Kyra said. "Now what?"

The agents with her no longer had free will, they were under Archer's control. When and how that happened, she was unsure, but if she attempted to attack Archer, they were stop her. She had to wait until the room got cold enough to cause the hybrids to either snap out of it or begin to sleep. It had to get very cold for that. EDC Headquarters was equipped to lower its interior temperature to minus forty Celsius if needed. It was supposed to be triggered should something like this ever happen. Being equipped for such an event was one thing, but even after endless drills, no one was prepared when it finally did happen. The agents should not have been taken by surprise as they were. That was likely due to Naomi's ability to control minds.

"We wait," Archer answered.

"For what?"

There was silence for a few moments before Archer turned to face her once more. "You honestly don't believe this is my big plan? No, divide and conquer."

"What does that mean? The vote? Yes, you're certainly painting us in a good light. I'm sure they'll call in every EDC agent possible to hunt down and capture hybrids. Congrats."

He laughed and it was a strangely frightening sound. "So small minded. The vote has been delayed. They won't proceed while there is an obvious danger so close. And where would they be evacuated to?"

Kyra's eyes widened in understanding. "The bunker."

"Aye, the bunker," he confirmed with a nod. "My colleagues are already waiting for them."

"Colleagues…" she echoed. She glanced toward the wall of monitors and the Armed Forces and police rushing about the secure Parliament Hill. Her focus went past them to the long shadows being cast by the buildings. It all clicked in at once. "The Shadows…they're going to possess the MPs…you're working with them!"

"No, they work for me," he corrected. "And once they have the MPs…we will control the Nation…and every nation one by one. No more wars, no more fighting. Humans will serve us, the hybrids will expand, the Celestials will return, and we will be King and Queen of it all."

Kyra shivered. The temperature was steadily dropping. It was already minus ten. Archer didn't seem to notice, and other than Naomi, not of the hybrids seemed visibly affected. Of course, they couldn't react while under Archer's control. She had to wait just a little longer and hoped the cold didn't impact her as much as it usually would. She had to deal with it every winter. Living in the mountain offered a certain amount of protection against the harsh winds but it still got brutally cold. Her fingers were already becoming numb as she ran her fingers over the hilt of the rifle she was still holding. She could shoot him and end it now but there was no guarantee it would kill him. Like the guards and herself, he could heal. And if there was even an ounce of truth to his claims about being a Celestial in human form…he could do a lot more. Nonetheless, she needed to get to the MPs before they went into the bunker. There was a total of three-hundred-thirty-eight Members of Parliament in the House of Commons. If they were all in attendance for the vote that was three-hundred-thirty-eight hosts for the Shadows. It would devastate the country. She needed to get to them, or at best, have someone stop them. Unfortunately, there was no one else. She was on her own, with only a few outside hybrids like Katie. There was no telling how far Archer's psychic reach went though. The two agents with her didn't fall under his spell until after they entered the command center. As far as she knew, the one she sent to the basement was still free of his influence. She could only hope those outside were not affected as well.

Despite how much she wanted to put an end to Archer here and now, there was no point trying to fight him. The increasing cold would put most of the hybrids into a form of hibernation, their bodies unable to handle it. Even with the harsh Canadian winters, the safety measures EDC set up would make it as cold as, if not colder, than the Arctic soon. If she didn't leave now, she wouldn't be leaving at all. Without a word, she turned on her heel and headed for the door.

"You can't escape destiny, Kyra," Archer called after her. "You can't escape fate."

She bit back a retort. Becoming his queen was not her destiny. She made her own fate. No one controlled the story of her life but her.

She encountered McIntyre in the hall. The agent was out of breath and visibly shaking from the cold, but he still had all his wits about him. Kyra grabbed his arm and pulled him in the other direction, back to the entrance they had come through.

"We need to leave," she told him in a stern, no-nonsense voice.

"What about the others?" McIntyre asked, instinctively pulling away from her.

"There's nothing we can do for them," she responded. "Archer enchanted them. If we don't leave now, he'll take control of you, too."

"But you…"

"He can't control me. Let's go. Move! We need to get outside and have the building quarantined." She pulled the heavy metal door open. "The cold will buy us some time, but it won't be long before Archer sends someone down to shut it off."

They stumbled into the warmth and sunshine outdoors. The sudden heat was like a slap in the face for both, but Kyra didn't have time to bask in it.

"Find the Lieutenant or whoever is running the operation and tell him what's going on. The hybrids are under Archer's control. They need to be put in isolation and iced until we can break his hold on them…not killed. They're innocent. Do you understand?"

McIntyre stared at her for a moment before nodding. "What about you?"

"I need to get to the bunker and rescue the MPs."

His eyes widened. "That will be impossible! Even in uniform you won't be able to pass the soldiers guarding them. You'll never make it."

"The boy's right," Archer purred as he stepped out of the building, followed by his two guards and Naomi. His followers were close behind, sluggish but not downed by the cold as Kyra had hoped. He glanced toward McIntyre. "Go...fetch your lieutenant. I'd very much would like a one-on-one conversation with them."

"Archer, don't do this," Kyra warned. "You'll start a war."

"And what if that is exactly what I want?" He gave a low laugh. "But by all means...try and save your precious MPs...or you can save the people here."

Kyra opened her mouth to protest but Archer made a gesture to his followers.

"Kill them. Every last one," he ordered, a long finger pointed toward the bystanders.

The people under his control moved toward them as if with a hive mind. It strangely resembled a zombie movie Kyra watched with her fathers one Halloween night in her youth.

Kyra stared after them. There was no way to stop all of them. Archer had put her in a situation with no solution. She either had to kill the hybrids to save the humans or let them slaughter the humans only to be killed by the Armed Forces and police. They would die either way and Archer could care less. The only ones he had not sent were his two guards and Naomi, the latter seeming just as shocked as Kyra.

"Archer..." Naomi whispered, her voice meek and submissive.

"Go...seduce the members of high command," Archer interjected before she could voice her concerns. "Keep them occupied while the onslaught takes the city."

Naomi's mouth opened and closed, an objection obviously on her lips. She didn't seem to be under his control like the others, due to her own power of mind manipulation. She glanced at Kyra, sighed, then dashed off to do as she had been ordered to. Kyra wanted to grab her and stop her before she could do his bidding, but there was already too much going on. It was impossible to decide what needed her focus more. She was trapped in a way she never had been before, her mind divided between three impossible tasks: saving the MPs, stopping the hybrids, and stopping Naomi. Then there was Archer, standing before her with his two goons, looking at her as if the three would devour her. Kyra had faced many obstacles throughout her life, but never had she felt so out of her element.

"You can end this, you know," Archer told her. His voice sounded seductive, like warm dark chocolate on a chilly winter night. "Submit to me. You are our Queen. Accept that role, save your precious humans."

It was tempting...to hand herself over to save the people around her. It was also too easy. Far too easy. Handing herself over would not stop Archer, he would only empower him more. Instead, she did what she should have in the command center; she stepped back, raised her rifle, and took aim.

Screams echoed across Parliament Hill as the hybrids began their attack, followed moments later by yelling and gunfire. Kyra blocked it out as she focused on Archer.

"Call them off," she ordered, her only warning.

Archer smirked, unafraid. He wasn't giving her much choice. Her finger slowly tightened around the trigger as she inhaled deeply then exhaled. She fired, the sound echoing all around them only to be lost amongst all the other gunfire. It should have been a kill shot, aimed directly at Archer's forehead. Instead, one of his goons took the shot for him, stepping right into the line of fire at the last possible moment. The man was nearly a head taller than Archer and the bullet slammed into his throat with a sickening wet sound. For a moment, the man stood there, utterly confused, before the flesh began sewing itself back together, proving Kyra's earlier theory about him and his twin having rapid healing abilities. That didn't bode well. She fired repeatedly with the same result. Short of beheading them, she couldn't kill them. If she couldn't kill them then there was little more, she could do than run and hope Archer had all the hybrids under his control chase after her. It was the only thing she could come up with that may have a chance of saving the humans.

The rifle fell to the ground next to her feet. Her heart sank and for a moment she wanted to give up, fearful she could never outrun them, but she didn't need to outrun them, just distract them. She needed to give the humans a chance to escape…even if it meant sacrificing her freedom. While the twins and Archer recovered, she dashed toward the group of soldiers and police fighting back the hybrids. She shoved them out of her way, yanked hybrids away from humans, then pushed her way through the retreating crowd, instinctively knowing the hybrids would follow her. Sure enough, she felt Archer's hold on them switch focus to her as they abandoned the people they attacked to chase after her. Now the question was where to lead them that could free them from Archer. The cold had not stopped them as she had hoped, but what else was there that could stop them?

The lab. Would they follow her back to the lab? It was a long shot. There could still be Shadows there and if they were working for

236

Archer then she would lead herself into a trap. If they happened to be against Archer…then maybe she had an ally. It didn't matter either way. The lab was the only place equipped to contain the hybrids.

Chapter Fifteen

T he radio chatter was frightening at best. Lucas listened closely, unable to make sense of it. There had been an attack on Parliament Hill as they had expected would happen. However, the scene that was being painted for them was that of a Zombie Apocalypse not a terrorist attack. Hybrids were attacking civilians while soldiers and police were trying to stop them only to be attacked as well. It ended as fast as it started with no explanation other than their focus moving to a better target. There was no word if Kyra was involved or not. If she was there, she was gone now.

Lucas removed the large headphones and slumped back in his seat. What in the world was going on? How many hybrids were there? For the longest time he had thought his daughter was the only one, only to learn there were hundreds, maybe thousands spread across the world. Now there were hundreds of thousands, each a walking time bomb if the attack on Parliament was anything to go by. Even with the attack over – for now – it was not safe to land. There was nothing they could do here. Elizabeth had sent a warning about the bunker to those protecting the Members of Parliament. It was the best they could do. The helicopter flew low over the city as they looked down to the streets, hoping to get some sort of indication of where Kyra could be.

He put the headphones back on. "Any idea where she may be?" He glanced toward Alex but his beloved shook his head.

"She's trying to lead them away," Liam reported from the seat next to Alex.

Lucas turned in his seat to face him. "Where?"

Liam made a face, his head tilted slightly as if someone whispered in his ear. "The lab...I think she's going to try capturing them there."

Alex stared at Liam in disbelief but Lucas nodded. It made sense. If hybrids had been held captive there before than it was strong enough to hold them again. Kyra wasn't going to be able to do it alone.

"Elizabeth?" Lucas asked.

She nodded. "There was a landing pad on top of the building," she said, already steering the helicopter back toward the building. "What's the plan?"

"If she's not there yet, set up a trap for the hybrids. If she's there...get as many of them caged as possible."

Elizabeth nodded. "And if she's part of all this?"

He took a deep breath and let it out slowly. "Capture her as well."

"Lucas..." Alex objected.

"Let's just hope she's still on our side."

He certainly hoped so. He refused to believe Kyra was truly a Celestial and possibly the cause of all this. The key was getting everyone into the void in the building where there had been cells. Whomever had gone out of their way to abduct them likely knew of their adversity to cold. He should be able to lower the temperature to near arctic levels. Maybe lower. He would have to be fast. If Kyra was already on her way, it wouldn't take her long to reach it.

The lab wasn't far from Parliament. Within minutes, Elizabeth guided the helicopter onto the landing pad. Lucas grabbed on of the wireless headsets then shoved the door open. Alex did the same and pulled the sliding door on his side open and stepped out, ready to do what was necessary to protect their daughter. Lucas gave him a pointed look. His mental connection to Kyra made him a liability. She could read his thoughts.

"Don't even start," Alex said, meeting the look with a hard glare. "I'm going with you."

"Alex…"

"I should go as well," Liam called, feeling his way along the opening.

"No," Lucas snapped. He knew he couldn't stop Alex but he'd be damned if he was going to let a blind youth with no combat training wander the lab. They had no idea what they were about to face. Liam was a walking target. "Stay with Elizabeth. Track Kyra and keep us updated on her location."

"But…"

"Liam, you're attached to her…better than I am," Alex reasoned as he slipped a small earpiece into his left ear, the only one that could hold such a device. "You can pinpoint her location faster than anyone. We need to know once she reaches the building. If she's on our side, you can let her know what the plan is. If not…we need to know what she's planning. Can you do that for us?"

The youth opened his mouth to object, then sighed and nodded.

"Channel twelve," Lucas told him, also inserting the small earbud into his ear. "I want updates every five minutes."

Liam nodded. "Yes, sir."

"I want you two checking in every five minutes as well," Elizabeth told Lucas and Alex sternly over the radio. The whirling of blades made it near impossible to hear her. "I'll keep the engine running. Get our girl and get out of there. The chatter is getting back. Over a dozen civilians have been killed and all human EDC agents in HQ are dead. The Armed Forces just gave the order 'Shoot to Kill.' They're hunting the hybrids. Including those that were EDC agents."

Alex's face paled but he nodded. It made Lucas all the more tempted to shove him back in the helicopter and tell Elizabeth to fly off with Alex and Liam, to keep all three of them safe while he dealt with Kyra and the hybrids. He didn't. He couldn't. Alex would find a way to convince her to bring him back. He and Elizabeth were best friends after all. Besides, Alex had a habit of thinking ahead and sometimes much more strategically than Lucas. He was already pulling up the blueprints on the tablet they had taken from Trenton base. While the levels that contained the cells were still missing from the prints, it gave enough information for how to reach them.

They entered the building through a heavy metal access door on the roof and headed down the steps to the top floor. By all appearances it was no different than any other office building with men and women in suits working in offices and moving about their daily business. Lucas ignored them and headed in the direction the elevators were located. He paused as he neared them, realizing Alex was not by his side. Turning, he spotted Alex striding toward a fire alarm. Before Lucas could ask what he was doing, his husband pulled the alarm. A moment later the blaring ringing of klaxons filled the building followed by a feminine voice over the loud speaker directing everyone in the building to the stairs to safely leave the building.

"Second time today," a man cursed as he stomped by. "The bloody alarm is broken." He glanced at Lucas and Alex. "Don't even bother trying the elevators. The moment the alarms go off they lockdown. Only way out is by the stairs."

Lucas's brows furrowed as he looked at Alex. "Brilliant," he grumbled with a shake of his head. "Simply brilliant."

"I was trying to evacuate the building before the hybrids showed up," Alex argued.

"And now they get a buffet," Lucas sighed. "And who's to say they aren't the cause of all this?"

Alex frowned at him. "Then all the more reason to get them out of here."

A sigh escaped Lucas. He shook his head. He couldn't get mad. Under normal circumstances evacuating the building was wise, but without the elevators the hybrids would be coming up the stairs and perhaps encountering the men and women mid way up. There was no way to reroute anyone, but perhaps the was another way for Lucas and Alex to get where they needed to, without having to shove their way past the office workers. He huddled next to Alex as the looked over the blueprint on the tablet. There was a service elevator in the west wing of the building, tucked between two large storage rooms and out of sight from the public, meaning most of the office staff either didn't know about it or had no access to it. The area appeared to be locked down and had heightened security compared to the rest of the building, with exception of the void. Perhaps it was the only elevator that went through the void. Perhaps the others went just outside it and had no access to those floors. It made the original assessment seem more likely, that the upper and lower floors were nothing more than offices. If that was so, then this elevator was likely the only one working right now and would take them directly where they needed to go.

Getting there was another challenge altogether. That whole section of the floor was under lockdown as it must be on each floor. Alex was went to work on the lock immediately, plugging in the tablet directly to the computer port on the side of the door and hacking the system. For once, Lucas had no complaints about his husband's skill at hacking into places, something Elizabeth had taught him after their first encounter with Celestials and those who worked with or for them. He would have to thank Elizabeth for keeping on Alex to learn because in no time the younger man had overridden the locks and they were inside the west wing. It didn't look like anything special when they stepped inside. In fact, it was rather bare, just a larger corridor with several doors and a large elevator to one end and numerous cameras along the ceiling. Alex flipped them off as they headed toward the elevator clearly not amused.

"You have got to be kidding me," he grumbled as they neared the elevator. It, like the door, was locked and didn't so much as have a button to summon it.

"Someone clearly doesn't want anyone using it," Lucas mused as Alex began hacking the system.

"Fuck them," Alex cursed, his focus on the tablet. It was rare to hear him swear outside the bedroom but the curse brought a small smile to Lucas's lips. He liked this side of Alex.

The elevator whirled to life in a matter of moments. Alex unplugged the tablet and stood. He took a step back and reached for his sidearm, ready for anything. Lucas did the same, but he drew his gun and aimed at the doors. Yes, they had summoned the elevator, but there was no telling what may be inside it.

They braced themselves for possible attack as the huge double doors drew apart...but there was nothing inside. The elevator was empty.

Giving the inside a once-over to be certain, Lucas nodded to Alex that it was safe, then keyed-in the void's uppermost level.

"We'll find the control room first," Lucas said as the lift began moving downward. "There should be environmental controls which will allow you to turn the place into a virtual ice box."

"And what are you going to do?" Alex countered, already not liking the plan.

"I'm bait." He gave Alex a hard look, silently pleading him to not interrupt and let him explain his plan. "We don't know how large this lab is. There appeared to be at least three floors of cells but it's likely much larger. I have a chance to outrun them if I need to, but with your leg...babe, it's getting harder for you to run long distances and next to impossible for you to run up and down stairs."

Alex's lips pursed but he held back the usual retort he would make when someone pointed out his disability. "I'm not going to take that as the insult it clearly was," he bit out.

"I'm stating a fact, not an insult. Alex, you're fast, there's no argument there, but in this case...I may not even be fast enough, but one of us has to be able to lock this place down while the other gets everyone in the hold...and gets Kyra out."

Alex stared at him for a long time then gave a curt nod. "You better get our baby out of there or I'll..."

His words faltered, unsure what sort of threat would work to guarantee their daughter's safety. Nonetheless, Lucas nodded. He felt the same way.

Despite not having a blueprint or layout of the void, finding the security room wasn't very hard. In fact, it was within the same corridor as where the service elevator was, on the other side area in which the service elevator was hidden. The door to it was ripped from its hinges and lay discarded across the hall in a twisted heap. Lucas's eyes widened in surprise. He knew hybrids were stronger than the average human but he had not met one capable of such a feat. The door, like those leading to the service elevator, were made of steel and extremely heavy. This looked as if someone had torn tinfoil off a ham sandwich. It made Lucas's decision to leave Alex in the security room all the more legitimate. He did not want his beloved facing off against whoever or whatever had done that. Hopefully, it was no longer in the building and not one of the hybrids following Kyra.

He didn't comment on the door and instead went directly inside the security room. It was a mess, computers overturned and monitors destroyed. How were they supposed to do anything in here? His mind raced for another option while Alex moved about the room, checking to see if any of the equipment was still useful. There had to be a manual environmental control. Something, anything that would keep the cell block cold and hybrids under control. He pulled open what appeared to be the main control panel and began reading down the list of fuses and switches, praying to find something that could help them. Everything but what he wanted appeared.

"I've got this," Alex told him as he straightened a computer tower that seemed to have the least amount of damage to it. "You should prep for the hybrids while I get the place back online."

"Are you sure you can hack into the system?" Doubt filled Lucas. The security room was completely trashed. It was unlikely Alex could take control of the complete system through one broken computer terminal.

"I have Elizabeth to walk me through it. We'll transfer control to the tablet and get things running. Go, there's not much time left."

Lucas nodded. Alex was right. He had to go now. Kyra and the hybrids could arrive at any moment…if they weren't already in the building. His gaze lingered on Alex as his beloved worked diligently to access the lab's security system. Dread filled him. Alex was able to care for himself but it didn't stop him from worrying. He didn't know what he would do if he lost his husband and child, but he couldn't bring Alex to the cell block with him. If the hybrids attacked they needed a quick retreat. Alex could get to the service elevator quickly from this location without having to outrun anyone.

He crossed the short distance between himself and Alex, wrapped an arm around his waist, and drew him into a slow passionate kiss. It felt almost like the first time they kissed many years ago, forbidden, and sweet, full of nervousness and unspoken words. He took his time to savour it. When they finished, he reluctantly pulled away and looked over the man he loved.

"I'll be back shortly," he promised.

"You better be." Alex wrapped one hand in the shoulder of his armoured vest and pulled him into another kiss. "Get our daughter back."

Lucas nodded. "I will. I love you."

"I love you, too."

It was hard to pull away from Alex, but with a reassuring smile, Lucas made his way to the door, gave Alex one last look, then made his way further into the void. The entire floor was empty. Not one person remained, as if they had all disappeared. No bodies, no lab technicians, no guards. They could have fled when the alarm went off but there would have been evidence they were there. It was as if someone had wiped the area after the hybrids had escaped. Yet, they had not taken the time to clean the security room as they had everything else.

He found a large heavy set of double doors with thin wired windows. Through them, he got his first look at the cells. It was large and looked like a high security prison only sterile and prison white. From his vantage, it, like the rest of the floor he was on, had been cleaned with impeccable precision. Unfortunately, the doors were locked and unlike Alex, Lucas had no clue how to hack the computer system that secured it.

"Babe, tell me you've bypassed security," he said into his headset.

"Just about…" Alex answered. "Got it. What do you need?"

"The doors to the prison wing are locked." He glanced above the door. There were numbers identifying it. "4.17B."

"One sec…found it. Stand back."

There was a loud metallic click then the sound of gears. The huge double doors swung outward, showing that they were much heavier than even the doors to the elevator. It was freezing inside, like an Arctic blast hitting him in the face. Frost decorated the rails and bars while ice formed in corners damp with condensation.

"Do you see this?" Lucas whispered into his mic to Alex.

"I have no visual," Alex answered. "What's going on?"

Lucas's gaze swept over the vast chamber. The whole chamber was a pristine white. It reminded him of when Alex had been kidnapped many years ago and taken to the Arctic in search of one of the underground temples. The same blinding-white and bone-chilling cold. He decided it best not to remind Alex of that. It could trigger a panic attack which neither of them needed at the moment. Not only had Alex been kidnapped, but he had also been raped, manipulated, tortured, and nearly killed, only to then be possessed by a Celestial and turned into its vessel. It was not something he needed to relive.

"They must have been preparing to recapture the hybrids. They already have the cells prepped and lowered the temperature." He walked further into the chamber and looked around. "They must have left in a hurry; almost all the exits are wide open. Strange how the door on our floor was locked. As if they were trying to keep the hybrids on the lower levels."

"Or protect the upper levels," Alex countered. "They may have expected to be swarmed."

Lucas hummed softly to himself. "It leaves too many exits…too many escape routes. We want the hybrids in here, not escaping. Do you know the most likely entrance they'll use?"

Alex sighed in his ear. "I don't know. If they're chasing Kyra then they'll probably come through the main doors. Kyra will head for the first set of stairs. She's not fool enough to try the elevator. So…east wing. It should be directly across from you."

"I see them," Lucas answered with a nod. "Alright, let's bottleneck them. Lock down every door expect this one and the bottom east door."

"I'm going to need you to read them off to me. I still can't access the entire security grid. How much time do we have?"

"Not nearly enough."

They would have to make do. There were four doors per level but only two on either side that appeared to be exits, with a half dozen cells or more between them. There had to be a quick way to do this. He took note of the numbers above the door he has passed through then headed toward the opposite one, pausing long enough to check the side door to see if it was an exit. It turned out to be a lab fit for an autopsy or lobotomy. Lucas shivered at such thoughts and hurried to the next exit. He didn't want to think of what may be behind the other doors. He could only imagine the horror the hybrids who had been captured must have felt. Guilt dug into his stomach. Many hybrids likely suffered here and he was about to trap a bunch of them here once more. Given the horror happening outside, he had little other choice. What else was he to do to stop the chaos and save the city?

"4.17A," he read to Alex once he reached the other exit. He pulled the doors closed and waited until he heard the motorized locks snap into place.

"Locked," Alex responded.

Satisfied, Lucas hurried down the steps to the next door. "4.16A."

"Got it. That means the other one would be 4.16B."

Lucas jumped in surprise as he heard the doors on the other side of the chamber slam shut.

"How many floors are below you?" Alex asked as the doors on the floor below Lucas began to slam shut and lock into place.

"Four," Lucas reported. He looked over the rail to make certain.

"Alright, I'll lock each of them except 4.12A. That will be their entrance. 4.17B is your exit."

That wasn't so bad, Lucas decided. He head back to the level he had entered on. It would give him the best vantage point. He could keep an eye on the hybrids as they entered and give him a proper idea of how many there were. There was no way to get an accurate count, not if they swarmed, but if they got them in and locked them in, then EDC could figure out what to do next. While the cold would slow them down, EDC may be able to flood the chamber with some form of knock out gas then put them on ice, in a deep sleep. Or, put them down for good if needed. He hoped it didn't come to that. Whatever was happening to them was not their fault. There had to be a way to sever their link to the Celestials. The aliens had to be the reason all this was happening. There had to be one close by, one powerful enough to corrupt so many minds all at once. He still blamed Archer. He had to have something to do with this.

He watched the remaining open door below, his chest tight with anticipation as he waited for Kyra. Time seemed to tick by minutes feeling like hours as his anxiety grew. What if the other hybrids captured her? What if she became like the others, out of control and feeding on humans?

"We may have a problem…" Alex suddenly announced.

Lucas's grip on the rail tightened until his knuckles turned white. "What sort of problem?" he asked, managing to keep his voice even.

Alex hesitated a moment. "This security software has infrared…I guess to distinguish between humans and hybrids…well there are a hell of a lot more hybrids than we originally thought."

250

A chill ran through Lucas at the report. "How many are talking about?"

"Hundreds…far more than we reported in the attack on Parliament. I have no idea where they're coming from." Alex gave a frustrated sigh. "Maybe the ones Kyra freed came back…it's makes no sense though. Why are they configuring here? They can't all be hunting her. They're moving fast. They've almost reached the Void."

This made things a lot harder. He wasn't sure how many people the prison could hold. Not only that, but they had to wait until the hybrids were inside the void before icing it. The hope was they would all try coming through the one entrance and get bottlenecked, slowing them down enough for Kyra to escape. Now he was uncertain. With so many they may swarm each level before even entering the void.

"You need to get out of here," Lucas said sternly, not leaving room for argument. "Your tablet should be able to control everything remotely now. Take it and get to the helicopter. "

"I'm not leaving without you."

"I'm not asking, I'm telling you." He inhaled sharply as he spotted Kyra rush into the prison. "We'll be right behind you."

For a moment it sounded as if Alex was about to object, but he didn't. "Don't take long."

"We won't," he promised.

He waited until the line went dead before giving a loud whistle and shouting Kyra's name. The young woman stumbled in surprise before glancing up at him, utter relief filling her face.

"Pappa!" she cried excitedly.

251

She glanced over her shoulder, fear evident on her face, before running to the nearest staircase, taking the stairs three at a time. Lucas aimed his rifle at the door, ready to take down anyone who came through and made a move on his daughter. He hoped a warning shot was all they needed. He didn't want to kill anyone if he didn't have to.

"Pappa, no," Kyra said, appearing next to him quicker than he anticipated. "They can't control themselves. Archer...he's in their heads. We need to lock this place down."

"I know," Lucas assured her.

He slung the rifle back over his shoulder. He wanted to hug her and promise everything would be okay, but the hybrids were pouring into the prison, shoving, and pushing one another in search of Kyra. It was almost like watching a Zombie film but it was happening in real life, where they were killing real people, whether they knew it or not. He grasped his daughter by the elbow and steered her toward the exit. Knowing Alex, he was probably still in the security waiting for them rather than leaving as he was supposed to.

He stopped short when the door suddenly shook, as if someone was trying to push it open. It was followed by a pounding sound and shouting.

"Alex..." he whispered over the mic.

"They just flooded this floor," his husband answered, fear echoing through their connection. "I'm pinned. You guys need to get out of there."

There was a loud crash in the background and Lucas's heart all but stopped. "Alex!"

"I'm fine, I just barricaded the door…" He paused for a long moment. "I may have found another way out. Can you get to the air vent?"

"What about icing the prison?"

"Forget it. Get into the air vent. In a building like this they're large enough for a grown man to crawl through. Get to the service area. It's clear. I'll meet you there. I've unlocked the lab closest to you. Get in there and lock the door. It'll buy you a few minutes."

Lucas glanced to his right as a white, heavy metal door swung open. His blood ran cold and he silently cursed Alex for choosing that lab of all the labs to open. It was one of the ones he had took notice of before, where hybrids had been experimented on. He could all but smell death wafting from it. It may be clean and pristine but there was no doubt in his mind that more than one hybrid had died in it. They had no other choice. It was only a matter of time before the hybrids broke through the door and more was stumbling up the steps trying to reach Kyra. He pulled his daughter into the lab, slammed the door shut and looked it, then pulled the shades over the narrow window on the door. It was unlikely, but perhaps the hybrids didn't see them enter.

"Do I even want to know what happened?" he asked while Kyra stood on one of the high tables and pushed open the metal access panel to the vent.

"Can we talk about it at home? It'll take more than the thirty seconds they need to break through," she countered. She gripped either side of the opening and hauled herself up with ease.

He followed her up but with far less grace or ease. It had been a long time since he had to pull himself up into such a small space. The air vent was large and surprisingly brightly lit, but it was still a little claustrophobic for his tastes. It reminded him of when he first started out as an Archaeologist and investigating temples. Very carefully, he closed the access panel behind him, hoping it would buy them some much-needed time.

The service elevator was only a few dozen feet away, but crawling to it on their hands and knees, it might as well have been miles away. They had to move slow to avoid making excessive noise, especially Lucas. Every time he put his full weight down, the vent creaked and he feared that one wrong move may cause the vent to give out under him. Having the rifle strapped to his back didn't help any. The barrel scraped against the metal of the shaft and would get caught when they turned down another path. Kyra would pause and wait for him, unwilling, like Alex, to leave without him. Eventually they made it to the service area. Alex was nowhere in sight.

"Alex?" Lucas called through his headset service once he and Kyra were on solid ground.

The sound of footsteps hurrying up the side stairs made Lucas draw his rifle. He stepped protectively in front of his daughter and aimed down the steps.

"Whoa…stow it, Lucas," Alex snapped as he came up the steps. "I was making sure this stairwell was secure."

Relief filled Lucas. He lowered his weapon. "And?"

Alex shook his head. "It won't hold for long. They'll find a way through the locks." His face softened upon seeing Kyra and he moved toward her, wrapping her in a loving hug. "Are you alright?"

The young woman nodded, hugging him back. "I will be."

"What is going on? Why are they after you?"

She sighed. "It's Archer...he..." She shook her head. "He's controlling them. He has it in his head that he and I are some superior breed, actual Celestials in human form. He thinks...it doesn't matter what he thinks. We need to break his hold over them."

"How?" Lucas asked. He gestured to the stairs, silently telling them it was time to go. They had no time to wait for the elevator, and there was no telling who may be on it or if the hybrids now had access to it.

"I don't know," Kyra admitted. "Kill him?"

"That's easier said then done," Alex pointed out as the made their way up the stairs. "If he is a Celestial then it's near impossible. Even in human form. Only a Celestial can kill a Celestial."

Lucas glanced at Alex. He didn't like what the younger man was implying. Kyra had been through enough already. They had to get her to safety, regroup with the remaining EDC agents, then hunt down and finish Archer off themselves.

He pressed two fingers to his ear piece. "Elizabeth, we have Kyra. We're on our way. Elizabeth?"

He stopped and tapped the ear bud. Something was wrong. He met Alex's gaze. There was fear and worry in them. Lucas nodded and together the three of them rushed up the stairs to the roof. It was unlikely the hybrids had made it there but there were other stairwells that led to the roof, ones less secure then the one they were in now. There was no other reason for Elizabeth not to answer.

Lucas took the steps two at a time, fearful that the hybrids may have overwhelmed Elizabeth and taken the helicopter. Or, she saw them coming and flew to a safe distance. Young Liam was with her. She would protect him...unless he turned as well. Every possible scenario played in his mind as he neared the roof access. If anything happened to her he would never forgive himself.

"Lucas, wait!" Alex called, struggling to keep up.

He pulled the heavy metal door open and stepped into the bright sunshine, rifle drawn. He looked around, expecting to see hybrids flooding the roof. Instead, it was empty. No hybrids. No helicopter. Nothing.

"Elizabeth, where are you?" he called through the radio.

"Sorry, Lucas. Eight O'clock...we're coming up to your left. We had to move. They called in air support," she finally answered, radio crackling with the whirl of the blades in the background. "We need to do a quick evacuation. We have jets incoming."

He looked in the direction she indicated. The sight of the helicopter brought a sense of relief. It would take only a few minutes before she landed.

A smile lifted his lips as Kyra and Alex joined him on the roof. They were going home.

The smile fell when he saw Kyra's eyes widened. Instinctively he turned, rifle at the ready, only to have it ripped from his hands and something long and sharp shoved into his stomach and upward. He stared at Archer, his mouth gaped open but no words filling the void. There was a knife in him. He didn't need to look down to know this. He felt no pain, it was slow to come, the shock of it making his body numb to it. Archer said nothing at first, just met his stare with a hard, cold one of his own, like a shark about to devour his prey. He shoved the knife deeper and Lucas felt the agonizing pain as it sliced upward, not doubt cutting through vital organs. The only emotion from Archer came in the form of a sick grin when he suddenly twisted the knife.

The former bartender leaned in close, his breath brushing against Lucas's ear.

"Don't worry. Alex will be joining you shortly," he whispered before yanking the knife out of Lucas.

He walked away as if nothing had happened, leaving Lucas to fall hard to the cemented ground.

"Papa!" Kyra cried out but Lucas could only fainted hear her words.

His heart pounded in his ears as he yelled for her and Alex to run. He tried to push himself to his knees, to stop Archer from attacking his family, but he couldn't. He was dying. He could already feel himself slipping away. All he could do was watch in horror as Archer reached for Alex. He tried reaching for the rifle. He had to stop Archer. He had to save Alex even if it was the last thing he did...

He couldn't reach it. It was too far away. Even if he crawled, he would never get to it in time. That didn't stop him from trying. He didn't need to though.

"Enough!" Kyra snapped, catching Lucas off guard by the forcefulness of her words. They held power, one that could be felt in the very air around them.

Lucas slumped on the guard and watched, unable to do anything else as his blood slipped from his stomach. His daughter stood protectively between Archer and Alex. No...that was wrong. Archer was no longer standing and Kyra no longer looked like herself, no longer looked human. She glowed with an ethereal light. It pulsed through her in time with her heartbeat. Raw, untamed power of pure, unadulterated light. She held Archer by the throat, lifting him clear off the ground as if he weighed nothing at all. He struggled in her grasp as she floated a few inches off the ground, whatever part of her that was human now gone.

Alex moved around her, seemingly unaffected by their daughter's change. He hurried to Lucas as he shrugged off his jacket. He bunch it up and placed it directly on the wound, pressing firmly to stop the bleeding.

"It's okay…it's okay," he assured. He wiped aside some of Lucas's hair as he stared down at him with wide, worried eyes. "Elizabeth is almost here. We'll get to a hospital."

A small smile lifted the corners of Lucas's mouth as he gazed at the man he loved with all his heart.

"Yeah," he answered, unsure if he agreed with his lover's optimism.

He looked back toward Kyra, unable to look away from her for more than a moment or two. Alex followed his gaze. The had watched her do many fantastical things through out the years but this…this was something altogether new. They watched with a twisted sense of fascination as Kyra's powers grew. Lucas could feel what she felt, sense her thoughts, understand her rage and fear as if he was somehow in her mind, much as Alex often could. Her words resonated through him, like a fist grabbing at his own heart.

"You wanted me to embrace my powers," she sneered, her focus entirely on Archer. "To become your queen. You thought we were equals." She held him higher, her grasp on his thought tightening. "You're nothing more than a pretender. You warped the minds of innocent people. Aligned yourself with the very creatures that would do away with us…you're nothing more than a pathetic traitor out for glory. You started a war you had no way or winning."

"Kyra…" Archer gasped. He clawed at her wrist but her grip was a strong as steel.

"Kyra?" another voice asked, this one timid and scared.

From the corner of his eye, Lucas noticed Naomi standing far too close to the edge of the building.

"Let me go or I'll make her jump," Archer warned.

That was the wrong thing to say. The rage Kyra felt intensified. With her free hand she waved toward Naomi, grabbed the young woman in a psychic fist and all but threw her to Lucas and Alex. Alex managed to catch her before she landed on Lucas and held her protectively to him.

"Tell me Archer," Kyra purred, her rage settling into something else, something almost seductive. "All these hybrids you *helped* find their power through sex…was it really consensual or did you fuck with their heads first? Paint yourself as some sort of Messiah? Use your power to make them dream of you, plant a pretty little fantasy in their heads of being ravished by you before finally having sex with them?"

"I…"

"Or did you actually rape them, hmm? Mind-fuck them when they had no way to stop you? Make them think it was what they wanted when all you wanted was to control them?"

"No…it wasn't like that."

"Use them until they no longer serve a purpose then do away with them like last week's trash." She choked him before he could answer. "I think your actions speak for themselves."

She threw him aside, treating him the same way as he had treated his followers…like trash. He stumbled on the asphalt before looking around desperately for an escape. He attempted to run to one of the many doors leading back into the building only to have them slam in his face. Desperate, he turned on Lucas, Alex, and Naomi, drawing a Browning 9mm from the back of his jeans. Before he could even aim it, Kyra was on him, ripping it from his hand and crushing it within her own. This time she gave him no quarter, no chance to argue or attempt to plead his case.

Her left fist smashed into his chest, tearing it open as if it was nothing more than a piñata. He stood before, mouth agape in horror, but she did not rip out his heart and feast on it as Celestials tended to do. She held it, her hand still in his chest.

"Death is too good for you," she told him. "You will suffer as the Ancients have suffered because of your actions and those that came before you."

Archer gave a blood curdling scream as his skin and clothing were slowly ripped from his body, hanging momentarily before turning to ash. The muscle and tissue followed as blood emptied from his body, floating, and moving around him and Kyra as if it had a life of it's own. Eventually even his bones began to change, as if his body was burning from some unseen flame, until nothing remained but his pulsing heart clenched tightly in Kyra's fist. She stared at it in fascination for a moment or two before crushing it. It too incinerated the moment she tossed it aside.

Relief flooded Lucas as Kyra's shoulders fell but it was short lived as a military helicopter flew up along side the building and gunfire erupted.

"No!" Lucas yelled, reaching out to the helicopter.

It wasn't Elizabeth. She was yelling in his ear, obviously in communication with the other helicopter and trying to stop the attack. They were firing solely on Kyra but in this form they had no affect other than reignite her rage. Despite what she had done to Archer, most of her rage was still bottled within. Now, with a new threat, she let it out. It came in the form of a powerful wave that lashed out at all around her like a powerful whirlwind.

It sent a nauseating burst of pain through Lucas. He grimaced but could not tear his gaze away from the helicopter. It had tried to land only to be thrown backward, the blades whirling for only a few moments before suddenly dying and the vehicle falling out of the sky.

The burst of power slammed into Elizabeth's helicopter as well and for one fearful moment, Lucas thought the same would happen to it, only to see young Liam kneeling next to the open side door, his eyes closed and hands thrust outward, as if to hold the raging power at bay. A moment later Elizabeth was landing as Kyra returned to her human form.

"We need to move. The EMP will only hold them so long. They'll call in more jets as soon as they realise what happened," Elizabeth told them as she pulled a gurney from the back of the helicopter. "Lucas…can you shuffle on here?"

He shook his head. It took her and Alex to get him onto it but they managed to do it without causing him additional pain. In fact, Lucas felt next to nothing, only a bone rattling cold. He said nothing though. They had no time. He was hoisted into the helicopter and secured to the floor. Alex and Kyra stayed next to him while Naomi found a seat next to Liam. They were airborne moments later.

A flash of bright orange light shooting down from the sky, followed by a resounding explosion made the helicopter rock dangerously.

"What was that?" Alex asked. He left Lucas for a moment to see what happened.

Kyra stared after him, the first signs of fear etched on her face.

Lucas watched them for a moment more, his vision growing fuzzy. He blinked once, twice, then saw something he had not thought he would ever be able to see again…his brother Owen, standing before him, his hand held out as if the help him. He felt no fear or regret as he reached up to take it. It was time.

Chapter Sixteen

T he fire burned late into the night. Alex had never personally cremated a body before, let alone a loved one, but it felt wrong to bury Lucas. After all, they were fugitives now. There was no telling how long they would be able to remain in their home in the mountains before EDC or the military came after them. Even the temple was no longer safe for them. However, it was the only place still secure against the Shadows. They were home now, the funeral pyre set on the beach a dozen feet from the water and far enough from the tree-line to not cause a fire. It was Lucas's wish to be cremated just as Owen had been. He had died during the laser blast from space which completely destroyed the lab, killed everyone inside and left nothing but rubble in its wake. Alex had only turned away for a moment but when he turned back Lucas was gone. He had tried to revive him but his wounds were fatal, the internal damage too severe. Kyra even tried to heal him, pouring all her remaining power into him, but it was no use. There was no bringing him back. Not this time.

He was thankful Lucas's body was covered with the quilt from their bed. It was hard enough setting his body on the pyre but to see his body actually burn would have been too hard. The shape of it was hard enough and the sickening smell of burning flesh filled the air for kilometers around. He would stay with Lucas until the process was complete, tending to the fire as needed. Elizabeth stood next to him, her hand wrapped around his, a solid wall of support as she had been since their childhood. Kyra sat on the beach, her knees pulled to her chest as she watched. Liam sat a few feet away from her. He hadn't said a word since their escape. He stayed by her side, along with Naomi. Naomi seemed confused, as if waking up from a dream. Eventually, she would have to be debriefed about what Archer had done to her and the others. She was the only survivor.

Eventually Kyra stood, wiped at her face, then walked away. One by one, Liam and Naomi got up and followed her. Alex let them go without a word. They were young and the pyre was likely to burn all night and perhaps into the next day. When it was over, he would collect some of the ash for a memorial, the rest would be raked into the river. He didn't know what else to do with them. It wasn't as if they had an urn to put them in and even if they did, there was no telling how long they could remain here before finding a new place to hide Kyra. Sooner or later, they would come for her.

"You didn't tell them," Elizabeth said after the three were safely out of earshot. "About the laser. That wasn't one of our weapons. There's no weapon on Earth that could do what it did."

"Cut into a building and have it implode, killing everything inside without so much as damaging a building or the street around it? No," he agreed. There was no manmade weapon that can do that. It was something else…something alien. Something Celestial. "They're back."

"Why? Why now? Why wipe out so many hybrids. I thought they were meant to merge with the human race."

He shook his head. "I don't know. Nothing Caldwell said makes sense. None of this makes sense. I should never have let Caldwell train her. I should have listened to Lucas and kept her here where she was safe and no one knew what she was. None of this would have happened if I had just listened to my gut."

Elizabeth squeezed his hand. "You couldn't have kept her here forever. Kyra is a free spirit. Just like you. Just like Lucas. You can't protect her, only prepare her. That's what Lucas would want."

He nodded and stared back into the flames. He would do everything in his power to prepare Kyra for the battle ahead. Without Lucas, that would be much harder than ever before. He wasn't the military expert Lucas was.

Kyra laid across the back of Lucas's old jeep, her ankles crossed and propped up on the back of the passenger seat. She stared up into the night sky. Thousands of stars twinkled high above, mixed with the bright sparks from the pyre. Ever since her pappa died, she had been calling out to Owen, praying that her uncle had taken Lucas's soul with him, that Lucas was now a Guardian. Neither had answered her call. It had been deathly quiet, not one Guardian answered her, as if those that remained now hid from her. It made her feel painfully alone, despite her family and friends being so close. The Guardians had always been a part of her, always been her guides and closest confidants. Now they had forsaken her, all because she had allowed Archer to use her.

She gave a sideways glance as Liam climbed into the Jeep next to her. He slid into the same position as her and stared blankly. "How are you holding up?" he asked.

"Do you want an honest answer?" she responded, unable to hide the sarcasm.

"No, I guess not." He sighed. "Look...I'm sorry. This is all my fault."

A hallow laugh escaped her. "Oh...and how's that?"

He was silent for a long time. She glanced at him, her curiosity piqued.

"The attack on my mom's bookstore...the Shadows...they weren't after you...they were after me."

She raised a brow.

He sighed. "I'm not a second-generation hybrid. I'm...I lied...we lied. My mom isn't a hybrid she's..."

She turned to face him, understanding dawning on her face. If he was saying what she thought he was saying then Marie was a Celestial, a real Celestial like Caldwell, hiding in a human form, as his father must have. He was just like her.

"Archer must have found out what we were and reported it to the Shadows. With mom out of the way he could claim he was Celestial-borne. His mind tricks weren't powerful enough to control her. And regardless what he said...she never slept with him. She's not that desperate for a man." He gave a small chuckle. "She would have sent him packing."

That was a lot to take in. "Why didn't you tell me before?" Kyra asked.

"The same reason you didn't tell me. It's no one's business but my own, but after everything that happened...I thought you should know the truth."

"So, what now? We get together and produce the next generation of Celestials?"

"Ew...no offense but I'd like to finish college and get into film before I even consider 'reproducing'. If I can even do that now without my sight. Life's too short."

She almost laughed and almost reminded him that they were practically immortal, but she didn't. She liked the fact that he was practical and thought of a life outside what they were supposed to be. It gave her hope for the future.

"Well, you're in the perfect setting for just about any film," she pointed out. "You direct, I'll film."

He laughed. "I may need to learn Braille to finish designing my computer-generated characters."

"We'll figure it out."

He glanced out toward the dense woods.

Then she felt it as well. Hybrids, a large group of them. Rolling over, she climbed out of the Jeep and headed toward to woods, ready for anything. She could hear them now; twigs breaking, voices mumbling...children crying. She began running, Liam by her side, keeping pace as if he could still see. No doubt he was following the signature of the other hybrids.

"Mom!" Liam cried as they neared the group.

"Liam?" Marie called back in surprise. She held a little girl in her arms as she and the other hybrids made their way down an old worn path towards the chalet. She handed the child to one of the other adults before embracing her son. "Thank the Ancients!"

"Marie!" Kyra said in relief.

"We got here as quickly as possible," the older woman told her. She pulled Kyra into the embrace as well. "I'm just thankful you both are safe."

She planted a motherly kiss on both their foreheads, stunning Kyra.

"We have some hungry and tired children. Is there a place we can go so they can rest?" Marie asked when she withdrew from them.

Kyra nodded. "Come with me."

Leading so many people onto her family property no doubt took Alex by surprise. Her father looked away from the funeral pyre in utter surprise as dozens upon dozens of frightened men, women, and children followed Kyra.

"Daddy, this is Marie, Liam's mother," she said by way of introduction. "She and the others were held captive in the lab. I managed to get them out before Archer turned the others. They need a safe haven."

"Doctor Jackson," Marie said. She shook his hand. "It's an honor to finally meet you. I..." She glanced at the pyre, understanding dawning on her face. "I'm so sorry to be meeting you under these circumstances."

"Thank you. Our home is open to all of you," he told her.

Elizabeth looked to Kyra. "There should be enough food and supplies in the Sanctuary. It would be safer for them down there."

MJ Spickett

Kyra nodded. She was right. Regardless of what had happened there early that morning, it was still the safest place for them and the only place large enough to safely sustain them all.

Elizabeth placed a hand on Kyra's shoulder. "I'll take them. You should stay here with your father."

Kyra opened her mouth to object but stopped and gave a curt nod instead. She watched as Elizabeth lifted one of tired children into her arms and led the newcomers down the path to the old mine that hid the underground temple. Alex wrapped an arm around Kyra and leaned against her.

"I guess all our preparations finally came in handy," he mused. "Lucas would be so proud of you."

She leaned into him and blinked back tears. "I should have listened to him. He tried to warn me about Archer."

"I know."

"Hm…Kyra, Dr. Jackson," Naomi called. She hurried toward them with a smartphone in hand. "You might want to see this."

She turned the phone so that they could see the monitor. It was a news report from Parliament with all the Members of Parliament in session. "They just had the vote. All protections for hybrids have been repealed…they just declared us less than sub-human…they're blaming the destruction of the lab and are now actively hunting us down."

"The Shadows," Kyra breathed. "They've taken control."

Alex shook his head. "Even without the Shadows, what Archer did…what happened to the lab…it's to be expected."

"They know about the temple. Without the EDC they'll come for us," Kyra said, worry, fear, and anger bubbling inside her. She looked toward where the hybrids were heading into the woods.

"Then we fight," Alex said firmly. "We defend our home and we protect those in our care. We do exactly what Lucas trained us to do. No matter the cost."

About the Author

☐ Canadian born and raised, M.J. writes primarily urban fantasy, erotic paranormal thrillers, young adult fiction, branching out into short screenplays as well as children's fiction. She enjoys mentoring young authors in the craft of story telling and writing.

To become an ARC reader and join our newsletter for chances to win swag and/or gift cards visit:

www.mjspickett.ca

www.ingramcontent.com/pod-product-compliance
Lightning Source LLC
Chambersburg PA
CBHW031609240626
47153CB00002B/686